A Chef's Kiss for Christmas

CHRISTMAS IN THE COTSWOLDS
BOOK TWO

HANNAH ELLIS

Published by Hannah Ellis
www.authorhannahellis.com
Postfach 900309, 81503 München
Germany

Cover design by dmeacham design

A Chef's Kiss for Christmas

Chapter One

Considering it had been two years since they'd broken up, Anna spent way too much time thinking about her ex-boyfriend. He was on her mind yet again as she strode down the main street in Chipping Campden. Christmas decorations had popped up the week before, and the golden glow from the twinkling lights illuminated the smattering of snow on the ground.

Warm air enveloped her as she entered her brother's hotel. Her eyes feasted on yet more festive decorations, which hadn't been there on her last visit. The Christmas tree in the lounge filled the room with the scent of pine, while strings of tinsel and fairy lights criss-crossed the ceiling.

Ivy smiled at her from behind the reception desk.

"How are you?" Anna asked, walking around to give her old friend a hug.

"Fine. Enjoying the calm before the storm."

"How do you mean?"

"November," she said, as though it was obvious. "It's got a weird feel to it, hasn't it? There's not much going on, but I know December will be crazy, so I feel as though I'm waiting for chaos."

"I know what you mean. December will be busy enough for me, with more work than usual. I can't imagine what it's like for people with kids."

"Poppy is already getting excited," Ivy said, about her six-year-old daughter. "She's started writing a letter to Santa."

"It must be so wonderful to still believe in Santa." Anna smiled, thinking of how simple and magical Christmas was when you were a kid. "I have the wreath for the front door," she said, holding up the shopping bag with the decoration she'd made at her brother's request.

"Leave it with me. I'll put it up later." Ivy took the bag, then gestured to the door, which led to the staff area. "Carla's here, by the way."

"I know. I messaged her earlier." She'd told her sister to meet her here – she had a favour to ask and was sure it would be easier to persuade her in person. "Did she seem to be in a good mood?"

"The last time I saw her she was in the kitchen, arguing with Warren. It's hard to say whether that means she's in a good mood or bad. I think she enjoys antagonising him."

"I think she does too." At one time Anna had thought her sister had a crush on the hotel's chef, but as her brother had pointed out, if Carla really had feelings for him, she'd have acted on them by now.

"Is Lewis around too?"

"In the office," Ivy told her, and Anna headed that way.

Not so long ago, she wouldn't have had to ask if Lewis was at the hotel. During daylight hours you'd never have found her brother anywhere else, but since his girlfriend, Erin, had moved in with him and he'd hired a general manager for the hotel, he took a lot more time off.

Halfway along the corridor, she reached the door to the office and gave a quick knock before opening it.

"Hi," she said to Lewis, who was looking very relaxed,

leaning back in his chair. She smiled automatically at the amusement in his eyes. "What are you smirking about?"

"These two idiots." He tipped his head across the room.

Stepping further inside, Anna did a double take. Both her sister and Warren were lying on the floor with their legs up the wall.

"What are you doing?" she asked, closing the door behind her.

"Your sister's being a weirdo, as usual," Warren said, but didn't open his eyes to look at Anna.

"Who said you could speak?" Carla snapped at him. "Concentrate on your breathing, or this will be entirely ineffective."

"It's ineffective anyway. I'm getting more annoyed, not less. Though maybe if you'd go away, all my anger would mysteriously vanish." His voice dripped with mocking, as it usually did around Carla.

"We're working on his anger management," Carla said, twisting her head to look at Anna. "I'm teaching him ways to calm his nervous system."

Anna drifted over to the two of them. Since Warren still had his eyes closed, she let her gaze linger on the hard line of his jaw, which was covered in stubble. His short brown hair was slightly mussed up in the way it often was – as though he'd been dragging his fingers through it.

When his lips twitched, she shifted her attention away, nervous that he'd catch her staring at him.

"You look ridiculous," she said.

Warren still didn't open his eyes. "What's really ridiculous is the idea that when one of those idiots in the kitchen winds me up, I'll lie down and put my legs up the wall instead of shouting at them."

"He only burned some bacon," Carla said. "There was no need to yell at him the way you did."

Warren's eyes shot open. "It was pancetta! And there was no

need for him to burn it. Not if he'd been concentrating instead of sending his girlfriend pathetic messages."

"Maybe you should have a rule about phone use in the kitche–" Carla didn't finish her sentence before Warren interrupted her.

"There *is* a rule," he boomed. "Liam broke the rule, which means food got burnt and he got shouted at. Which is a logical sequence of events, so I'm not sure what your problem is."

"I just think there could be a more harmonious atmosphere in the kitchen. It'd be good for everyone."

"Then maybe someone should have a word with Liam about concentrating on the job... oh, wait, I did that!" When he slid his legs down from the wall, Anna shifted out of his way, then went to sit on the couch while Warren slumped into the chair opposite Lewis.

"Is everything organised for the weekend?" Lewis asked him.

"Just about," Warren replied. "Hopefully it will all run smoothly enough."

"What's happening at the weekend?" Carla asked, still lying on the floor.

"Nothing." Warren shifted in his seat. "But I'm not working, so I need to make the menu idiot-proof."

"His parents are visiting," Lewis said, then cocked his head. "Is that why you've been in such a bad mood all week?"

"I haven't been in a bad mood!"

Carla snorted.

"No more than normal," Warren muttered.

"How come we've never met your parents?" Carla asked.

"Why would you have done?" Warren replied.

Carla moved her legs down the wall and sat up. "Have they never visited before?"

"Nope."

Anna sat forward as curiosity niggled at her. "Are they staying here, in the hotel?"

"No."

"There's still a room free if they want to stay," Lewis said.

"No, thanks. They have other accommodation sorted."

"Why?" Carla asked from her cross-legged position on the floor.

"They're just staying somewhere else, that's all."

"You'll bring them into the hotel, though?" Lewis asked. "I guess they'll want to see where you work."

"And meet your friends," Carla added, eyes sparkling. "We could all have dinner together."

Warren rubbed his brow. "Or we could *not* do that."

"Don't you get on with them or something?" Anna asked.

He shrugged. "We get on fine."

Anna had so many questions. If she were brave like Carla, she'd just fire them at him and not care if it annoyed him. Since she was certain it *would* annoy him, and she absolutely wasn't brave like her sister, she held her tongue.

"So that's why you're stressed?" Carla said, popping up and positioning herself behind Warren to massage his shoulders. He grimaced and swatted her away.

"I'm not stressed."

Lewis rested his elbows on the desk. "I hope the Michelin people don't visit while you're away."

"For goodness' sake! We're not getting a Michelin star. Why do you keep going on about this?" Warren attempted to shrug Carla off him. "The conversation is getting really boring."

"It's nice when you're humble," Carla told him, ruffling his hair before moving away from him. "We all think you'll get a Michelin star, even if you don't."

"The review they gave you in the Michelin Guide was amazing," Lewis said. "We're definitely on their radar."

"That doesn't mean anything."

"You're a chef," Anna said, confused by how defensive he

always got when the subject came up. "Getting reviewed by Michelin is definitely a big deal."

His features softened. "Yes, but it doesn't mean we'll get a star. Can we please change the subject?"

"Let's talk about your parents again, then." Carla plonked herself beside Anna on the couch. "Do you need a buffer?"

"A what?" Warren asked.

"Someone to come out with you and your parents, so it's not so intense. I could pretend to be your girlfriend."

"I don't think that will be necessary, thanks." His voice was firm, but Anna caught the uncertainty in his eyes, as if he were pondering the idea.

"What's going on with *you?*" Carla asked, slapping Anna's thigh as she changed the subject again.

"Oh, I have news!" She'd decided to phrase her favour as an exciting opportunity and hope her sister wouldn't catch on to her real motives. "We're invited to the Christmas ball at the Grange Hotel. It's free food and drinks, and we can stay over in the hotel for free, too." The perks of her best friend's dad owning the hotel.

"*I'm* invited?" Carla asked, eyes wide with excitement. Exactly the reaction Anna had hoped for. "I've always wanted to go. What am I going to wear?" She paused for breath. "Wait, when is it?"

"A week on Saturday. It'll be so much fun." It was an annual event that Anna had always enjoyed. At least until she and Hayden had broken up. It had lost its magic somewhat since then.

Carla's eyes widened once again, but the excitement had been replaced by something else. Panic, or annoyance maybe. "I'm away. You know I'm away! Why on earth did you just get me all excited for nothing?"

"Where are you?"

"House sitting, remember!"

"Oh." It rang a vague bell. "The house isn't that far away, is it? Can't you still come?"

"It's a bit of a trek. Also, I can't leave the dogs alone all night. I wouldn't even want to leave them for the evening, really. And I wouldn't be able to drink or stay late, so it wouldn't be that much fun." She glared at Anna. "I can't believe you made me get all excited."

"Sorry," Anna said, neglecting to mention that she was just as disappointed as her sister.

"How come I was invited?" Carla asked. "You always go with your old gang from school."

"Yeah," Anna said weakly. "But Frannie said I could bring someone if I wanted."

"So I wasn't specifically invited?" Carla pouted. "Hang on... is Hayden going?"

"I believe so," Anna said, clocking Warren and Lewis following the conversation and wishing she'd had it in private.

Carla gave a knowing look. "I take it he's bringing a date?" She didn't wait for confirmation, but ploughed on with her theory. "So Frannie said you can bring someone because she's worried about you feeling awkward around Hayden and whichever bimbo he's with now."

"She just said I could bring someone," Anna murmured.

"She'll have meant a guy. But I guess you already know that. You just invited me for moral support."

"You are great at moral support," Anna said.

"Of course I am. But you should take a guy. Imagine the look on Hayden's face if you turn up with a hot guy!"

While she definitely enjoyed the idea, it was ridiculous. Mostly because of the slight obstacle of not having a guy to take with her.

Carla's eyes flickered with mischief before her head turned slowly in Warren's direction.

"No!" He gave a weird, strangled laugh. "Keep me out of your scheming."

"Go on," Carla whined. "Take her to the party. There's free food and drinks, and Anna will look totally hot in her evening gown. I don't see how you can say no. I'll even sweet-talk your boss into giving you the night off. You'll have a great time."

Warren was already out of the chair, holding his hands up in a defensive gesture as he headed for the door. "I have to get back to work," he said before darting out of the room.

With her cheeks burning, Anna dropped her head into her hands.

"You're welcome!" Carla said cheerfully.

"For what?" Anna glared at her sister. "You totally embarrassed me."

"It's a great idea to take Warren. Hayden will go nuts when he sees you with him. And it'll stop your friends from shooting you pitying looks all night."

"They don't do that," Anna said, not sure why she was lying. It wasn't as though she hadn't already confided in her sister about how uncomfortable she felt when they were all out as a group.

Carla continued to grin. "I only wish I could be there to see Hayden's face when you arrive with Warren."

"Did you miss the part where Warren refused?" Lewis asked, swivelling contentedly in his chair.

"He refused because *I* asked." Carla gave a dismissive flick of her hand. "He always says no when I ask him something, but Anna only has to look at him and the big grumpy oaf agrees to anything."

"That's not true," Anna said firmly.

"What about the other week when I asked him to make me a sandwich, but the kitchen was already closed and he outright refused? Then you walked in and mentioned you were hungry and he was back in the kitchen like a shot."

"Maybe because I asked politely, instead of bossing him around like you do."

"Exactly!" Carla said. "All you have to do is ask, and he'll go to the party with you."

"No." Anna shook her head, but an image flicked into her head of walking into the party with Warren by her side. It certainly would put an end to all the pitying looks. And it would be nice not to have to be so self-conscious around Hayden and his latest girlfriend.

"You're considering it, aren't you?" Carla asked eagerly.

"No." This time she shook her head more firmly. "Absolutely not."

The room fell silent, and she could feel both of her siblings watching her. They could read her far too easily.

After a moment, she pressed a hand to her forehead. "Do you really think I could convince Warren to go with me?"

Carla nodded enthusiastically and emitted an excited squeal of delight.

Chapter Two

Returning to the kitchen, Warren felt much calmer. Hanging out with the Carrington siblings had that effect on him. It definitely wasn't anything to do with Carla's weird legs up the wall nonsense.

Maybe he could be a little hard on the kitchen staff, but if the food wasn't up to standard, it was him it reflected badly on. After working so hard to build himself and the hotel an outstanding reputation for the food, it irked him when anyone in the kitchen wasn't a hundred percent focused on their job. Mistakes happened, but mistakes that could easily be avoided riled him up.

He offered Liam a rueful attempt at a smile when he walked back in to find him prepping the vegetables for the dinner service. At the back of the room, Sarah was unloading the dishwasher.

Warren went straight to the food storage, wanting to check again that everything was organised for the weekend so the rest of the staff should be able to manage easily without him. For his regular day off, they kept the menu simple, and they managed fine. That was always a Monday, though, when the restaurant wasn't busy. He couldn't remember the last time he'd taken a weekend off.

"Hi," the quiet voice said, interrupting his thoughts and startling him too.

It took him a moment to register how unusual it was for Anna to come into the kitchen. Then it dawned on him why she'd tracked him down there.

"Oh, no!" He raised a hand to his face as though he could block her out. "No, I'm not doing it. Please don't ask." He could say no to her sister all day long, but with her delicate features and the constant shimmer of vulnerability in her eyes, Anna was a different matter entirely.

"Please," she said, dragging his hand away to look him in the eyes. "I'm desperate."

"If you don't want to see your ex at the party, just don't go," he suggested.

"I considered that. But we have the same friendship group, and I don't want to miss out on events because of him."

Warren exhaled a long breath, already resigning himself to the fact that he'd be going to this Christmas party. Given the fact that his boss was her brother, he couldn't use work as an excuse to get out of it.

"I had an idea," she said, the pleading note in her voice hitting right at his core.

"What is it?" he asked hesitantly.

"I could be your buffer."

He screwed up his features. "What?"

"When your parents are here. Like Carla suggested."

"I don't need a buffer." That was a lie. He definitely needed a buffer.

"You're worried about it, though, aren't you? I don't know what the situation is, but I know families can be difficult..."

He almost laughed at that, since she was probably the last

person who would understand how difficult families could be. Her family was perfect, as far as he could tell.

"Having a third party around always makes things easier," she went on, tucking her dark hair behind her ears. "People behave better with someone else there. Also, your parents will ask me questions about my life, which will take the focus off you. It'll be less intense."

Annoyingly, she made some solid points. It would be easier if someone else were around. "You'd really come for dinner with my parents?" Given how painfully shy she was around new people, he was surprised at her volunteering.

"Free dinner, right?" she said sheepishly. "Parents always like me, too."

He rubbed a hand across his forehead. Anna was exactly the sort of person his parents would approve of. She was beautiful and graceful. On top of that, she was intelligent, but also mild-mannered. If she had a degree and were more career-minded, his parents would think she was absolutely perfect.

"You really are desperate for a date to your party, aren't you?"

"Yes." She interlocked her fingers and pressed her knuckles against her chin. "Please will you come?"

He sighed dramatically. "I'd have to check with Lewis about taking the night off."

"He already said it's fine," she told him, her eyes sparkling as she beamed. "You can tell your parents I'm your girlfriend if you want. It's not as though they visit often, is it? Or you can just introduce me as your friend. Whatever you want."

Warren smiled, not sure he'd ever heard Anna talk so much. "I'll think about it," he said. "Now go away and let me work."

"Okay. Thank you." She turned to leave, then swung back around. "When is the thing with your parents?"

"They arrive tomorrow afternoon."

"So I'll have dinner with you tomorrow night? How long are

they staying? It's just dinner, right? Because I'm busy on Saturday. I need to be up early so I won't be able to stay too late tomorrow night."

"You were the one who wanted to make a deal," he said, amused. "Now you suddenly have a load of terms?"

She winced. "It is just dinner, isn't it?"

"Yes. Dinner tomorrow night." That would at least ease the initial tension of his time with his parents. "And I'll make sure you're not out too late."

Her needing to leave would actually be a good excuse to get away from the evening he'd been dreading.

Chapter Three

Bracing against the freezing wind outside Anna's building the following evening, Warren couldn't fathom how he'd even agreed to Anna coming to dinner. Her meeting his parents would complicate things in ways he hadn't quite considered until he'd set off for her flat.

Because, while the idea of his parents asking Anna questions to keep the attention from him was great, inevitably Anna would have questions for them too. Since he'd moved to Chipping Campden four years ago, he'd been very careful not to talk too much about his life before that.

It was one reason he got on with Lewis so well. Lewis didn't ask a lot of questions – he'd always accepted Warren as he was. The whole Carrington family had. Even when he was being grumpy, and sometimes outright rude, they still treated him like part of the family.

Having dinner with his parents meant Anna was bound to find out things about his past, and he'd really rather keep that to himself.

He rang the bell and waited for her to buzz him into the building. He'd been to her place with Lewis and the rest of the family before for an occasional dinner or other gathering, but arriving alone felt odd.

When she buzzed him in, he trudged up the stairs, then lifted an eyebrow when she appeared in the doorway.

"I'm nearly ready," she said while pushing an earring through her ear. Her hair was tied up, with a few loose strands framing her face and drawing attention to the flawless skin at her neck.

A hint of blusher highlighted her cheekbones, and her subtle eye makeup drew attention to the blue of her irises.

"Are we driving or walking?" she asked, plucking a pair of black heels from the rack.

"Walking. I got a taxi over here since I thought I might need a drink or two with dinner, and it's just down the road – that new Italian place."

She paused, then returned the shoes and took a pair of boots instead. "I won't wear heels then."

"The thing is..." He got distracted watching her drag the zip of her knee–high boot over her skin-coloured tights. It left a small gap between the hem of her skirt. Bent over, her black V-neck sweater offered him a good view of her cleavage. It took him longer than it should have done to drag his gaze away.

"What's wrong?" she asked, oblivious to him ogling her.

"I was just thinking that you don't need to come after all."

She frowned but reached for her coat, apparently undeterred. "We made a deal."

"I'll still come to your party. You just don't need to come to dinner."

"I'm hungry." She took a step back along the hall and picked her dainty handbag from the sideboard. "Also, I got all dressed up. I'm coming."

"It's a stupid idea," Warren said firmly. "They probably won't even believe we're a couple. And I just don't need you to come. Okay?"

She stopped and glared at him. "I realise you're stressed about spending time with your parents, so I'm going to let this go."

"Let what go?"

She frowned again, then picked up her keys and shoved them into her bag. "You being surly and mean. I'll ignore it since you have a lot going on at the moment."

"I'm not being mean. I'm doing you a favour. Sparing you from an uncomfortable dinner."

"It'll be fine," she said, pulling the door behind her as she stepped out into the hallway. "Stop panicking. I already told you I'm great with parents. Come on."

He followed her. "You really shouldn't come."

"We don't have to say I'm your girlfriend," she huffed. "We can say I'm a friend."

He hurried to keep up with her as she descended the stairs. "I didn't even mention you were coming. I'm not sure how I'll explain that I decided to bring a friend at the last minute."

"I'll make something up," she said, holding the external door for him. "Stop stressing."

"But–"

"What are your parents called?" Anna cut in.

He fell into step beside her, confused by how difficult it was to dissuade her from coming. Why did she have to choose today to be assertive?

"Jen and Dennis," he said.

"Is there a big feud I should know about?"

"How do you mean?"

"A reason you don't see them often, and barely speak about them, and are freaking out about having dinner with them?" She gave him a sidelong look. "Are they horrible people? It doesn't matter if they are," she added quickly. "I'll still have dinner with them. It would just be easier to know."

"I don't think I've ever known you to talk so much," he remarked, striding along beside her.

"I'm nervous, and I'll feel better if I'm prepared."

"If you're nervous, don't come!"

Her lips twitched upwards. "If I let nerves stop me from doing things, I'd probably never leave the house. Please, just answer my questions."

He squinted, trying to remember what she'd even asked. "They're not horrible people," he said. "But they're not like your parents."

"In what way?"

"They're not warm. My dad is likely to ask what you earn and your level of education. Those are the things they care about."

"Okay." She looked thoughtful. "Good to know. Did you fall out with them? Is that why they never visit?"

He stared ahead, watching snowflakes flutter past the streetlight and ignoring the question.

After a moment, she sighed loudly. "Let's try some easier questions. Do you have siblings?"

"Yes," he said, feeling his shoulders tense.

"How many?"

"One sister."

"I take it from the tone that you don't get on?"

"She's even more annoying than your sister."

Anna snorted a laugh, and the sound made Warren's shoulders drop slightly. He hadn't even noticed how tense he was until then.

"You really don't need to come if you'd rather not," he said, half wanting her to bail, and another part of him hoping she'd stick to her guns and insist on joining.

"I'm coming. I only need to know whether I'm your girlfriend or just a friend?" Her cheeks flared with heat. "I mean, what are we telling your parents?"

He looked ahead to the restaurant, thinking of how satisfying it would be to introduce Anna as his girlfriend. Finally, he might impress his parents. It would be a pathetic way of going about it, though.

At the door to the restaurant, he took a deep breath. "I guess we'll stick to being friends."

Chapter Four

Anna had chosen her outfit strategically, knowing she always felt more confident when she was well-dressed. She'd got an extra confidence boost when Warren had gawked at the sight of her.

His grumpiness irked her, but she blamed his mood on his nerves.

Walking into the warmth of the restaurant, she pulled her shoulders back and corrected her posture. Tempted as she'd been to back out when Warren had given her the opportunity, she didn't want to risk giving him a reason not to uphold his end of the deal.

It was just one evening, and the one good thing about spending so much of her life awash with nerves was that she was also adept at hiding them.

She stepped aside to let Warren pass. He headed for the smartly dressed couple in a booth at the side of the room.

Anna tugged her gloves off and unwound her scarf while he greeted his parents with quick, perfunctory hugs. After the snippets he'd told her about his family, she was intrigued to meet them. And to find out more about Warren, too.

It was actually weird how little she knew about him, considering he felt like part of the family half the time.

"I brought a friend," Warren said, when his mum looked quizzically at Anna. "Sorry, I forgot to mention it earlier."

"He didn't forget at all," Anna said smoothly. "I only invited myself half an hour ago. I hope you don't mind, but he said you were visiting, and I was dying to meet you."

"How lovely." His mum offered a bemused smile. "I'm Jen."

Anna introduced herself as she shook her hand, then did the same with his dad.

"It's always good to meet Warren's friends," Dennis said amiably.

Anna caught Warren's eye roll, but not the words he muttered under his breath. While his parents slid back into their seats, Warren took her coat and hung it with his own at the end of the booth. He motioned for her to sit, then slid onto the bench beside her.

"It's lovely and cosy in here," she said, rubbing her hands for warmth as she glanced around the room. "It only opened a couple of months ago, and I kept thinking I should try it. I've heard good things about the food."

"It's nice and convenient for our hotel," Jen said.

Anna nodded vaguely, choosing not to ask why they weren't staying at Lewis's hotel. "Is it your first time in the Cotswolds?"

"We've been before, but not for years and not to this part." Jen smiled. "It's good to have an excuse now that Warren is here."

Except he'd been living there for years. Again, Anna held her tongue.

"How do you two know each other?" Dennis asked.

"I'm Lewis's sister," Anna said.

"Oh." His mum pinched her lips together, then opened her mouth to speak before Warren cut her off.

"Lewis is my boss at the hotel."

"Ah." They both nodded their understanding, but Anna could have sworn they really weren't much wiser about the situation.

"So your brother is the manager of the hotel?" Dennis asked.

"He's the owner," Anna replied.

Dennis's eyebrows rose. "That's impressive."

"Yes." She chose not to disclose exactly how Lewis had acquired the hotel, deciding they probably wouldn't be impressed to find it involved a healthy dose of luck. "He's done very well for himself. But he always says it's partly because of his brilliant staff." She shot Warren a glance and smiled.

"You still enjoy working there?" Jen asked Warren.

He nodded. "I love it."

"And what do *you* do?" Dennis asked, eyes on Anna.

"I work part-time at a florist's."

The conversation was interrupted by the waitress coming to take their drinks order, and then by their focusing on the menu to decide what they wanted to eat. A quick glance at Warren told Anna he wasn't concentrating on the menu, despite having his eyes fixed on it.

His jaw looked painfully tight, and he held his shoulders so rigidly that she had the urge to massage the tension out of them. When he glanced up and caught her staring, she whipped her gaze away, cursing the way her cheeks flashed with heat.

❄

Anna's blush made Warren smile, and he felt himself relax a little. At least until they'd ordered food, and his dad manoeuvred the conversation straight back to where they'd left off.

"Did you say you only work part time?"

Warren breathed deeply through his nose. There was no way Anna's erratic work schedule would impress them. Which wouldn't matter if they were better at hiding their disdain of anything that didn't meet their approval.

"I only work part time at the flower shop," she explained. "But I also have a lot of freelance work."

His dad's eyebrows rose keenly. "What kind of freelance work?"

"I have an online shop," she told him. "Selling cards and gifts. I also sell at craft fairs pretty regularly."

"I see," his dad said with a condescending smile.

"It's pretty small at the moment," Anna said. "But that's how all businesses start, isn't it?"

His mum tapped a nail against her wineglass. "Do you have plans to expand?"

"My idea is to have my own flower shop eventually," she said, then paused and sipped her wine, while Warren tried to figure out if that was true or if she was just trying to impress them. "I have a degree in business and marketing," she added.

Warren's eyes widened. When he'd told her what his parents were like, he hadn't expected her to outright lie. He was surprised she had it in her.

"I always had the idea of opening my own flower shop, but I decided it'd be best to get some experience first. It almost feels cheeky getting paid to gather knowledge for when I open my own place. I don't tell my boss about my plans, of course."

"Do you have a specific timescale for opening your own place?" his dad asked.

"I keep an eye on the property market, waiting for the right premises to come along. I'm only twenty-five, so I don't feel there's a big rush. The more experience I have when I branch out, and the more money I've saved, the more likely I am to make a success of it." She shrugged. "Maybe I could even have a chain of shops one day."

"Interesting plans," his mum said, with a nod of approval.

"Sounds like you've got a good head on your shoulders," his dad intoned. "I'm sure you'll do well."

Anna caught Warren's eye. He could barely contain his surprise. For someone so meek and mild, she could put on quite a show of confidence when she felt like it.

Smoothly, she asked his dad about his work, which got him talking about his recent business deals. More impressive than her earlier performance was the way Anna feigned interest in everything his dad said.

The conversation flowed easily, filling the space until their food arrived.

"I don't know about yours," his dad said, winding tagliatelle onto his fork, "but my food is divine."

"It's good," Anna said, popping a piece of ravioli into her mouth. "I think I'm spoiled with food these days since I eat at the hotel quite a bit. Warren makes amazing fresh pasta." Glancing up at his parents, she smiled softly. "You must be very proud."

Warren wanted to laugh at that. Even more so when his mum murmured that, of course, they were proud of him.

What else could they say? That he was their biggest disappointment?

He knew that's what they were thinking, but they'd be nothing other than polite in company. Which was exactly what Anna had said – that family would always be on their best behaviour around other people.

He refused to look at his parents, but took a swig of his beer and decided that whatever Anna needed from him at her party next weekend, he would play the role to perfection.

When the desserts arrived, Anna turned to Warren. "What have you got planned with your parents tomorrow?"

"I booked tickets for Blenheim Palace in the afternoon."

His mum would no doubt love it, and with so much to see, it should make conversation easier.

"It's beautiful," Anna said to his mum. "The palace is all decorated for Christmas, and there's a light trail around the gardens. You'll have a great time."

"Why don't you come with us?" his mum said.

"She's working tomorrow," Warren said, answering for her since she'd just taken a mouthful of tiramisu.

"That's a shame," his mum said. "At the florist?"

Anna shook her head. "There's a craft fair. I'll probably be there for most of the day."

"What will you be selling?" his mum asked.

"Tomorrow it will be mostly Christmas wreaths and handmade Christmas cards. I also have handmade soaps and candles, which sell well."

"That sounds lovely." His mum smiled over her coffee.

"I'm looking forward to it. I have a table at this fair every year."

"Maybe we could call in." His mum looked questioningly at Warren, who searched for an excuse. He'd promised Anna it would only be dinner.

"We don't have anything planned in the morning, do we?" his mum pressed.

"I thought we'd go for a drive," Warren said. "There are some pretty little villages to explore."

"I'd really like to see the craft fair."

"You should," Anna said, giving Warren a reassuring look before addressing his mum again. "They have food and drink vans in the car park. You can get mulled wine and hot chocolate, and it's a gorgeous atmosphere. Not that I get to enjoy it much. I'll be stuck behind my table all day."

"Let's go," his mum said decisively.

"We can call in, I guess," Warren said. If Anna didn't mind, there was no reason not to.

"It's over at the community centre just outside Bibury. I can send you the details. It'd be good to see you there." Her eyes brightened. "I'll be able to send you off to get me a hot drink and snacks. It's usually so busy that I hardly have time to move out from behind my table."

His mum dabbed at her mouth with her napkin. "That's the plan for the morning, then."

Anna checked her watch as she pushed her empty dessert plate away. "Sorry, I'm going to have to head off. I have to be up early."

"I'll walk you home," Warren said, then offered to get the bill, only to be waved away by his dad.

He held Anna's coat out for her, and she glanced at him over her shoulder. "I'm fine getting home alone if you want to stay longer."

"I'll walk you." Not only because he didn't like the idea of her walking alone in the dark, but also because he had no desire to hang around with his parents. The evening had passed reasonably easily, and he was keen to get out while the going was good.

There was a round of goodnights, and his mum even hugged Anna before they left.

Outside, he broke into a smile.

After spending weeks dreading their visit, the first evening had gone surprisingly well.

Chapter Five

Anna breathed a sigh of relief the moment they left the restaurant. It had actually been much more pleasant than she'd expected, but that was the upside to having a mind that insisted on predicting worst-case scenarios. Most social situations weren't as bad as she expected them to be.

When the cold air hit her, she automatically tucked her arm into Warren's, and only felt a burst of self-consciousness at the action once she'd done it. While she always felt pretty comfortable around him, she didn't have the tactile relationship that Carla had with him. But she wasn't a tactile person in general.

After the evening schmoozing with Warren's parents, she felt very at ease with him. Also, judging by the look on his face and the way he clamped her arm against his side, he didn't seem to mind.

"What are you grinning about?" she asked, his smile infectious.

"You!" A loud chuckle erupted from him. "You were brilliant."

Warmth pooled in her stomach. "I told you parents always like me."

"They loved you."

"I see what you mean about them being a little uptight."

"A *little?*" he said mockingly.

"They're definitely more formal than my parents."

"You can say that again. You had them wrapped around your little finger, though. That was quite a performance."

"I kind of enjoyed myself," she said, realising it was true. It was oddly satisfying to try to get his parents' approval. Surprisingly easy too.

"I have to say you lie amazingly well."

She frowned and slowed her pace to look at him. "I didn't lie. I may have twisted the truth in places, but there were no actual lies."

He arched an eyebrow. "You have a degree in business and marketing?"

"Yes." She loved the surprise on his features.

"Where did you study?"

"Cardiff."

"I never knew that," he said, a faraway look in his eyes. "I don't think I did anyway."

"I'd already finished university and moved back here when you started working at the restaurant."

He gave a subtle shrug. "I suppose I didn't really get to know you until I'd been here for a while."

"No."

"So you're really going to open your own flower shop?"

She smiled. "I said it was an *idea,* not that it was a plan, so I wasn't lying. It was a partial truth."

"You also said you'd been looking for premises."

"I have been. Doesn't mean I'm going to do anything about it."

"Why not?"

"Because the price of property around here is insane."

"And you don't think a flower shop is financially viable?"

"I guess it could work, but the initial costs would be daunting."

"Lewis would give you the money," he said, as though it was an obvious solution.

"I don't want to take money from Lewis. He already bought me a flat."

"Take a loan from him, then. Also, since you own the flat outright, you must be able to save easily…"

"Yes." She paused, because if she really wanted to open her own shop, she could find a way. "I guess I'm just comfortable with things the way they are."

Warren scratched at his collarbone as they approached the door to her building. "You're not a fan of your boss, though, are you?"

"No." It wasn't exactly surprising that he knew that tidbit. She often complained about Martin. "Actually, he's fine. He's mostly just annoying with my hours."

"How so?"

She stopped outside her place and slipped her arm out of Warren's. "I'm forced to take time off whenever his daughter is home from university because she wants to work in the shop. So in December, and most of January, I won't be working there at all."

"That seems unfair."

"Yeah. But it also works out well because I'm free for the Christmas fairs. And I'm doing some wreath-making workshops this year."

"It'd be cool to have your own shop with space to offer workshops, too."

Anna narrowed her eyes. He'd landed directly on her favourite business idea. "It would," she agreed, then pondered whether to say more. "There's a building that's just become available next to the chemist. It would be perfect."

"You've looked at it?"

"No. Just saw the listing online."

"Are you going to view it?"

She shook her head. "If it were available to lease, I might have done, but it's for sale."

"Get Lewis to buy it for you," Warren said excitedly.

"Just like that," she said, amused by his enthusiasm.

"Not just like that." He looked at her seriously. "It's like you said, you've spent years gaining experience in how to run a flower shop. You could do it."

"I told you I'm comfortable as I am. Setting up a physical shop would be a lot of stress." That's the story she told herself, anyway. She was fairly sure that if she examined it too closely, she'd find it was mostly fear holding her back.

Warren took a step back and shoved his hands into his pockets. "Thanks a lot for coming tonight."

"You're welcome. Maybe I'll see you tomorrow if you bring your parents to the craft fair."

"I reckon I'll have to. I'm sure Mum has her heart set on it."

Anna glanced over her shoulder. "Do you want to come inside and wait for a taxi in the warmth?"

"No, that's okay, thanks." He checked his watch. "I think I'll wander over to the hotel and see if Lewis is around for a drink."

"I'd be surprised if he's still there."

"I'll check," he said, with an odd look on his face.

"Oh!" Anna realised exactly what he was up to. "You just want to check they didn't burn the kitchen down without you there to keep an eye on things."

Guilt flashed in his eyes. "I'm reasonably confident there won't have been any major incidents. I just want to check they cleaned properly, and that things are organised for tomorrow."

Bunching her shoulders against the cold, Anna shot him an amused look. "Maybe you should have a little more faith in your staff."

"Maybe if they've left the kitchen in an appropriate state, I will." He scowled jokingly, then leaned to kiss her cheek. "Thanks again for tonight."

He waited while she opened the front door, and she wished him goodnight before ascending the stairs to her flat, smiling as she went.

Getting out of her comfort zone now and again really wasn't so terrible.

Chapter Six

The community centre was busy from the moment the doors opened. Some sellers travelled long distances to show their art and crafts at the popular fair. It was a great place to shop for unique Christmas gifts, and the clientele it attracted were more than willing to part with their money. Anna rode a rush of adrenaline until lunchtime, when she felt her energy levels drop.

She'd heard nothing from Warren, and wondered if they'd decided to give it a miss. Or possibly that they'd come in and been put off by the crowded room.

Glancing across the room after selling her eighth Christmas wreath of the morning, she spotted Warren watching her from near the entrance. He smiled at her, then rolled his eyes as his mum said something in his ear.

Catching Anna's eye, Jen waved demurely and mouthed something which Anna had no hope of deciphering. She nodded regardless and turned to greet a couple of old ladies admiring her Christmas cards. They each bought half a dozen, and Anna had just given them their change when Warren arrived at her table.

"In case you didn't catch it, Mum said she's going to have a look around and she'll come and see you after."

He squeezed behind her table and parked himself on the chair amid her boxes of extra stock.

"You didn't want to look around?" Anna asked.

A smirk teased the corners of his mouth. "It's not really my thing."

"So you're just going to sit there and watch me?"

"Is that a problem?"

"No. I guess not." Aside from the fact that she felt incredibly self-conscious with him there.

"I'd like to point out that it's your fault I'm here," he said teasingly. "If you recall, you invited my parents."

"I didn't think it would entail you sitting there and watching me."

"Any excuse for a break from my parents. I told Mum I was going to help you out for a while."

"Good. I could use an assistant." She caught his eye and grinned.

"You know I'm not good at customer service. That's why your brother keeps me hidden away in the kitchen as much as possible."

"That makes sense," she said cheekily, before being drawn away from the conversation by an older gentleman asking about her Christmas cards. When he'd bought a packet of them, Anna turned to find Warren's gaze on her.

"Why are you looking at me?"

He shrugged. "Is it always so busy?"

"Not always *this* busy, but it's not unusual. People love craft fairs. Especially at this time of year, when they can get their Christmas goodies." She moved to find more Christmas cards in a box on the back wall and replenished the display rack on the table.

With a steady stream of customers, she focused on them and

told herself she was being paranoid and that Warren wasn't staring at her the whole time. Except that every time she glanced behind her, his eyes were on her.

He didn't even pretend not to be looking at her.

Finally, she turned all the way around and held his gaze until a grin stretched over his face.

"Why are you staring at me?"

"I wanted to see how long it would take for you to tell me to stop it." He tilted his head. "How come you just let people annoy you and not say anything?"

"I don't."

"You do. I see it all the time. Even when it's your siblings annoying you, you hardly ever say anything."

"That's not true. I tell Carla to stop annoying me all the time." She was fairly sure she did anyway, but, come to think of it, there was a possibility she only thought it rather than saying it.

The amusement in his eyes said he knew she was doubting herself. "Stop annoying me," she said pointedly and turned back to the room, but there was finally a lull in customers, so she had nothing to do.

"Stop it!" she said again, certain she could feel his eyes on her. "I've hardly eaten today, and I'm pretty hangry, so you really shouldn't annoy me."

"I don't know," he said mockingly. "I think it might be fun to see you snap."

"It wouldn't," she said without looking back at him.

When he spoke again, he was right beside her. His breath sweeping over her ear made her jump. "Want me to grab you some food?"

"Would you?" Usually she'd bring a sandwich and snacks but in her rush that morning she'd forgotten to pack anything and had been hoping things would slow down enough that she could ask one of her neighbours to watch her stall while she nipped out to the food vans. Having Warren go for her would be great.

"Any special requests?"

"Anything. Whichever queue is the shortest. I just want food."

"Oh, my goodness." Warren's mum appeared on the other side of the table. "Your wreaths are gorgeous."

"Thank you," Anna said, while Jen admired her collection.

"The cards are beautiful, too." She lifted one with a robin on a snowy postbox. "Did you draw this?"

"Yes," Anna said meekly.

"What a talent," she said, then twisted her lips. "I've seen them before." Her eyes flicked to Warren. "You always send us one of Anna's Christmas cards."

"Yeah," he said sheepishly. "I'm just going to find some food for Anna. She hasn't eaten."

Jen tutted and eyed Anna sympathetically. "Why don't I keep an eye on things here while you have a break? Get something to eat with Warren and have a look around."

"Umm..." Anna glanced around the room, which was quietening down. "Are you sure?"

"Of course." Jen looked at her husband as he ambled over. "We can play shop for a while, can't we?"

"I don't see why not."

Anna scanned her table. "Everything has price tags on," she said, then pointed at her money tin. "There's cash in here, and I have a card reader if anyone wants to pay by card... which you probably won't know how to use..." She frowned.

"We'll encourage people to pay with cash," Jen said. "Or ask them to come back in a little while."

"Thank you." Anna grabbed her coat and followed Warren out from behind the table. "If there's a problem, just call Warren."

"Will do," Jen said, and looked quite entertained by the idea of looking after things.

Wandering through the hall, Anna had a quick look at the other stalls, but her rumbling stomach led her out to the food trucks pretty quickly.

"That was nice of your parents," she said, once they had burgers and hot chocolates and stood by a high table at the edge of the car park.

"Yeah."

She covered her mouth with her hand while she chewed her burger. "Do you buy my Christmas cards?"

"Yeah." Warren took a large bite of his burger and spoke with an amused glint in his eyes. "They sell them at the reception desk at the hotel. Way more convenient than having to go shopping."

She rocked sideways to knock her shoulder against his.

"I'm only joking. I buy them because they're really good."

"Thank you," she said shyly. "How's it going with your parents?"

"Surprisingly painless so far."

"How often do you see them usually?"

"I usually take a week off in January and go down to London."

She eyed him sceptically, thinking of Lewis's claims that Warren hardly ever took time off, and how she was sure she'd never gone a week without seeing him around the hotel.

"You take a week off?"

He smiled. "Maybe four or five days."

"And you spend that time with your parents?"

He bobbed his head from side to side in an ambiguous gesture. "I don't stay with them or anything. But I usually have dinner with them once or twice. I see my sister, too."

"That's all you see of them throughout an entire year?" She couldn't quite hide her shock.

"I usually do a quick visit for my nephew's birthday, too."

"So you see them twice a year?"

"For the last few years, yeah."

Her curiosity was well and truly piqued. "You saw more of them before that?"

"Yeah." His voice rang with mocking. "For quite a long time, I had to live with them and see them every day."

"Obviously!" She glared at him but had the impression he was purposefully making jokes to avoid a serious conversation.

"I already told you," he said resignedly. "My family isn't like yours. Seeing each other once or twice a year works fine for us."

"Is there a reason they're visiting you now, when they've never been before?"

He was about to bite into his burger, but paused and looked thoughtful, as though he wasn't sure of the answer.

"I don't know. There's probably a reason. I can't imagine they just decided they wanted to see where I live." He shrugged. "That's what Mum claimed."

Certain that he wouldn't appreciate a sympathetic response, Anna kept her thoughts to herself and concentrated on the rest of her burger and the rich hot chocolate.

"Feel better for that?" Warren asked when she polished it off and wiped her lips with a napkin.

"Much," she said. "It was delicious. Thank you."

"You're welcome. Do you want to have a look around?"

She gave a small shake of the head. "I think I'll just get back. I'd feel guilty about leaving your parents for too long."

They were about to go back inside when Anna spotted a familiar face. Grabbing Warren's arm, she dodged behind him.

"Who are you hiding from?" he asked, looking around.

"Frannie. The one whose party we're going to. Well, it's not her party. Her parents own the hotel. She invited me to the party."

"And you're avoiding her, because?"

"Because if I see her now, I'll have to introduce you."

"She's going to meet me next weekend anyway, isn't she?"

"Yes, but I don't want to introduce you now. I'm not mentally prepared." She took his arm and set off back inside. "I don't even know what I'm going to tell them about you."

"I thought you were going to tell them I'm your boyfriend."

"I was," she muttered, stopping in the foyer of the community centre. "Now I think it might be a stupid idea. I thought it would be easier if Hayden thought I was seeing someone, but that means lying to my friends, which I'm not keen on."

"You could just say I'm a friend," he suggested. "But I'll flirt with you all night to annoy your ex."

"It's not even about annoying him. I just don't want everyone to see me as an object of pity."

He lifted an eyebrow as his gaze bored into her. "I really can't imagine that."

"They think I can't move on from Hayden."

"You're not over him?" he asked, his voice tinged with surprise.

"I am," she said, but didn't sound convincing even to her own ears. "I just didn't meet anyone else like he did, so I guess they think I'm not really over it."

"Did you already tell your friends that you're bringing someone?"

"Yes. I messaged Frannie last night. But I was vague about our relationship." She glanced at the door, keeping an eye out for Frannie. "Let's get back to your parents. I can figure out a plan for the party later."

The crowd had thinned in the large hall, but it still took them a few minutes to reach her table at the back of the room. Warren's dad was deep in conversation with the woman selling knitted baby clothes on the next table, while his mum straightened out the wreaths.

"There you are! I sold a wreath. I'm very proud of myself.

Not that I should be. They're so pretty they practically sell themselves."

"Thanks so much," Anna said. "I really appreciate it."

"Did you get something to eat?" Jen asked.

"Yes. That should keep me going for the rest of the afternoon." Anna was about to slip around the table when movement in her peripheral vision caught her attention.

"Hi!" Frannie said, waving enthusiastically as she approached. "I've been looking for you." She kissed Anna's cheek and gave her a quick squeeze. When her eyes went to Warren, Anna's cheeks heated.

"Sorry," Frannie said. "I'll come back later when you don't have customers."

As much as Anna wanted to let her go, that would make things pretty weird when Frannie met Warren next weekend.

"Actually, this is Warren." She waved her hand towards him in a weird flourish.

Frannie sucked in a gasp. "The mystery man!" An approving smile flittered onto her lips as she looked Warren over. "It's so great that you can come to the party." She gave a small shake of the head and extended her hand. "Sorry, I'm Frannie. Lovely to meet you."

"I'm looking forward to the party," Warren said with a genuine smile.

"It's going to be great." She put a hand on Anna's arm. "I look forward to the Christmas ball all year, don't I? It's always a fantastic atmosphere." Her gaze shot back to Warren. "Anna didn't mention if you'd be staying the night?"

Internally, Anna grimaced. She hadn't mentioned to Warren that it was an overnight event – or even considered that. Not that she needed him to stay; just having him there for the party would be enough.

"Unfortunately, I have to work on Sunday morning, so I'll

probably have to drive back after the party." He gave Anna a look, apparently unsure whether he was saying the right thing.

"You're still staying, though, Anna? You can't miss out on Sunday brunch." She beamed at Warren. "Most people will be nursing hangovers. It's quite entertaining."

Anna nodded. "I'll stay. I was going to ask Kylie for a lift home on Sunday." She'd be going her way anyway, so she couldn't imagine it being a problem.

"It's a shame you have to work," Frannie said to Warren. "What is it you do?"

"I'm a chef," he said, looking oddly nervous as his eyes darted to his mum.

"And you have to work on Sunday morning?" Frannie asked.

"Breakfast at the hotel restaurant," he explained.

"Oh, right, of course. That makes sense."

"He was lucky to get Saturday evening off," Anna put in. "His working hours are fairly antisocial." An excuse that would come in handy if she was going to keep up the pretence of their relationship. No doubt any invitations from her friends would include him in the future.

Jen leaned across the table behind them, adjusting a wreath on its stand and drawing attention to herself, leaving Anna no choice but to introduce them.

They exchanged polite conversation for a few minutes, while Anna caught Warren's eye and tried to convey her panic about the situation. In return, he only looked amused.

Eventually, Frannie spotted someone she knew across the room and excused herself to speak to them.

"We should get going," Warren said to his mum. "It's a bit of a drive to Blenheim, and the tickets have specific time slots."

She retrieved her coat from the chair behind her and waved at Warren's dad, who'd drifted to look at the other tables nearby.

"Thanks so much for your help," Anna said again.

"You're welcome." Jen came around the table and hugged her lightly. "It's been really lovely."

Anna smiled at Warren's dad and told them to enjoy the rest of their visit.

"I'll speak to you during the week," Warren said, as his parents drifted away. "To get the details for next weekend."

"Yeah." Anna said, but was distracted by Frannie, who openly watched them from across the room. "She's looking at us," she muttered, stepping closer to Warren.

"Who is?"

"Frannie."

"Is that a problem?"

"I'm fairly sure she already thinks you're my boyfriend," she whispered, trying to get her story straight in her own head. "It's probably for the best. If I want Hayden to think you're my boyfriend, my friends will need to think so, too."

"I already thought that was your plan," he said with a shrug.

"Yes. But it means you need to act like my boyfriend. To make it believable."

"Am I supposed to conjure flowers or something?" he asked mockingly.

"No!" Stepping closer, she put a hand on his arm and lifted onto her toes to press her lips against his.

It was only a fleeting kiss, and one which might have looked more convincing if he hadn't looked so surprised. Hopefully, Frannie wouldn't notice that detail from a distance.

"What was that?" Warren asked quietly.

"I kissed you. So she'll think you're my boyfriend."

"Hmm." He lowered his face to hers. "Just out of interest, did my parents also witness your public display of affection."

Her eyes went over his shoulder to where his parents were waiting. His mum caught Anna's eye and smiled delightedly.

"Yeah." She pressed her lips together. "I think they probably did, but it was only a peck. It could have been a friendship thing."

"Not sure they're going to buy that."

"It doesn't really matter anyway, does it?"

"I guess not." His eyes flashed with amusement. "I'll talk to you soon."

Anna watched him walk out, her heart thundering with the realisation that she'd just kissed him. It hadn't exactly been earth shattering, but it was the first time in a long time since she'd kissed a guy. She supposed if she was intent on passing him off as her boyfriend, she'd probably be kissing him again.

It wasn't a terrible prospect.

"Anna!" Frannie appeared, rushing towards her. "He's gorgeous!"

All Anna could manage was a murmur of agreement.

"I wasn't sure from your messages if you were dating or if you were bringing a friend."

"It's early days," she said, hating the lie.

"You've already met his parents," she pointed out. "So not that early. How come you didn't mention him before?"

"I suppose I didn't want to jinx it."

Frannie clutched her arm and squeezed. "I'm so happy for you. He seems lovely."

"He is."

"Oh, my goodness!" Frannie sucked in a breath. "Hayden is going to flip out when he sees you at the party with Warren."

The thought of it made Anna feel much more relaxed about lying to her friends. Not that she wanted to make Hayden jealous. She didn't even think that was possible.

It would just be nice if he didn't look so smug when he introduced Anna to his latest fling.

Chapter Seven

They made it almost the entire way to the palace before Warren's mum brought up the inevitable.

"How long did you say you've known Anna?" she asked from the back seat, her tone almost convincingly casual.

"For as long as I've lived here, but I only got to know her properly over the past couple of years."

For his first couple of years in Chipping Campden, he'd been certain he wouldn't stay long. He'd kept his head down and focused on his job. With hindsight, it should have been obvious that he and Lewis would end up becoming friends, given how much time they both spent at the hotel.

He might also have guessed that being friends with Lewis would mean the entire Carrington family would adopt him as a friend by proxy, but he'd never realised some families operated like theirs.

"She's lovely," his mum said, clearly dying to say more. "I'm glad we got to meet her."

In the passenger seat, his dad nodded. "You've done well for yourself there. I admire her determination. It seems she has a solid plan for growing her business. Hopefully, some of that might rub off on you."

Warren's grip on the steering wheel tightened.

"Dennis," his mum hissed, a warning note in her voice.

"What?" his dad grumbled. "Anyone with an ounce of business sense knows that working for someone else is a mug's game. He may be too proud to admit it, but Warren knows it too."

"I like my job," Warren said through gritted teeth. "I don't want to run my own business."

"You're lining someone else's pocket when you could fill your own."

Warren dragged in a breath, thinking about Carla's anger management strategies. "Not every decision in life should be decided by money."

"You can also set your own hours. That way, you wouldn't have to miss out on things like a night away with your girlfriend."

It took Warren a second to figure that he was referring to the Christmas party with Anna. He hadn't even registered that his dad had been listening to that conversation.

A voice in his head told him to bite his tongue and not let his dad get to him, but he couldn't keep his thoughts to himself.

"So you having your own business meant that you could organise your own schedule exactly as you wanted it?" he asked. "Am I supposed to assume that you just didn't want to see your children when they were growing up?"

"We had plenty of family time," his dad said, in a tone that suggested he believed it.

"Selena and I were practically raised by hired help," Warren argued. Which was actually fine. The house had always been more relaxed when his parents weren't around, but it was ridiculous for his dad to claim that being self-employed offered so much freedom when his life proved the exact opposite.

"Your dad and I might have spent a lot of time building up

the business when you were younger," his mum said. "But it paid off in the long run."

"We built something really special for you and your sister," his dad said, his voice laced with pride.

"It's a shame it's not something I want," Warren growled. No amount of breathing exercises would stave off the anger that pulsed through his veins.

His dad rubbed his forehead. "I see your stubborn streak hasn't diminished at all."

"Can we please not argue?" In the rearview mirror, Warren caught his mum's look of defeat. "He made his choices. Let's just leave it at that."

Again, Warren bit his tongue. It had been years since he'd decided not to go into the family business, and he'd never regretted that decision for a moment.

What he regretted was agreeing to his parents' visit. And especially the tiny part of him that had stupidly hoped they might finally have accepted his choices.

"Look at that!" His mum pointed to the palace, which loomed ahead.

Awash with golden Christmas lights, the imposing building was a striking sight, which thankfully kept his parents in a stunned silence while he followed the traffic into the car park and found a spot.

As he'd hoped, the following conversations revolved around the sights and sounds in the palace. This year, the elegant rooms had been elaborately decorated with a Sleeping Beauty theme, and it even had the effect of relaxing Warren a little. The light trail in the grounds was perfectly pleasant too, and he enjoyed watching his mum's enthusiasm.

They strolled around the Christmas market in the courtyard, and Warren cast a glance at the Santa's grotto. Nicholas Carrington would be posing as Santa again, and in other circumstances, he'd nip in and say a quick hello. He smiled, thinking of how Nicholas would chastise him if he found out Warren had been nearby and hadn't called in. He made a mental note to drop it into conversation the next time he saw him, specifically so he'd get a lecture.

"You look happy," his mum said, her cheeks rosy from the two mugs of mulled wine she'd drunk.

"Do I?" he asked, amused by his mum clutching his arm. She was only ever tactile when she had alcohol in her.

"Thinking about your girlfriend?" she asked quietly. Subtlety wasn't her strong suit after a drink, and she'd obviously been dying to confirm his relationship status all day.

He should probably put her straight on the matter, but he had a mental vision of her chatting to her friends at her Pilates class and filling them in on her visit. He supposed it wouldn't hurt to give her the pleasure of being able to brag that her son had a lovely girlfriend.

He could imagine it clearly. *Still doing that terrible job, but at least he's got a nice girlfriend.*

"Maybe," he finally replied, to avoid outright lying.

She squeezed his arm, eyes dancing with excitement.

"We should go," he said. "You need food to soak up some of that alcohol."

"Stick in the mud!" she said affectionately. "Work hard, play hard. You know, that's always been my philosophy."

He waved his dad over, and they wandered back to the car. The alcohol seemed to have subdued them, and it was a pleasantly quiet drive back to their hotel.

They were amiable enough over dinner at their hotel as well, but mostly because Warren let his dad rattle on about business as though they hadn't had almost the same conversation the previous evening.

At least the food was delicious. Warren had heard great

things about the chef, and the food lived up to the hype. His mind wandered once or twice to his own kitchen, and he fought the urge to message and check that everything was going okay. Anna might have been right that he should have more faith in his staff.

"This has been lovely," his mum said, reaching over to squeeze Warren's hand and clueing him into the fact that his dad had finally stopped droning on. "I wish we could see more of you."

"It's been nice," he said. "I'll try to visit in the new year."

"Yes. Your sister would love to see you."

Warren wasn't convinced that was true. He wouldn't mind seeing his nephew, though. His sister's four-year-old was the one person who made his visits bearable.

"We're also going to the house in Bath before Christmas. Selena will be there with little Josh. He's at a lovely age. You should join us."

"Is Phil going?" he asked, not sure of the last time he'd seen his brother-in-law.

"No." His dad lifted his napkin from his lap and scrunched it on the table in front of him. "I need someone I trust to keep an eye on the business."

"Of course," Warren said.

It was a dig, and not a subtle one, but he refused to rise to it. He only wished his dad would be content with having his daughter and his son-in-law in the family business and get over the fact that Warren had no interest in it.

With dinner winding down, he reminded himself that the visit was almost over and he'd got through it with minimal drama.

"You could bring Anna with you," his mum said, drawing his attention.

"Where to?" he asked, entirely lost.

"Bath. I'm sure Selena will be keen to meet her."

"December is busy with work," he said.

"You could just come for a day or two," his mum suggested. "It'd be a nice relaxing break for you both."

It wouldn't, and it amazed him that his mum lived in a fantasy world where she genuinely believed it could be relaxing for him to spend time with them.

"I'll send you the dates," she said, patting his hand. "Chat it through with Anna and let me know."

"I won't be able to take time off work." He didn't want her getting it into her head that this was a possibility.

"We'll see." Judging by her smile, she wouldn't be deterred on the matter, and it felt easier to let it go. "I'm afraid I'm going to have to leave you and get my beauty sleep," she said, then yawned in what seemed to be a deliberate gesture.

"I should get going anyway," he said, and felt a pang of relief that the ordeal was almost over.

"Stay and have a drink with your dad. He'd like that. Wouldn't you, Dennis?"

"Let's move to the lounge," his dad said, standing.

"I actually need to go," Warren protested. "I have an early start tomorrow."

"It's only nine." His dad clapped him on the back. "I want to have a drink with my son. Come on."

Since arguing felt futile, he kissed his mum goodbye and promised he'd see her soon, then followed his dad into the lounge area.

"What's your preference for whisky?" he asked, sinking into a leather wingback by the fire.

"I don't drink whisky," Warren told him wearily.

"Don't be daft. I want to drink a whisky with my son." He waved the waiter over and ordered two glasses of Glenfiddich.

Warren didn't bother arguing further. If his dad wanted to throw money away, so be it. Not that the whisky would go to waste. His dad would polish them both off, despite having consumed the best part of a bottle of wine with dinner.

The waiter returned, and Warren dutifully clinked his glass against his dad's before setting it down.

"I have a proposition for you," his dad said without preamble.

Warren felt a headache coming on and rubbed his temple. "If it involves me coming to work for you, I'll stop you now to save you from wasting your breath."

His dad held a hand up. "Let's not get ahead of ourselves. Be sensible. At least listen to what I'm offering."

"There's nothing you could offer that would interest me," he said, smiling at the absurdity of the conversation. "As impossible as it is for you to understand, I like my life. I enjoy my job."

"You enjoy making a point," his dad said, shaking his head. "Enough is enough, though."

"I'm not trying to make a point." He closed his eyes. "I was never trying to make a point. I just wanted to do something else."

"There's no shame in admitting you were wrong," his dad said as though Warren hadn't spoken.

"Wow," Warren said, stretching his neck and fighting the urge to walk out. "Why are you here, Dad?"

"How do you mean?"

"I mean, why did you come to visit me? Was it just so you could try to talk some sense into me?"

He took a measured sip of his drink. "Your mother thinks it's time we sorted things out. I agree with her, of course. Hence the olive branch."

Warren blinked slowly. "I'm sorry – was there an olive branch?"

"I'm offering for you to come back to the family business. Even after everything that's happened."

"How big of you," Warren said, his words heavy with sarcasm.

"Come on now. Your mum has her heart set on us making amends. Do the right thing. For her sake, if nothing else."

For a moment, all Warren could do was stare at his dad. Then he exhaled a long breath and stood up.

"Goodbye, Dad," he said as he walked away.

Chapter Eight

Following the craft fair at the community centre, Anna's day ended with her being physically tired but mentally alert. She tried calling her sister, thinking a natter with Carla would help, but she got no answer.

Going to bed would no doubt entail staring at the ceiling for hours on end, and she couldn't face that. Instead, she grabbed her coat and headed for the hotel. It would be a first if she didn't find someone there to chat to. She could prop up the bar for an hour and then go to bed when there was a better chance that she might actually sleep.

On the front desk, she was greeted by Tom, the general manager. As a fairly recent addition to the team, he was the member of staff Anna knew the least.

"Hello," he said in an overly cheerful tone, which suggested he didn't recognise her and assumed she was a guest.

"Hi," she replied. "I take it my brother isn't here?"

"Oh." Recognition hit his features. "No, he isn't."

"I don't suppose Carla's here?"

"I haven't seen her today."

"Ivy?" she asked hopefully.

He nodded. "Working on the bar."

"Perfect. Thanks." She walked through the lounge and into the restaurant, where a few tables were occupied. "I'm glad you're here," she said, sliding onto a bar stool opposite Ivy. "I had a weird day and I can't get hold of Carla."

Ivy pushed a wayward strand of red hair behind her ear. "I love being a backup sister."

"Sorry!" Anna grimaced. "That was rude. I didn't even say hi or ask how you are."

"I was being genuine," Ivy said brightly. "I do like being your backup sister. Also, I'm bored to tears. Please tell me about your weird day." She turned to get a bottle of wine from the fridge and raised a questioning eyebrow before pouring Anna a glass.

"I met Warren's parents," she said eventually, twirling the glass on the mat.

"Really?" Ivy's eyes lit up. "What are they like?"

"Posh."

"No way!"

"They are. I swear. His mum's okay. His dad's not particularly likeable. They're nothing like Warren."

"Where did you meet them? I knew they were visiting this weekend, but I got the impression we wouldn't get to meet them."

"I went for dinner with them," Anna said, then tilted her head. "There's a chance they think I'm Warren's girlfriend."

"What?" Ivy's eyes looked as though they might pop out of her head. "Keep talking, please!"

"It's a long story," she said, then did her best to explain as succinctly as possible.

"So you're pretending to be a couple," Ivy stated ten minutes later, her eyes sparkling with delight. "And you're going to a Christmas ball together. I feel as though I know where this is heading. Except–" She cut herself off and shook her head.

"What?" Anna asked.

"Nothing. I just can't really imagine you and Warren together."

"We're not together. It's all pretend."

"Until it's not," Ivy said. "Is Carla okay with you pretending to date Warren?"

"Why wouldn't she be?"

"Because she flirts with him like crazy. I wondered if she has a thing for him."

Anna twisted her lips. "I've wondered the same, but she suggested I take Warren to the party."

"She must be fine with it, then." Ivy turned her head as the door behind her burst open and Warren stalked in. "Speak of the devil," she muttered under her breath before saying hello to him.

He didn't seem to register Ivy's greeting as his gaze swept over the dining room. Anna smiled, waiting for him to catch her eye, but he didn't look in her direction.

"What's wrong with you?" Ivy asked.

"Nothing." He frowned deeply. "Why?"

"Because you're not supposed to be working. Why are you here?"

His eyebrows knitted together. "Thought I'd see what kind of mess they're making of things in the kitchen."

"Everything's fine," Ivy told him, but he was already striding to the kitchen. She rolled her eyes. "Just when I thought it was going to be a boring, uneventful shift."

The kitchen door had only just swung shut behind Warren when a crash of broken crockery erupted from the kitchen.

"That's not good," Ivy mumbled and rushed away.

Chapter Nine

Alone at the bar, Anna was on high alert. She didn't have to strain much to catch the raised voices. The atmosphere in the dining room changed in an instant, and a quick glance told her that most of the diners had paused their conversations to listen to the commotion in the kitchen.

Automatically, she hopped off the stool and crossed the room.

If she thought the atmosphere in the dining room was tense, it was nothing compared to the kitchen.

"It doesn't matter," Ivy whisper-shouted at Warren, while Liam and a junior chef looked terrified beside them. On the other side of the room, a young waitress picked up pieces of what looked to be a broken plate.

"What's going on?" Anna asked quietly.

"Warren is causing chaos," Ivy replied. "That's what's going on."

"It's fudge cake with hot chocolate sauce," Warren shouted. "How could you forget the sauce? It's not that difficult. What else have they screwed up when I wasn't here?"

"Everything was fine," Ivy replied.

"Well, it's not fine now. They're ruining people's desserts." He swung around to the two guys, who both took a subtle step back. "You can get out of the kitchen, the pair of you!" He flicked his hand. "Go home."

Ivy stepped in front of him. "You can't just send them home."

"I can," he growled at her. "You can leave as well. Apparently, I have desserts to make." He turned on the two chefs who hadn't budged. "I said *go home.*"

"Wait!" Anna said, raising a hand and gesturing for Liam and his colleague to stop. "You're not going anywhere. Please make the desserts. Don't forget the chocolate sauce." She turned to Warren. "*You* need to get out of the kitchen."

He glared at her. "*Excuse me?*"

"You can't be in the kitchen when you're in this mood." She pointed to the back door. "Get out. Now."

He opened his mouth, but she cut him off.

"Please, Warren. Just go."

"She's right," Ivy said, touching his arm.

He shrugged her off and strode to the back door, throwing it open so hard that it bounced back on the hinges.

"You take care of the kitchen," Anna whispered to Ivy. "I'll deal with him."

"Sounds like a good deal to me."

Quietly, Anna closed the back door behind her and descended the handful of steps to the car park where Warren was pacing.

"They're a bunch of idiots," he said, jabbing a finger towards the kitchen. "I can't even leave them alone for one evening without them making a mess of things."

"They were doing fine," she said, eyes following him as he walked back and forth.

His whole body radiated anger. "He only had to put two things on the plate! How could he forget one of them?"

Anna let the silence linger for a moment. "Did you throw a plate?"

"No. She dropped it."

Things weren't as bad as they could've been then. "What's going on?" she asked.

"He messed up the order."

"I know that, but I'm fairly sure it's not actually the chocolate sauce you're upset about. You were furious before you even went into the kitchen."

He clenched and unclenched his hands. "I feel like punching something."

"There's a wall over there," she said, pointing.

Finally, he stopped pacing and stared at her. "You think I should punch the wall?"

"God, no." She shook her head. "That would hurt. I was thinking you could lie down and put your legs up the wall. According to Carla, it will stop you from wanting to punch things. Or people. Whatever it is, you feel like punching."

His laughter wasn't exactly the heartfelt kind, but he seemed to relax a little.

"What's going on?" Anna asked again.

He pushed his palms into his temples before dragging his hands through his hair. "My dad asked me to go and work for him."

"I assume you said no."

"Of course I said no."

"Then why are you so angry?"

He looked her right in the eyes, and she could practically see the moment the anger left him. His voice was so quiet it was almost a whisper. "I'm just so sick of being a disappointment. It's exhausting."

Her heart squeezed, and the lump in her throat was almost painful.

"I'm sorry," she whispered.

He threw his hands up, and the vulnerability was gone in an instant. "It doesn't even matter. They'll be gone in the morning. I won't have to see them again for a while."

Anna wished she had something helpful to say, but the thought of not having her parents' support was so foreign she could barely fathom it.

"I need to get back in there," Warren said, gesturing to the kitchen.

"No way." She stepped into his path when he moved to go around her. "You're not going back in there. They'll manage fine without you. Just go home."

His eyes were fixed on the back door. "It's the only place I feel useful."

"You won't be useful in there now. You're just going to upset people."

His gaze stayed on the kitchen door, but eventually he blew out a defeated breath. "Yeah. Okay. I'll go home."

"Are you driving?" she asked, looking around for his car.

"Yeah. My car's at the front. Do you want a lift?"

"Please," she said, deciding it was a good time to call it a night. "I'll grab my coat and meet you at the front."

As she pushed the door and walked into the kitchen, all eyes whipped to her.

"He's gone home," she said as she walked through. She caught Liam's eye and grimaced. "He said to apologise to you all for shouting... and to thank you for doing such a great job while he's not here."

"Sure he did," Liam said, but gave her an appreciative smile all the same.

Ivy had gone back behind the bar and moved over to Anna when she scooped up her coat.

"What just happened?" she asked, narrowing her eyes.

"He's in a bad mood. But he's gone now."

"That's not what I meant."

"What then?"

"You told him to get out of the kitchen," Ivy stated.

"Yeah, so?"

She raised an eyebrow. "You told him to get out, and he left."

"And?" Anna said, aware that Warren was waiting for her.

"Nobody bosses Warren around in the kitchen. And anyone who tries gets booted out of the kitchen themselves."

With no answer to that, Anna shrugged.

"Are you going?" Ivy asked.

"Yeah."

"Are you going with Warren?"

"He's driving me home," Anna said impatiently.

"Okay." Ivy held her hands up in a defensive gesture.

"It's not what you think. We're just friends."

Ivy nodded. "Is he okay?"

"I think he had an argument with his dad. I'm sure he'll be fine once he cools off."

"I'll talk to you soon," Ivy said, moving along the bar to the customer, who was trying to get her attention.

Anna tugged her coat on as she walked through the hotel and put her hat on as she stepped out into the cold.

Warren pulled the car away as soon as she got in, and neither of them spoke until they were outside her place.

"Are you okay?" she asked, unclipping her seatbelt.

"Yeah." He leaned onto the steering wheel. "Sorry about before."

"I'm not sure it's me you owe an apology to."

"They're used to me," he said absently.

"Doesn't mean it's okay."

His gaze slid to her, and he arched a lone eyebrow.

"You can probably hold off on feeling bad about that for this evening," she said, wincing.

A flicker of amusement crossed his features. "Thanks for dragging me out of there."

"What are fake girlfriends for?" She smiled softly. "Frannie completely believed you're my boyfriend, by the way."

"My parents also think you're my girlfriend. You even got invited on a family holiday."

Her eyes widened. "Are you serious?"

"Yeah, but don't worry, it's not happening. They really like you, though."

"I hope that won't end up being awkward for you. Sorry for kissing you in front of them."

"I don't see why it will be awkward. It's not as though I see much of them."

"Will you see them tomorrow before they leave?"

He shook his head. "No. They'll head off straight after breakfast and I'll be back at work, thank goodness."

"Maybe you should ask them to call in at the hotel – clear the air if you won't see them for a while."

"No." He looked at her fondly. "We're not that kind of family. If we argue, nobody cares about clearing the air. We ignore each other, and the next time we see each other, we pretend it never happened."

"That doesn't sound like a great system."

"It works for us." He shifted in his seat. "What's the plan for the party next weekend?"

"Are you sure you want to come?"

"I didn't think I had a choice."

"You have a choice." After being worried that he might back out, she was wondering if it was really a good idea to have him there. "I won't hold you to it if you don't want to come."

"Don't you want me to come?"

"I do. But I also feel bad about lying to my friends."

"I feel as though I should come, otherwise I will be forever in your debt."

"Why?" she asked, with a bemused grin.

"Because you helped me out with my parents."

"I didn't really do anything."

He frowned. "Am I coming on Saturday or not?"

Closing her eyes, she had an image of Hayden flirting with his latest girlfriend and felt slightly nauseous. "Yes, please. Is it okay if you pick me up? If you drive there, you can drive back whenever you feel like it. I'll stay the night and come home on Sunday."

"Fine by me. Just let me know what time I should pick you up."

"I'll message you." She smiled before exiting the car.

With a busy week ahead, she hoped to avoid too much overthinking about the party.

And with any luck, with Warren there, she might even enjoy herself.

Chapter Ten

Not so long ago, Warren couldn't go a day without seeing Lewis around the hotel, but with the new general manager, Lewis spent far more time away from the place. Apparently, having his girlfriend living with him made home a more appealing place to spend his time.

It was Wednesday before Warren saw him. He'd been in the office all morning, so Warren took him a plate of food once the restaurant quietened down after lunch.

"Thanks," Lewis said, looking up from the computer. "I lost track of time."

"You're welcome," Warren said, sliding the plate onto the desk and setting cutlery beside it. "How's everything?"

"Good. Just catching up on admin." He set the keyboard aside and moved the plate in front of him. "How are things with you?"

"Fine." He flopped onto the couch.

"How was it with your parents?"

"I survived."

"I heard you took Anna out for dinner with them."

"Yeah. I was going to talk to you about that. It was her idea.

In return, I'm supposed to pretend to be her boyfriend at that Christmas party." He'd mentioned it to Lewis in passing to check it was okay for him to have the night off, but they hadn't talked about it beyond that.

"I still can't believe she got you to agree to that. It's good you're going though," he said, popping a chip into his mouth.

"Is it?" Warren was secretly looking forward to it, but had been a little apprehensive about Lewis's thoughts on him posing as his sister's boyfriend.

"The breakup with Hayden hit her pretty hard, and at one point I was worried she might cut off all of her friends to avoid seeing him."

"What's he like?" Warren asked, not sure what Anna's type would be.

Lewis seemed to mull it over. "I always liked him. He's one of those people who can chat to anyone. Easy to get on with. I don't know exactly what happened when they broke up. Anna didn't talk about it much, but she was devastated. I always suspected he might have been seeing someone else, but I don't know for sure."

Warren disliked the guy already. "So you're cool with me pretending to be her boyfriend?"

"Yes." Lewis chuckled. "Why wouldn't I be?"

"I don't know."

A smile pulled at Lewis's lips. "There's a rumour going around this place, by the way..."

"What now?" Warren said, rolling his eyes.

"I heard you came storming into the kitchen on Saturday night and caused chaos. And Anna marched you out of there and sent you home."

Warren winced. "There may be a grain of truth in that somewhere."

"All true then?" Lewis asked.

"Yep."

"What happened? You weren't even supposed to work on Saturday."

"I got into an argument with my dad and took it out on Liam and Sam."

Lewis sucked in a breath and had that look he got when he was trying to find a tactful way of making a point.

Warren moved from the couch to sit in the chair opposite Lewis. "Just say it."

"What?" Lewis asked.

"Whatever you want to say as my boss, but don't feel comfortable saying because we're friends. I'm now just your employee."

Lewis only hesitated for a moment. "You know I think you're a brilliant chef. The food coming out of that kitchen is top-notch... but the kitchen could be run better."

Resisting the urge to defend himself, Warren gave a curt nod of acknowledgement.

"You need to trust the rest of the staff to manage the kitchen when you're not there. If they can't, it's a problem. I also don't think them being terrified of you makes them better at their jobs..."

Warren opened his mouth to cut in, but closed it again quickly.

"They can respect you without being scared of you."

Again, Warren nodded while he fought the urge to fidget. It felt like getting into trouble at school. He swallowed hard. "My parents' visit has stressed me out..."

"I realise that," Lewis said. "But your personal life shouldn't impact the kitchen. Especially considering you weren't even supposed to be at work on Saturday. And your attitude in the kitchen isn't exactly a new thing."

"Yeah," Warren agreed weakly. He really couldn't argue that point – he was only thankful Anna had been around to de-escalate things on Saturday.

"It'd be good if the atmosphere in the kitchen was more harmonious," Lewis added. "I think you've got a good team in there. You should work on bringing the best out of them instead of crushing their spirits."

Warren tapped on the arm of the chair. "I'll work on it," he said quietly.

"Thanks." Lewis let out a heavy breath. "I hate being the boss sometimes."

"It's fine," Warren said, but the atmosphere was far too tense for him to hang around. "I should get back to work." He stood and headed for the door.

"Thanks for lunch," Lewis said.

Warren managed a tight smile, but felt as though he only breathed properly again once he'd closed the office door behind him.

The mental chatter was fairly incessant as he walked back to the kitchen. He didn't make eye contact with anyone, but went straight to the back door and stepped outside into the freezing air. Standing at the top of the steps, he leaned on the rail and released a long exhale, which fogged in front of his face.

Pulling out his phone, he opened his preferred review website and found the list of reviews for the restaurant. He scrolled through the latest ones with his jaw tight. He only relaxed when he saw they were all positive. Lots of them referred to the food as exceptional or excellent.

Previously, the food and the reviews were all Lewis seemed to care about as far as the kitchen was concerned, so Warren wasn't sure what had provoked Lewis's lecture on the way the kitchen was run. The fact that he probably had a point didn't make it easier to swallow.

He turned when the door opened behind him.

"Sorry," Liam said. "I have a question about the new specials... if you have a minute."

The sous chef looked nervous, and for once, that didn't sit

well with Warren. "Sure," he said, and gestured for him to go back into the kitchen. "Just give me a minute."

"Sorry," Liam said again and disappeared back inside.

Warren spent a few minutes staring out across the frosty car park before he pulled himself together and went back inside. Calmly, he got everyone together and talked them through the specials again, then set Liam and Tom to work on the evening prep while he sat at the counter at the back with his laptop and went through the food order for the weekend.

As usual on a Wednesday, they weren't overly busy at dinner-time, but had a steady stream of guests. He'd just sent out desserts for a table of four when Lewis wandered in.

"Hey," Warren said. "I thought you'd left ages ago."

"No. I'll be in London for the next couple of days with Erin, so I wanted to make sure I was on top of everything here."

"It's Erin's work Christmas party, is it?" Warren remembered him mentioning it, but hadn't registered when it was happening.

"Yeah." Lewis glanced awkwardly around the kitchen. "We're good, right?" he asked quietly. "I feel weird about before."

"We're good," Warren said.

Lewis nodded nervously. "Great, because I would like to switch fully back into friend mode..."

Warren chuckled, assuming he was so uncomfortable because he wanted to ask a favour. "What is it?"

"Nothing really, just that Carla has been messaging me all afternoon. She says Anna's stressed about seeing Hayden at the weekend."

Warren nodded. "I'll look out for her."

"Yeah?"

"Of course I will. By the way, I heard it being referred to as a ball. I take it I shouldn't go in jeans?"

"It'll be fancy. Trousers and a shirt, at least. Possibly a tie and jacket too."

"Good to know."

Lewis smiled widely. "Have fun at the weekend. Thanks again for looking out for Anna."

"No worries." After what he'd heard about Anna's ex-boyfriend, he was actually looking forward to being her date for the evening.

Chapter Eleven

Warren didn't ring the bell on Friday, just messaged Anna to say he was outside. As she put her coat on, she glanced around, sure she'd forgotten something. She was about to open her bag to check when the impatient blare of a car horn stopped her. Considering how many times she'd been through her bag, she probably hadn't forgotten anything. Nothing vital anyway. She was just stalling.

Warren's car blocked one lane, and his hazard lights flashed, illuminating the layer of frost that covered the road.

Anna opened the back door and set her case on the seat before getting into the passenger seat.

"Did you really need to honk the horn? Couldn't you just try being patient?"

His eyes sparkled. "I'm blocking the road – and I'm not blessed with patience. Besides, I knew it would annoy you, so I couldn't resist."

"Fairly sure it annoyed my neighbours too," she told him.

He glanced into the back. "I thought you were only going for one night. Also, am I appropriately dressed?"

She looked him over, realising she hadn't mentioned a dress code, but happy to see the suit trousers and bright white shirt.

"I've got a tie and jacket if it's really fancy..."

"No, I think you're fine in the shirt."

"So, are you staying for a week, or what?"

She beamed. "I might have packed too much, but I couldn't decide which dress to wear." The one she really wanted to wear was quite revealing and a little out of her comfort zone, so she might chicken out and opt for the more demure one instead.

"How are you going to get home tomorrow?"

"I'll get a lift back with my friend Kylie."

He nodded and pulled the car away, instructing her to put the address into the navigation system.

"Anything I need to know about your friends?" he asked when they were well on the way.

"Not really," she mused. "We all went to school together. At secondary school, the six of us were really close. We did everything together. There's Frannie, whose party it is, or her parents' party, really. Frannie's together with Jake. Then there's my ex, Hayden, and Dev and Kylie. Kylie's boyfriend will probably be at the party, too. He's lovely."

"So it's only Hayden who we hate?"

She rolled her eyes. "I don't hate him. I hate that he always brings his latest girlfriend anytime we all get together, and I hate everyone giving me pitying looks as though I must be insane with jealousy."

"So you're bringing me along to make him jealous?"

"No. I just didn't want to deal with the pitying looks." That was her primary reason for bringing him, anyway. She didn't exactly hate the idea of making Hayden jealous.

"How long were you and Hayden together?" Warren asked after a couple of minutes of uncomfortable silence.

"Three years. We both went to university in Cardiff. That's when we got together. We broke up a couple of years ago."

When she thought back, she suspected Warren would have met Hayden at some point, since they used to hang out at the hotel bar from time to time. But Warren used to keep to himself back then, so she couldn't say for sure.

"Why did you break up?"

She inhaled deeply, knowing this was the real reason she was always so self-conscious whenever she met up with her friends. The shame of him ending things still lingered. Because the breakup was very much one-sided. She'd adored Hayden and had been heartbroken when he'd split up with her.

And then he'd quickly started turning up at their get-togethers with a string of women who were everything Anna wasn't – loud and fiery and full of confidence.

"Things just didn't work out," she said vaguely. "We kind of drifted apart."

He let out a thoughtful hum. Clearly he had an opinion on that, but there was no way she was going to prolong the conversation by asking. He could keep his opinions to himself.

She sighed and leaned her head against the cold window. Maybe bringing Warren was a terrible idea. If he thought she'd brought him to make Hayden jealous, everyone else might think the same. She might be about to elevate the pitying looks to a whole new level.

"Are you nervous?" Warren asked, giving her leg a nudge.

"No."

"Really? You're quiet."

"I'm always quiet," she said.

"More than usual."

"I probably shouldn't have invited you. It's kind of pathetic that I can't hang out with my friends without obsessing about what they think of me." She pushed her head back into the headrest. "If you want, you can just drop me off."

"Tempting as that is, I got all dressed up. Besides, you didn't let me back out when I got cold feet about bringing you to dinner with my parents."

"True. Maybe we can take the same approach, and I'll introduce you as my friend. It will save complicated conversations down the line."

"One minor problem," Warren said, casting her an amused glance. "You already told Frannie I'm your boyfriend, and you proved that by kissing me in the middle of a crowded room."

Anna dropped her chin to her chest. "I'm an idiot."

He laughed, and the sound brought an instant smile to her face.

"It's a free bar, right?" He nudged her leg again. "We can get drunk and have a laugh."

"I don't think I've ever seen you drunk," she said, eyes lingering on his profile while he concentrated on the road. She'd been around him at lots of parties, but she'd never seen him anything other than slightly tipsy.

"I don't really drink much," he said.

Her smile stretched wider. "Me neither. So I don't suppose your plan is going to work out. Especially since you have to drive home tonight."

"True. But we can enjoy the free food and one or two free drinks and pretend we're party animals."

Part of her wished she were the sort of person to get drunk and party the night away. It might be nice not to be hyperaware of every single moment.

"It'll be fine," he mused.

"Trying to convince me or yourself?"

He pouted dramatically. "What if your friends don't like me?"

"I can't imagine they will," she said, unable to resist teasing him.

"What?" He slapped a hand against his chest. "With my wit and charm, how could they not?"

She felt all the tension leave her.

"You don't need to laugh quite so hard," he said, grinning. "I can actually be quite charming when I want to be."

"I imagine you probably can," she said. "Can't imagine you being witty, though."

He mock-scowled. "Now you're being mean!"

Shaking her head, she pointed out the turn, which he almost missed. A few minutes later, they were crawling along the driveway to the Grange Hotel. On either side of them, trees were draped with twinkling lights. Up ahead, the glow from the windows of the imposing red brick building acted like a beacon, drawing them in.

A ripple of anticipation swept through Anna. After weeks of dreading the evening, she felt suddenly very calm about it.

Chapter Twelve

Once she'd checked in, Anna directed Warren to the hotel bar, leaving him there while she went to find her room. She'd considered taking him with her, but suspected getting ready would cause her some stress and she'd rather not have Warren around to witness her panic over her wardrobe choice.

The new dress she'd bought during the week had felt like a good idea in the shop, but as she slipped into the silky satin number, she felt hyperaware of the way it clung to her. In front of the mirror, she adjusted the midnight blue material, as though she could somehow make the slit which ran up her thigh less prominent.

It would be a formal affair in the ballroom, so she wasn't overdressed, but usually she'd choose an outfit to blend in rather than draw attention.

At least she'd thought to bring a shawl. The shimmery silver material covered her arms but did little to tone down the cleavage on display.

Having Warren with her meant she'd draw attention anyway, at least among her friendship group, so her outfit probably didn't matter much. She didn't like to ponder why exactly she felt so inclined to wear something so revealing. Not since that would inevitably lead to her thinking about her lingering feelings for Hayden. She'd rather not go there.

Briefly, she considered changing into the other dress, which she'd feel more comfortable in, but forced herself to be brave and stick with her choice. The pep talk she gave herself while applying her makeup was ineffective, and she was a nervous wreck when she finally left the room to find Warren.

❄

With a bottle of beer in his hand, Warren wandered back out of the bar and across the entrance hall. He poked his head into the large ballroom where staff in crisp black and white uniforms were putting the final touches to a space that featured a large dance floor circled by tables dressed in white tablecloths and sparkling silver cutlery. A canopy of fairy lights glowed between the ceiling beams, and festive foliage twined around sconces on the walls. Matching foliage made striking centrepieces on the tables. Backing away, he scanned the entranceway, which was vaguely intimidating in its elegance.

Slowly, he wandered back to the bar area, which was filling up with people. Gentle Christmas music blended with the chatter in the room. The women mostly wore elegant cocktail dresses, and the men ranged from bow ties and dinner jackets to more casual shirts with top buttons open.

He glanced at the door, looking for Anna, then headed for the end of the bar, thinking it looked a good place to loiter while he waited.

He didn't get far before hearing his name. A woman was waving at him, and he automatically moved in her direction.

"Hi," she said as he got close to her and her group. "We met last weekend. I'm Frannie – Anna's friend."

He smiled. "Sorry, I didn't recognise you for a second. You

look different." She'd been all wrapped up in her winter clothes the first time they met, which was a striking contrast to the strapless dress she wore now.

"True." She looked down at herself and grinned. "I'm not usually so dressed up."

"You look great," he said. "It's good to see you again."

"You, too." She grabbed the guy next to her, pulling him to her side. "This is Jake, my boyfriend. He's also an old school-friend of Anna's."

Warren shook his hand. "Anna told me about you."

"Did she mention *me?*" an excited redhead asked from across their little circle.

"Kylie?" he asked, hoping he'd remembered the names correctly.

"Yes!" She beamed at him. "I've been hearing about you as well, though Anna's been coy. She hasn't said much."

"Probably because she can't get a word in," the guy beside Kylie said, then extended his hand to Warren. "I'm Dev. Nice to meet you."

"You, too."

"Where's Anna?" Frannie asked.

"She's upstairs getting changed. I got shooed out of the way."

"She sent me a photo of her dress," Kylie said, pressing a hand to her chest. "I can't wait to see her in it." Her eyes shot to Frannie. "Where's Hayden?"

"Late as usual," Frannie replied.

Jake lowered his voice. "Probably waiting for what's-her-name to finish trowelling her make-up on."

"Don't be mean," Frannie said, giving him a disapproving look.

"He's not bringing her anyway," Kylie said. "They split up."

"Who's he bringing then?" Jake asked.

"No one," Frannie said. "I told you earlier he's coming on his own."

"Did you?"

"He told me he was coming alone," Dev added. "I'm not sure I believe it though. Also, what are we going to talk about if he doesn't bring an inappropriate date?"

"Shush," Kylie said. "He's here now."

Warren followed her gaze to the tall guy who sauntered in wearing a perfectly fitted three-piece suit. He had an air of confidence about him as he walked through the crowd, greeting a couple of people as he went.

Warren hung back while his friends greeted him with hugs and handshakes.

"Don't take this personally," Frannie told him when she released Hayden from a tight embrace. "But my great aunt Sandy is waving at me. I need to mingle before dinner."

"Have fun!" Jake said, with a definite hint of sarcasm in his words.

Frannie laughed. "You're coming with me. I can't deal with my elderly relatives alone."

"No," he grumbled. "I don't even have a drink, Frannie. Let me get a drink!"

Ignoring his protests, Frannie dragged him away.

"Speaking of drinks," Hayden said.

"I'll go." Dev grinned. "My round!"

"Oh, my god!" Kylie glared at him. "You're going to make that joke all night, aren't you? It's not even funny." She cast Warren a weary glance. "It's a free bar. Dev thinks he's hilarious." Her eyes widened, and she looked at Hayden. "This is Warren, by the way."

"Hey." Warren shook his hand. "Nice to meet you."

"We'll go to the bar," Kylie said, taking Dev's arm. "Do you need another?" she asked Warren.

He held up his bottle, which was almost full. "I'm fine, thanks."

"I think I'm going to have champagne," Kylie said happily. "I'll grab Anna one too. She should be here soon."

As they wandered away, Warren took a swig of his beer.

"How do you know Kylie?" Hayden asked while his eyes scanned the room.

"I don't. I only just met her."

"Are you a friend of Frannie?"

"No. I'm here with Anna."

The way he suddenly had Hayden's attention was almost comical.

"How do you two know each other?"

The feeling of rivalry that overwhelmed Warren wasn't exactly rational. This guy had hurt Anna, though, and that didn't sit well with him. If he could annoy Hayden, he'd do it at every opportunity.

He opened his mouth to tell him they were dating, but stopped when he spotted Anna across the room and lost his ability to focus on anything other than her.

In the dark, sultry dress, she looked absolutely breathtaking. From the corner of his eye, he was vaguely aware of Hayden waiting for an answer, but he couldn't drag his attention from Anna. His chest fluttered when her gaze collided with his. A smile touched her lips and brightened her eyes.

"Here she is," Warren muttered as she made a beeline for them. He caught the way Hayden's eyes widened when he laid eyes on Anna. The hunger in them was wolfish and not subtle in the slightest.

"Hi." She greeted Hayden first, giving him a perfunctory hug while keeping her eyes on Warren and looking for all the world like she was entirely uninterested in Hayden.

Stepping close to Warren, she smiled shyly. "Do I look okay?"

He stifled a laugh at the world's most absurd question.

"Stunning," he said quietly, deciding this was a great opportunity to answer Hayden's question about how he knew Anna without uttering a word to him. "I'm definitely the luckiest man in the room tonight," he said, gazing into Anna's eyes and watching the blush that brightened her cheeks.

He lifted her chin and swept his lips against hers in a kiss that was far too fleeting.

"I take it you two have already met?" she said, eyes flicking to Hayden.

"Yes," Warren said. "Frannie spotted me and introduced me to your friends."

Hayden's jaw was tight as he stared at Anna. "I didn't realise you were seeing someone."

"Yes," she said, a hand resting on Warren's arm. "Where's…" She appeared to be thinking, but Warren was certain it was just for show. "Nicola, isn't it?"

"She's not here," Hayden said. "We broke up."

"Sorry to hear that," Anna said, her eyebrows pulling together. "Are you here on your own?"

"Yes. Kylie said Mike wasn't coming, so I thought it would be just the six of us, like old times." He rubbed the back of his neck. "I didn't realise you were bringing someone."

"Anna!" Kylie shrieked behind them. "Bloody hell. You look fantastic."

"Thank you," Anna said, accepting a glass of bubbly from her friend. "You look amazing too."

"This old thing," Kylie said, dropping her hip dramatically as she looked down at herself. "I thought it looked good until I saw you walk in. You have better accessories than me as well. It's all very unfair."

Warren caught the puzzled look on Anna's face as her hand went to her necklace. He also caught the mischievous wink Kylie directed his way.

"I think she means me," Warren whispered in Anna's ear.

"Oh." She rolled her eyes at Kylie, then took a long sip of her champagne.

Feeling the nerves radiating from her, Warren put a protective hand on her back.

He felt an inexplicable spark of pride when she moved closer to his side.

Chapter Thirteen

Seeing Hayden and Warren together had thrown Anna. On top of her uncertainty about her choice of dress, her nerves were now completely in tatters and the party had only just started.

Hayden not having a date with him was pretty shocking. Apart from the first couple of times they'd all hung out after the breakup, he always had a date with him. It was fairly ironic that the first time he came alone, she had a date. Maybe only a fake date, but Hayden certainly didn't know that. Not after the way Warren had greeted her. He almost had *her* convinced he was besotted with her.

"Are you okay?" Warren said close to her ear as they walked through to the ballroom to find their seats for dinner.

"Yes." She cast him a sidelong glance. "Do I seem really nervous?"

"No," he said, but she didn't believe him for a second. "Maybe a little."

"I'll be all right. It just takes me a while to settle into social situations." She took another sip of her bubbly as they reached the table for the seven of them. "I never understand people who are at ease in a crowd."

"Are you looking at me?" he asked lightly.

"Yes. You're always so chilled out."

Hayden had always been a social butterfly too – which had sometimes felt like a good thing. He could carry conversations while she stood beside him and smiled. It also meant she'd socialised more than she'd liked. He was invited to everything and hated to miss out on a party.

"I wouldn't say it's my comfort zone," Warren said. "But I guess it also doesn't bother me."

She pulled out a seat, and they sat side by side. "I made the centrepieces," she told him out of the side of her mouth, while her friends discussed who was sitting where and shuffled to take their seats. "The rest of the decorations in the room, as well."

"Wow."

"I wasn't boasting," she whispered. "It's just something you should probably know. I spent a lot of time working on it this week."

He looked around the room. "I'd boast if I were you. It looks great."

"Thank you."

"I tend to think of a florist as selling pretty bunches of flowers. I never really thought about decorating entire event venues."

"I love events like this," she said, eyes roaming the room. "It's a lot of work, but not as much pressure as a wedding."

"It looks amazing."

Kylie groaned beside Anna. "Are we still talking about your dress?" she joked.

"No," Warren told her. "I've moved on to raving about how great her decorations are." He tipped his head at the wreath in the centre of the table.

"They do look great," Frannie agreed. "I know you get

annoyed about your boss messing you about with your hours, but it's so good that you had the time to do all this."

"Maybe it's time you quit and set up your own shop," Warren suggested, flashing her a knowing look.

"Are you still thinking about that?" Hayden asked, catching her eye across the table.

"Not really."

"Liar," Warren said, grinning.

"I'm not lying!" She glared at him with mock outrage.

"I reckon it's time you stopped kidding yourself and turned your *idea* into a plan."

His reference to their previous conversation amused her, and she couldn't help but grin at him.

"Urgh!" Kylie groaned. "You already have your own private jokes. How sickening!"

"Sorry," Anna said, laughing at the way Warren continued to stare at her with a silly smirk on his face. Finally, she nudged his leg and told him to stop it.

"You'd be great with your own shop," he said, his voice turning serious as he reached for her hand, entwining their fingers in her lap.

"Keep telling her that," Frannie said. "She doesn't listen to me."

"What do you do?" Dev asked Warren, redirecting the conversation.

Once he'd talked about his job for a while, he asked what everyone else did for a living.

It kept the attention pleasantly away from Anna. She tried to focus on the conversation, which included a lot of banter, but mostly her mind was on Warren's hand, which remained resting in her lap until the food arrived.

Only then did he untangle their fingers. As he flashed her a quick smile, she felt a wave of gratitude that he'd agreed to come with her, and that he seemed to know exactly how to put her at ease.

Maybe it was also because Hayden hadn't brought a date, or maybe it was the alcohol, but as the conversation flowed around her, she found herself relaxing far more quickly than usual.

Chapter Fourteen

Having Warren beside her felt like a shield. The anxiety Anna normally felt at an event like this was drastically diminished. On top of that, she was having so much fun with him that she forgot to think about her complicated feelings for Hayden.

Which meant she was entirely unprepared when she walked out of the ladies' and almost collided with her ex.

"Hi," Hayden said brightly.

"Hi." Tension gathered in her shoulders as the usual discomfort she felt around him crept back in. "Are you having a good night?"

"Yeah. It's great."

She smiled limply and was about to walk around him when he spoke again.

"Warren seems nice."

"He is." Her lips pulled into a genuine smile. "He's great." He'd slotted easily into their little group, which was impressive given how long the rest of them had known each other.

"You seem happy." His gaze held hers with an intensity that made her uncomfortable. "Are you?" he asked softly.

She swallowed hard, hating him for asking her that now. For years, she'd been miserable, and he hadn't cared. Or he hadn't seemed to, anyway. Maybe he *had* felt some guilt, and it would be a relief for him to see her happy. Part of her didn't want to give him the satisfaction.

She reminded herself that the whole point of bringing Warren was to make everyone think she'd finally moved on.

"I'm very happy," she replied, then pointed along the hallway. "I should get back."

"Yeah. Sure." He gestured to the gents and continued in that direction.

In the foyer, Anna paused at the doorway to the bar area, checking to see if Warren was still getting her a drink.

She spotted him immediately, leaning against the end of the bar, chatting with a waitress. The slender blonde woman beamed at him, clearly enthralled by whatever he was saying.

Heat rushed over Anna's skin, and she clenched her jaw. Since they weren't actually together, she had no right to be jealous. Maybe he'd been playing the part of her boyfriend a little too well, given how prickly she felt about him flirting with someone else.

It wasn't jealousy, though – it was annoyance that he was being so open about it. If her friends noticed him flirting with the waitress, it would make things very awkward.

Pinned to the spot, all she could do was stare as he continued joking with the pretty blonde.

Eventually, Hayden's voice broke her from her trance.

"You okay?" he asked.

"Yes." Hopefully, he didn't notice the manic edge to her smile as she moved away from the door, trying to block his view of Warren. Ironically, it was probably her odd reaction that made him look.

"How come you're loitering out here?" he asked, giving no sign he'd seen anything untoward.

"Warren's getting me a drink. I was waiting for him."

"Right," he said, one eyebrow twitching. "I'll see you back inside."

He'd only just wandered back to the ballroom when Warren arrived beside her.

"One glass of wine," he said, holding it out to her.

"Thank you." She took a sip to calm her nerves. "I don't want to sound annoying and whiny," she whispered. "But can you please not flirt with the waitress where all my friends can see."

His features crumpled. "What?"

"I could see you from here."

His lips twitched in amusement before his smile fell away. "Oh, you're serious?"

"Yes." She took a step away. "If my friends see, they'll wonder what on earth is going on."

"I wasn't flirting. I was asking her about the food."

"Yeah, sure. I could see her eyelashes fluttering from here."

His eyebrows shot up. "Are you jealous?"

"No!" Her hands felt suddenly clammy, and she felt a jolt of irritation at the smirk that played at his lips. "I'm not!" She glared at him, but it only seemed to amuse him further.

"Come on." He tipped his head towards the ballroom. "I promise not to flirt with anyone except you."

She opened her mouth to argue, but decided she'd probably only make things worse.

Sitting back at the table, Warren checked his watch.

"You can go if you want," Anna said quietly. "I guess you have to be up early tomorrow."

"Yeah." He dragged his teeth along his lower lip. "I don't really want to leave before dessert, though."

"That's a wise decision," Frannie said, leaning onto the table and catching Warren's eye. "The chef makes the most amazing desserts."

"That's settled then." Warren shuffled his chair closer to Anna's and draped his arm along the back of it. "I'll stay a little longer."

Goosebumps rippled over Anna's skin when his fingers rested lightly on the exposed skin at her shoulder.

She hoped the dessert didn't come too quickly.

Chapter Fifteen

"Is it annoying to eat out as a chef?" Dev asked Warren when they were tucking into the desserts. "Are you constantly thinking about how you'd have cooked it better?"

"Only if the food's really bad," Warren replied, making them all chuckle. He shook his head. "Most of the time I'm just happy I didn't have to cook."

"You like your job, though?" Kylie asked.

"Yes." He glanced at Anna. "Not that I'd dare say anything else. She might tell my boss."

Again, they all chuckled while Anna gave his arm a playful shove. "You *do* like your job, though," she said, with a questioning lilt to her voice. She'd always assumed he did, but maybe he wasn't actually that fond of it. Which could explain why he lost his temper so much with the kitchen staff.

"I love it," he said, looking directly at her. His gaze flicked to the table at large. "It feels like a privilege to do what I love for a living."

He swiped his fork over his dessert plate, scooping up the last piece of rich chocolate cake with the final smear of cream. While she waited for him to polish it off, he aimed it in her direction instead. The hush that descended over the table told her that all eyes were on them as he fed her the last of his dessert. Warren wiggled his eyebrows at her, easing her nerves as her lips closed around the fork.

She didn't dare look at her friends and had just moved her hand to wipe the crumbs from her lips when Warren brought his hand to her face. His thumb dragging over her lower lip made her breath catch in her throat, and she completely forgot to breathe when he moved in and laid a gentle kiss on her mouth.

"I really wish I didn't have to work tomorrow," he said, eyes locking with hers as he pulled away.

"Can't you call in sick?" Kylie piped up beside him.

His acting skills were impressive. For a moment, even Anna believed he was considering it.

"I can't," he finally said, looking genuinely pained.

Standing, he shook hands with the guys around the table. Kylie and Frannie both stood to hug him, which was a sure sign he had their approval.

"I'll talk to you tomorrow," he said when he bent to Anna. His hand rested on her shoulder again, sending a shiver up the back of her neck. Her heart rate soared as he leaned in to kiss her.

Again, it was only a soft brush of lips, but it sent a buzz of excitement all the way to her toes.

"It was really great to meet you all," he said when he straightened up, fingers still caressing her shoulder. "Enjoy the rest of your night."

Through the cheerful goodbyes from her friends, Anna inhaled deeply. He was supposed to be her boyfriend, so it wasn't as though it was a bad thing that her friends noticed how much a couple of kisses affected her.

And they definitely noticed.

That much was clear from the way Kylie and Frannie beamed at her.

"He's so lovely," Kylie said, reaching over and squeezing her hand. "He definitely gets my seal of approval."

Frannie looked a touch emotional. "You're absolutely smitten, aren't you?"

"No," she said weakly, forgetting that's exactly what she'd wanted them to believe and instead focusing on convincing herself that she didn't have actual feelings for him.

As far as fake boyfriends went, it turned out he was quite a good one.

It was all for show – she reminded herself – nothing more.

"Oh, no," Frannie muttered. "Aunt Margaret is looking over here. Shall we all hit the dance floor? It'll save me from having to make small talk with more elderly relatives."

While Dev protested half-heartedly against dancing, Anna turned in her seat – her eyes finding Warren as he neared the door at the far side of the room.

It was a shame he'd left before the dancing. Although her notion of him sweeping her around the dance floor was probably too wild of a fantasy, anyway. She couldn't imagine he'd have indulged her in any slow dances, no matter how much he'd thrown himself into the role of devoted boyfriend.

He'd just reached the doorway when the waitress he'd been talking to caught up with him and grabbed at his elbow. Confusion wrinkled his brow as he turned to her, but was quickly replaced by a warm smile.

They exchanged a few words before he followed her to a nearby table. Hastily, she wrote on a notepad and tore the paper off for him. As he slipped it into his pocket, Anna's stomach knotted tightly. Her breath caught in her throat as Warren squeezed the waitress's arm.

As she watched him head for the door again, she registered the silence from her friends. Presumably it would be too much to hope that they hadn't witnessed that.

Slowly, she turned back to them. All eyes were on her as she forced a smile.

"What just happe–" Dev was cut off by Frannie, who elbowed his ribs.

"Are you okay?" she asked, tilting her head.

They'd all seen, then.

"I'm fine!" Anna said, her voice overly bright. "Did you say you were going to dance?"

"We should all dance," Kylie said, springing from her chair. "Come on?"

"I'm just going to finish my drink." Anna pulled her glass towards her. "I'll catch you up in a minute." Her friends all had those pitying looks she'd been desperate to avoid. "Go on," she said, making a shooing motion. "Liven up the party."

Kylie gave her shoulder a squeeze, then took Dev's arm and pulled him towards the dance floor. The rest of them followed, leaving Anna to stare at her wineglass and remind herself that Warren wasn't really her boyfriend and she shouldn't be upset by his interaction with the waitress.

Admittedly, it was slightly humiliating that her friends had seen it, but that was her own fault for lying to them about her relationship status.

"Come and dance," a soft voice said, snapping her from her trance. Hayden stood with his hand out and a wealth of sympathy in his eyes.

"I'm not really in the mood."

"That's exactly why you should dance." He took her hand, and she let him pull her onto the dance floor, where an increasing number of couples danced to the slow music.

It didn't even occur to her to protest when Hayden slipped an arm around her and pulled her close. He held her other hand in his, and they swayed gently.

"Are you all right?" he asked after a moment.

"Yes." She tried to sound perky but failed. Stupidly, she'd got caught up in Warren's flirting and had blurred the line between what was real and what was pretend.

"Just because he took her number doesn't mean he's going to call her," Hayden said quietly.

Anna's eyebrows shot up. She'd assumed they'd just ignore that little incident.

"Maybe he was just being polite," Hayden suggested.

"By taking the waitress's number?"

He shrugged. "He might not have wanted to hurt her feelings, so just took the number. It doesn't mean he's intending to use it."

"Do you think so?" Anna asked, stupidly hoping that was true.

Hayden didn't reply, but pulled her closer, resting his cheek against her temple.

"Is it serious between the two of you?"

She gave a small shake of her head. "I don't think so. It's still new."

"I'm sorry, anyway."

She pulled back to look him in the eye. "It's not a big deal, so you can stop looking at me like that."

"Like what?"

"Like you feel sorry for me."

"I don't feel sorry for you." He pulled her closer again, speaking quietly in her ear. "I think you can do better, that's all."

"You just said he might not have any intention of calling her."

"Because I don't like seeing you upset. But it really wouldn't have been impolite to tell her he has a girlfriend."

Anna shook her head and tried to step away, but his arm tightened around her back. "I'm sorry," he said, and his earnest gaze made her relax in his arms.

Gently, they swayed to the music until Hayden spoke again.

"I know things have been weird between us since we split up, but you're still one of my closest friends, and I care about you a lot."

"Thank you," she whispered.

"If Warren doesn't know what a good thing he's got, then he doesn't deserve you."

She huffed out an ironic laugh. "That's rich, isn't it?"

His eyebrows dipped a fraction. "I messed up, and I know it. I should never have..." His eyes drifted to somewhere over her shoulder.

"What?" she asked.

"Nothing. Never mind."

"Hayden! Tell me what you were going to say."

Finally, his gaze bounced back to her. "I should never have split up with you," he said so softly she wasn't sure she'd heard correctly.

She opened her mouth, but couldn't find any words. Once again, Hayden's attention moved over her shoulder. He held her hand tighter when she turned to look.

Through the crowd on the dance floor, her gaze collided with Warren's.

The fierce look he gave her made her heart beat erratically.

Chapter Sixteen

Warren was halfway across the car park when he rooted in his pockets for his keys. He pulled out his phone and the slip of paper from the waitress, then had a mild panic that he'd lost his keys before remembering he'd asked Anna to stash them in her bag. Turning, he shivered in the freezing air and took the front steps two at a time.

Anna and her friends were no longer sitting at the table and his eyes scanned the room, looking for them. He stopped short when he spotted Anna dancing with Hayden.

Internally, he grumbled about how it hadn't taken Hayden long to take Warren's place beside Anna. The creep had his hand very low on her back, too.

After taking a few steps, Warren stopped again. Anna looked pretty comfortable with her face touching Hayden's. Warren's chest tightened at the sight.

If she'd brought him to make her ex jealous, it seemed to have done the trick. He felt the muscles in his jaw tense as he watched them sway together.

He caught the moment Hayden looked his way and saw the

flash of guilt in his features. Not that the idiot seemed overly concerned.

Warren crossed the dance floor and had almost reached them when Anna spotted him. Her surprise at the sight of him was quickly replaced by irritation.

"What are you doing?" she hissed quietly. "I thought you were leaving."

"Clearly." Pointedly, he looked at her fingers, which were entwined with her ex-boyfriend's.

Hayden stepped in front of Anna. "It's probably best if you do leave," he said, his quiet tone not disguising the hint of a threat.

Frowning in confusion, Warren looked to Anna.

"Please just go," she said. "We'll talk tomorrow."

He wanted to point out that he didn't have his keys, but somehow that felt irrelevant. What on earth had happened in the last three minutes?

"What's going on?" he asked.

Hayden took another step between them. "She's upset. Just leave it for now."

"Why are you upset?" He kept his eyes on Anna and resisted the urge to physically move Hayden out of his way.

"It's okay." Anna put a hand on Hayden's arm as she stepped around him. "Just give us a minute." She pulled on Warren's elbow and led him off the dance floor.

"What's going on?" he asked before they'd got far.

She spoke out of the corner of her mouth. "They saw you with the waitress."

"So?" At the edge of the dance floor, he turned to face her.

"So you took her number," she snapped at about the same time he noticed her friends had followed them.

"Are you okay?" Kylie asked, moving to stand beside Anna.

When Frannie took up position at her other side, Warren

couldn't decide whether to be annoyed or amused by how protective they were.

"I didn't take her number," he said, taking a step towards Anna.

He could just about feel her male friends breathing down his neck.

"We all saw you," one of them said. He didn't bother turning to see who it was. Partly because he couldn't drag his eyes from Anna, who looked genuinely upset.

In fairness, the whole point of him being there was so they didn't feel sorry for her being alone. Having her supposed new boyfriend chatting up a waitress in front of them probably wasn't helpful.

With his eyes locked on hers, he fumbled in his pocket and drew out the paper.

"It's not her number," he said, holding it out. "I was asking about the sauce with the duck. She said she didn't dare ask the chef because he was so busy, but she gave me the details of his YouTube channel."

Anna looked at the paper, then angled it to show her friends.

"He does have a YouTube channel," Frannie said, wincing. "It's really good."

"Great," Warren said through gritted teeth. "Can you all stop looking at me as though I'm the devil?"

"Sorry," Jake said, moving to his side and clapping him on the back. "We may have jumped to conclusions there."

"Obviously." He could see how it had looked dodgy. It genuinely hadn't entered his head that anyone would think that, though. "Why on earth would I flirt with the waitress?" he said, looking Anna up and down and not caring about the way she squirmed under his scrutiny.

"Sorry," Frannie said, grimacing as she ushered the rest of them away.

"Oh my god," Anna whispered, covering her face with her hand. "That was so awkward."

"Awkward how fast your ex made a move," Warren muttered.

"He didn't make a move," she said, but didn't look as though she even believed it herself. "He was just concerned."

"Was that the plan all along?" Warren asked, trying to keep his voice level. "To make him jealous?"

"No." She shook her head but looked unsure of herself.

"It doesn't matter either way," he said. "It just would've been nice to know."

"I wasn't trying to make him jealous. I didn't really think that would be possible." Her eyes flicked across to her group of friends. She swallowed hard when her attention shifted back to Warren. "How come you came back?"

"You have my car key."

"Oh." Her eyes widened, and she took her handbag from her shoulder. "Yeah, I do."

"Couldn't get far without that," he said, shoving it into his pocket. "It's a good job I came back, anyway. Did you really think I'd taken the waitress's phone number?"

Slowly, she nodded. "Obviously, you're free to chat up whoever you want. It would just be better if you didn't do it in front of my friends, since they really believe you're my boyfriend."

He blew out a breath. "Sorry."

"It's not your fault. I should never have lied to my friends. This whole charade is ridiculous."

"I think we did an excellent job of convincing them," he said, smiling at her.

"A bit too good. It might have been better if you *had* taken the waitress's number. At least that would save me from having to make up an excuse about why we broke up."

"You could just wait a couple of weeks and then tell them

you had to dump me because the sex was too good... claim you couldn't focus on anything else and it was messing up your life."

She snorted a laugh and called him an idiot.

"So am I forgiven for speaking to the waitress?"

"I wasn't annoyed with you for speaking to her," she protested. "Just for making me look even more pathetic in front of my friends."

"I don't think any of them think you're pathetic," he said and meant it.

"Sorry they all turned on you."

"You're smirking," he said. "Which makes me think you're not really sorry at all."

"It was just quite funny now that I think about it."

He rolled his eyes, then shrugged his coat off and slung it over the back of the nearest chair.

"I thought you were leaving," Anna said, but thankfully didn't look concerned that he wasn't going anywhere.

"I can't leave now." He slipped his fingers into hers. "Your friends think I upset you. What kind of boyfriend would I be if I didn't stay and make it up to you?"

"They know it was a misunderstanding," she said.

He arched an eyebrow. "Are you going to dance with me or not?"

A slow smile spread over her face. "Go on, then."

Chapter Seventeen

When they danced, Warren wasn't gentle with her like Hayden had been, but swirled and twirled her until her cheeks ached from laughing.

Finally, as the music switched to a slower pace, she flopped against his chest.

"I think they'll all be satisfied that you stayed to cheer me up," she said, resting her cheek on his shoulder as they swayed with the music.

"You're a terrible dancer," he said into her hair.

"Yeah. That makes two of us." She laughed when he poked her side, then grabbed his hand to adopt a proper dancing stance.

She was already warm from the dancing, but the heat of his hand seared through the thin fabric at the back of her dress, and his breath sweeping over her hair felt like a desert breeze.

"I guess you need to go home," she said when the song ended.

"I probably should." He took her hand and led her from the dance floor. "Promise not to make up vicious stories about me with your friends the minute I leave?"

She swatted at his arm, then yawned when he picked up his coat. "I think I'm going to call it a night and go up to bed."

"Good plan. I always think it's best to leave before the end of a party. It gives an air of mystery – as though you've got better places to be."

"So you never stay until the end of parties?"

He shook his head and leaned close to her ear. "Not because I'm in any way mysterious. I just don't particularly like parties."

"You did a good job of pretending tonight."

"I quite enjoyed this one."

"I should say goodnight," she told him, linking arms with him and heading towards her gang, who were flinging themselves around at the edge of the dance floor. "We're going!" she called over the music when they got near.

"Decide to stay after all?" Jake asked Warren.

He opened his mouth, then glanced at Anna.

"I don't blame you," Dev said, swinging his hips to the music. "Make the most of that hotel room!"

"He's drunk," Kylie said merrily. "He's not wrong, though. Enjoy the rest of the night." She gave an exaggerated wink, then fell about laughing.

"Night," Hayden said, passing them and heading to the bar.

As she watched him go, Anna's brain flicked back to what he'd said earlier – that he should never have broken up with her.

Had he been drunk, or just trying to cheer her up? He hadn't *seemed* drunk, but she didn't spend much time with him any more, so maybe she wouldn't be able to tell.

Warren squeezed her fingers. "Let's go."

They were halfway up the stairs when she realised he was going the wrong way.

"I thought you were going to your car. You don't need to walk me to my room."

"I know, but I think it's suspicious if I leave now. If I were really your boyfriend, there's no way I'd leave you to stay here alone."

"You might if you had to work in the morning," she said, feeling slightly tipsy despite only having drunk two glasses of wine.

"I'd call in sick."

She squinted, unsure if he was really planning on staying the night or if he was just walking her to her room.

"Not that I can get away with calling in sick," he added.

"I don't suppose you can." She stopped outside her door and fished in her bag for the key card, burying her disappointment that he hadn't genuinely been suggesting he was going to take a sick day.

He had his phone in his hand and began typing a message. "I can probably get someone to cover for me at breakfast."

Tapping the card against the lock mechanism, she watched the light turn green, then pushed at the handle.

"Are you really not going to work in the morning?" she asked, still not sure what was going through his head.

"They can manage breakfast without me," he said, following her into the room.

She grinned as she plonked herself onto the edge of the bed and kicked her shoes off. "I'm just imagining their glee at getting to work without you breathing down their necks."

He gave her leg a gentle nudge with his own, then continued to the table by the window, where he stopped and rubbed his hands together. "Now we can really get this party going!" He glanced over his shoulder and flashed a mischievous grin.

"If you're thinking of hitting the mini bar, I don't think there is one."

He rolled his eyes. "Who needs a mini bar when we have a selection of assorted teas?"

She laughed loudly and flopped back onto the bed. "Is that

what you do when you mysteriously slip away from parties before the end – go home and drink tea?"

"It's not just tea," he told her, walking to the bathroom with the kettle in his hand. "There are also biscuits. Never let anyone tell you I don't know how to party."

Happily, she stared at the ceiling, only moving to roll onto her side when he'd returned and clicked the kettle on to boil.

"Did you have a good night?" he asked, dropping into the chair by the window.

"I did. Way better than I expected." Her mind flicked back to dancing with Hayden, and she thought again about what he'd said. When she snapped back to the present, Warren was staring at her. "I really shouldn't have lied to my friends. I don't know how I'm going to get out of this now."

"I'm sorry if I was too convincing. What was your original plan for explaining your return to single status after the party?"

"I didn't really think about it. Pretending you were my boyfriend seemed like a good idea when Carla suggested it."

"How often do you hang out with your friends?" he asked, sinking back in the chair. "Could you just drag me along with you often enough to keep up the pretence?"

She pulled a face at him. "I think I'll confess to the girls. The guys can think whatever they want. Or I could become a recluse and never socialise again."

"I like your thinking. I often dream of a hermit life."

"No you don't!" She laughed. "You love socialising. It's effortless for you."

"It's okay every now and again," he said, sifting through the tea bags. "What flavour do you want?"

"Anything," she said, then watched as he tore the packet of the teabag. "Are you really staying over?"

He cast her a quick glance. "I thought I might, if you don't mind. It's not very appealing to drive home in the dark. Plus, Dev was very effusive about the brunch tomorrow."

"It is a good brunch," she agreed.

"So it's okay with you if I stay?"

"Yeah," she said uncertainly.

"Don't look so nervous," he said, pouring water into the mugs. "I'll sleep on the floor. Or if you'd rather, I'll drink my tea and go."

"You're welcome to stay." She hadn't for a moment felt nervous at the prospect of him staying.

It had been a swirl of excitement that had swept through her stomach.

❄

Warren genuinely wasn't a fan of driving in the dark. That had been part of his reasoning for staying over at the hotel. If pressed, he might admit that it also had something to do with how much he enjoyed the pretence of being Anna's boyfriend, and the prospect of continuing their act at brunch the following morning.

He slightly regretted the decision at two o'clock in the morning when he woke on the floor and couldn't get comfy again. Dragging himself into the armchair, he dozed there for a couple of hours before giving up and lying hesitantly on the bed beside Anna. He kept his distance and stayed on top of the covers.

She'd suggested he sleep in the bed too, but had said it with enough uncertainty that he hadn't even considered taking her up on the offer.

Now, he waited a moment, but when she didn't stir, he let his body relax into the soft mattress and was asleep again in no time.

The next time he woke, it was to sunlight spilling through the gap in the curtains.

"Morning," Anna said as he squinted against the light.

He blinked a few times until she came into focus. With her hair spilled around her on the pillow and the light slanting onto her face, she looked angelic.

"Sorry," he said groggily. "I managed on the floor for a while, and the chair for a bit... then I gave up and opted for comfort."

"It's fine." She repositioned her head on the pillow. "I said you could sleep in the bed too."

"What time is it?" He turned to the digital clock beside the bed, putting a hand across the top of it to block out the daylight enough to read the numbers. "I never sleep that long," he said, surprised to find it was already mid-morning.

"It's good to be lazy sometimes." Sitting up, she discreetly adjusted her pyjama top. "I should get showered."

"Are we supposed to be at brunch at a specific time?"

She shook her head. "There's a buffet until eleven. Kylie messaged and said she's just getting up. Frannie and Jake are already downstairs. I guess Dev and Hayden are still sleeping."

She disappeared into the bathroom, and Warren settled back down on the pillows, not sure whether he'd prefer not to bump into Hayden at breakfast, or if he'd like him around so he could make it clear Anna was off-limits.

He groaned at the thought. Because she wasn't off limits at all. She was free and single and could do whatever the heck she liked.

Chapter Eighteen

The hotel dining room was reasonably busy, but they spotted Frannie and Jake straightaway, sitting with Kylie and Dev.

"Morning!" Anna said cheerfully.

Dev winced. "Not so loud," he said, clutching a mug of coffee with both hands.

"How's everyone feeling?" Warren asked.

Frannie smiled. "I think we're all doing pretty well, except for Dev. Hayden didn't look too hot either," she added as an afterthought.

"I'm surprised he's up." Anna glanced around for him. Usually, he'd be the last to bed at the end of the night and the last to emerge the following morning.

At least today she didn't have to endure the torture of watching him arrive with his girlfriend and force herself not to imagine what they'd been up to in their hotel room.

"You just missed him," Kylie said. "He grabbed a quick coffee and headed off. Apparently, he's in the middle of some big work project that he needed to get back to. He said to say goodbye."

Anna forced her lips into a smile, then turned to Warren. "Are you hungry?"

He nodded, and they meandered through the tables to the buffet at the side of the room.

As they took a plate each, Warren leaned close to her ear. "Are we happy that we missed Hayden this morning or not?"

The question amused her and also made her ponder her feelings on the matter. "It's a relief," she said, taking a bread roll from a basket. "Without him around, I can relax and enjoy breakfast with my friends."

He followed her to the hot buffet items. "Does it make me a bad person that I'm a little disappointed I don't get to watch him squirm with jealousy at the sight of us together?"

Anna smiled as she spooned scrambled eggs onto her plate. "I really don't think he was jealous."

"Then you need to get your eyes checked." He added sausages to his plate and served her a couple. "I wonder if that's why he left early – so he didn't have to watch us pawing at each other over breakfast."

"I don't think we'd really have been pawing at each other."

"I definitely intend to paw at you."

She laughed as she reached the end of the buffet table and poured them both orange juice. "Hayden's already left, remember? We can cool down the act."

"I thought you were mostly concerned with making sure your friends don't give you pitying looks."

"I suspect they might pity me if you inappropriately grope me during breakfast."

Suddenly, he was right in front of her, staring down at her with hunger in his eyes, which she'd swear had nothing to do with the food.

"I was thinking along the lines of affectionate touches." He ran his fingers down her upper arm in a way that made her breath catch. "Your friends are watching," he said, right before he gave her a lingering kiss.

When he picked up his orange juice, she fought to get her butterflies under control, then followed him across the room. He was right that her friends were watching. When they all whipped their gazes away and fell quiet, it was clear they'd been talking about them, too.

For once, Anna didn't mind being the subject of their conversations.

❄

After a lively brunch, Anna and Warren fell into a comfortable silence for the drive back to Chipping Campden.

Staring out of the window, watching the rolling fields slip by, Anna reflected on how much easier the party had been with Warren there. And how much she'd enjoyed it.

"What have you got planned for this week?" he asked when they were almost back at Chipping Campden.

"I have another Christmas market next weekend," she said. "And the online shop has been getting a steady stream of orders, so I'll need to work on replenishing my stock – making more wreaths and candles. Oh, and I have a thing tomorrow evening..." Her stomach plummeted at the thought of the event which she'd spent the last few weeks wishing she hadn't agreed to.

"A thing?" Warren asked, lifting an eyebrow as he slowed at the traffic lights.

She gave a small shake of her head. "A wreath-making workshop."

"Like the one you did at the hotel last year." He frowned. "You're doing it again this year, aren't you?"

"Yes. Although I wish I hadn't agreed to it. The one tomorrow is a private party at someone's house. It's the woman's sixtieth birthday, and she thought wreath-making would be fun to do with her friends. When she emailed me about it a month ago, it seemed like a good idea."

"And it doesn't any more?"

"No. I hate doing this stuff."

"I thought it went really well when you did it at the hotel last year?"

"It was fine in the end, but public speaking really isn't my thing, even when it's a small group."

"I'm sure you'll be fine."

"I'll be a nervous wreck." Her stomach already felt queasy and would likely stay that way for the next thirty-six hours until it was over and done with. "I always think it's unfair that Carla got all the confidence, and I got none. I'd like to be brave like her – she's not scared of anything."

Warren pulled the car away again, joining a queue of traffic. "I wouldn't describe Carla as brave. Cocky and self-assured maybe, but not brave."

"I think being cocky and self-assured makes her brave."

He shook his head. "If nothing scares you, there's no need to be brave. But I happen to know that Carla isn't the least bit brave. If something scares her, she doesn't do it."

"Maybe," she conceded. "I just don't think there's much that scares Carla." She chewed her lip as she pondered it, but couldn't come up with anything.

Warren grinned. "She's scared of driving on the motorway."

"That's true. But I'm not sure that really has a huge impact on her life."

"Apart from that one time it took her a week to drive to London on A roads."

Anna laughed loudly. "It wasn't a week."

"Perhaps not, but it took her way longer than it needed to. She also recently called me at ten o'clock at night, freaking out about a spider in her bathroom."

"She's terrified of spiders," Anna said, nodding.

"My point is that if something scares her, she avoids it. You do things even though they scare you. I think that makes you the brave one."

She shook her head. "I'd still like to have her confidence."

"Her confidence makes her loud and annoying," Warren said, eyes on the road ahead.

"Hey!" Anna gave his arm a gentle punch. "Don't be mean."

"It's true," he said, amused. "Don't pretend you don't agree."

"Sometimes she might be a bit much to deal with," she agreed. "But I'm her sister. I can say these things. You shouldn't."

He grinned as he geared down at the junction.

"Did she really call you to come over and remove a spider from her flat?"

He nodded once. "Personally, I think being nervous about making a speech or standing up in front of people is perfectly normal. Freaking out over a daddy longlegs is pathetic."

"It is a bit ridiculous." She could imagine Carla making a big drama of it.

Her attention went to the familiar sand-coloured buildings that lined the main street through Chipping Campden. A few minutes later, Warren turned onto a side street and then onto her road.

"What time do you have to be at work?" she asked.

"I'll go straight there."

She felt a tinge of disappointment when he stopped the car in front of her building. "Thank you for coming with me."

"You're welcome. I enjoyed it."

"I'm glad. I kind of wish I'd started taking fake dates to these events ages ago. It was fun."

"What will you tell your friends? Are you going to confess?"

She bit down on her lip. "I'm not sure. I'll probably tell the girls the truth. The other option is to say we broke up, but then I'll be stuck with the pitying looks again."

"They seem like a really nice bunch."

"They are. I'll figure something out."

"So we're done with our pretend dating?" he said, tilting his head.

"Yeah. I guess so."

"That was the easiest relationship I've ever been in. No drama." His lips twitched. "Apart from you accusing me of flirting with the waitress."

She smiled weakly. "I suppose this will be an amicable breakup too."

"I hope we'll stay friends," he said, mock serious.

When she waved him off, she couldn't help but think that the end of a fake relationship shouldn't really leave her feeling so disheartened.

Chapter Nineteen

On Monday, with her mind on her wreath-making workshop, Anna had little time to dwell on romantic issues. Once or twice her mind flitted to Hayden, but instead of missing him, as she usually did, she was just confused. Since she hadn't heard from him, it seemed unlikely he'd really meant what he'd said about it being a mistake to break up with her.

She was loading her car with several boxes of wreath-making supplies when a jolt of nerves hit her. Why had she agreed to do a private event? Surely she should have learned her lesson after Lewis coaxed her into running a class at the hotel last year. She'd sworn then that the nerves weren't worth it.

Closing the car, she dashed upstairs for a final bathroom trip, then checked herself in the hallway mirror. Her black woollen mid-calf dress was demure but practical. The green scarf gave a splash of colour, while her fur-lined ankle boots were comfortable and cosy.

She looked the part. From her professional appearance, you'd never know what a bag of nerves she was on the inside.

It was too late to back out now, she told herself, pulling on her coat and straightening her shoulders.

Besides, the workshop she'd done at the hotel had gone well, despite her nerves.

Because she was brave. Warren had said so, and he wasn't the type of person to say things he didn't mean.

I'm brave and I can do this. She repeated the mantra in her head as she walked calmly downstairs and got into her car. Amazingly, the words helped, and the overwhelming sense of dread had turned to a manageable flutter of nerves when she pulled up in front of the large house.

Checking her phone, her eyes landed on a notification. Intrigued, she opened the message from Warren.

Have fun tonight.

It was short and sweet and made her smile. Having fun seemed like a manageable goal for the evening – or at least something she had more control over than what the group would think of her and her wreath demonstration.

After sending a quick reply to thank him for the message, she shoved her phone into her bag and exited the car feeling surprisingly in control.

❄

Messaging Anna had felt like an entirely sane idea until Warren hit send. It was very tempting to delete the message, but a deleted message would look way more dubious than the three words he'd sent.

There was nothing wrong with the content of the message – telling her to have fun was nice of him. It was the fact that he'd messaged at all that felt suddenly idiotic. He and Anna didn't have the sort of relationship where they exchanged random messages. He scrolled back through their previous messages – mostly exchanges of bland birthday wishes and the annual 'Happy Christmas' message. In between were a couple of messages asking if the kitchen was still open at the hotel, but he suspected Carla sent them when he'd been ignoring her messages.

A reply came back from Anna with a simple thank you. He waited, but she didn't send anything else. What was he even expecting?

Thankfully, the waitress came into the kitchen with the first dinner order of the evening, and he slung his phone into the drawer and got to work.

After swapping shifts with Liam to take the weekend off, he soon remembered why he rarely worked on Mondays. The restaurant was only half full for the entire evening, and with no urgency in the kitchen, time dragged. Three hours suddenly felt like a full day.

Leaving the commis chef to deal with the last few desserts, he drifted to the back of the kitchen and took out his phone. He was wondering how Anna had got on when the screen illuminated with a message.

It was amazing, she wrote, as though she'd been reading his mind. *I had such a good time.*

His mind was chewing over how to reply when his thumb went to the top of the screen and hit call. He stepped out of the back door and smiled at the sound of her voice.

"So it went well?" he asked.

"Yes. It was brilliant. Thank you so much."

His smile stretched wider at her exuberance. "What are you thanking me for?"

"For telling me I'm brave," she said, her words brimming with joy. "And for telling me to have fun. Weirdly enough, I'd never thought of that before. Which seems daft now."

"What do you mean you never thought of that before?"

"I mean, I'm usually stressing about whether people will enjoy it, and whether they'll notice that I'm a bundle of nerves. But I got your message right before I went in there, and I just thought, *yeah, I'm going to enjoy it.*"

"And it sounds as though you did."

"Yes! They were such lovely women. I don't know why, but I got it into my head that they'd be a bunch of rich, snobby housewives."

"They weren't?"

"They weren't *snobby,*" she said, amused. "They were lovely and down to earth, and they were really interested in me. When they finished making the wreaths, they were asking what else I do, and they went on my online shop to browse. All of them placed orders for other things. Mostly Christmas cards, but a few wanted wreaths as gifts. They were so enthusiastic about my online shop."

"It's not surprising," he said, warmth filling his chest at the sound of her so happy. "You're very talented."

The brief pause told him she was uncomfortable with the compliment.

"Thank you," she said, then sighed. "I'm on such a high. I don't know why I always assume the worst. Before I left home, I was dreading it and wondering why I'd agreed to do it."

"How many more of these events have you got lined up?"

"I've got one at the old people's home in Bourton-on-the-Water, and the one at the hotel on the 23rd."

"Maybe you'll be more confident about those now."

She let out a tinkling laugh. "I don't think I'll ever really be confident, but maybe I won't be quite so terrified."

"I'm really glad it went well," he said, shifting his weight.

"Me too."

Silence fell, and he suddenly felt self-conscious – chatting on the phone wasn't something they'd usually do.

"Sorry," she said. "Are you at work?"

"Yeah, but it's fine."

"Don't burn anything because of me. I heard there's a rule about phones in the kitchen."

"There is." Grinning, he inhaled a lungful of freezing air. "I should probably get back in there."

"Thanks for calling," she said softly.

"I'll talk to you soon."

He ended the call and stretched his neck, craning to look up at the star-studded sky while kicking himself for calling her.

"Don't go there," he muttered to himself as he turned to go back inside. "It was all fake, and it'll never be anything more."

Chapter Twenty

The phone call from Warren played on Anna's mind long after she hung up. Their friendship had never included chatting on the phone, but it had felt wonderfully natural.

After spending the next morning preparing the orders from the previous evening, she set off to hand deliver them, as promised. It took longer than expected since the women all wanted to chat to her – one even insisted she come in for coffee and cake.

Arriving back home at lunchtime, she felt the urge to tell Warren about her morning. That seemed like a bad sign. As did all the time she spent thinking about him. When she contemplated confiding in her friends, she remembered that as far as they were concerned, she was in a relationship with him.

With an urgent need to rectify that, she sent a group message to Kylie and Frannie, asking when they had time to hang out.

Relief washed through her when Frannie suggested they have a drink at her place that evening. Chatting everything through with her friends was exactly what Anna needed.

A few hours later, she hid her surprise when Jake answered the door – she'd thought it was a girls' night.

"Hey," he said, kissing her cheek. "How are you?"

"Fine." She slipped her coat off and struggled to find space for it on the rack. In the end, Jake took it and slung it over the banister.

"I may have too many coats," Frannie said, wandering out of the living room to greet Anna with a hug. "Don't worry, Jake's going out soon."

"Thanks," Jake said, mock frowning.

"I was *very* concerned," Anna said, while secretly relieved that she could speak to the girls privately.

"Kylie and I are on white wine," Frannie said, heading to the kitchen. "Is that good for you?"

"Perfect." Anna went into the living room, where Kylie was sprawled on the couch.

"Everything okay with you?" Anna asked her.

"Thank goodness for wine, that's all I can say."

"Work busy?"

"Yes. It's a hectic time of year in the marketing world. You must be busy at the moment, too?"

She nodded. "I did a wreath-making workshop at a private party last night and spent this morning delivering orders. And this afternoon assembling more wreaths."

Frannie reappeared and handed Anna a glass of wine. "I'll bet you're making time for your new relationship, though?"

Anna gulped her wine. She should probably get the conversation over and done with, but she was aware of Jake being around somewhere.

"Warren's so lovely," Kylie crooned. "And it's great that you were friends first. When you have that foundation for a relationship, it makes it solid really fast. Don't you think? You definitely seem very together already. You'd never know it was a new relationship. There's no awkwardness between you."

"There isn't," Anna mused, then grimaced. She heard the creak of the stairs and decided Jake was probably out of earshot.

"I actually wanted to tell you something... it's a bit uncomfortable..."

"We're sorry again about jumping to conclusions about him and the waitress," Kylie said. "He won't hold it against us, will he?"

"No. It's not an issue."

"And things are good between the two of you?" Frannie asked.

"Yes." She grimaced again, then shook her head. "Well, not really."

"What's the problem?" Kylie asked, sitting upright.

Anna put a hand over her face. "Before I tell you this, you need to know that I'm truly sorry. I did something stupid, and I've been feeling terrible about it."

"You're freaking me out now." Frannie pressed a hand to her heart. "What did you do?"

"I lied about Warren," she said in a rush. "He's not actually my boyfriend. I just asked him to pretend for the party."

Kylie gave a manic shake of the head. "Are you joking?"

"No. It was really stupid."

Frannie wrinkled her nose. "Why would you do that?"

"Because I assumed Hayden would bring someone." Anna released a pent-up breath. "I'm so sick of everyone looking at me like I'm pathetic because I never moved on from him. And I get it, because it *is* pathetic. But I got stressed about the party, and I made a deal with Warren. I went along to a dinner with his parents that he was panicking about, and in return he came to the party."

"That was all pretend?" Kylie asked, wide-eyed.

"Yes. I hate that I lied to you."

"You and Warren aren't actually together?" Frannie asked, her words filled with disbelief.

Anna shook her head. "Please don't hate me."

They were silent for one horrible moment.

"Of course, we don't hate you," Kylie said.

Frannie stuck her bottom lip out. "I hate you thought you needed to pretend in front of us."

The door opened and Jake burst in. "I'm sorry, but I can't keep out of this conversation any longer."

"Jake!" Frannie hissed. "Were you listening the whole time?"

"No one was whispering, and in case none of you have noticed, we don't exactly live in a mansion. There isn't a room in the house where I wouldn't be able to hear you. But never mind that. Why are you focusing on Warren not actually being her boyfriend instead of asking the important questions?" He plonked himself on the arm of the couch, body angled towards Anna. "You're not over Hayden?" he said loudly.

"I *am* over him," she said uncertainly. "Kind of. I just never really moved on, did I?"

"*Didn't you?*" Jake asked, features scrunching.

Frannie glared at him and hissed his name again.

"You weren't asking good questions," he told her. "I don't understand what's going on." Again he looked at Anna. "You're telling me *you're* the one who hasn't moved on, and you think we pity *you?*"

Anna shrugged. "It always feels awkward when we're all out together. That's why I invited Warren."

"But that makes no sense," Jake said.

"I just thought if it looked as though I was with someone..."

"Yeah, yeah. I understand that bit." He leaned forward, jutting his chin out. "What I don't understand is how you got to the conclusion that we feel sorry for you. Because as far as I'm concerned, it's Hayden who never moved on." He looked at Frannie. "It's Hayden we feel sorry for, right? I feel as though I'm in some weird parallel universe now."

"Why would you feel sorry for Hayden?" Anna asked, eyes flicking between Frannie and Kylie while she waited for them to tell Jake he was confused.

"Because he never got over you," Kylie said, as though it was obvious. "He's practically a workaholic, and whenever we all meet up, he has to bring some random woman as a buffer."

"No," Anna said, her brain firing wildly.

"*Yes!*" Frannie argued. "Whereas you always turn up as though you haven't got a care in the world. You even chat with his random dates as though it doesn't bother you to see him with someone else. Plus, your business is booming, and you've been doing great since you two broke up. He's just been a sad mess."

Anna shook her head, trying to make sense of the conversation. "He was the one who broke up with me," she pointed out. "He didn't want to be with me any more."

Her three friends stared at her, and she had the feeling she was missing something.

"But when he realised he'd made a massive mistake, you refused to take him back." Kylie's eyes sparkled. "Which I think is awesome, by the way. I wish I were that strong."

"I don't know what you're talking about," Anna said. "He never wanted to get back together." Her mind flashed back to the party and him saying he wished they'd never broken up. That was the first time she'd had any inkling that he regretted the breakup, and she'd put that down to alcohol and a spark of jealousy over seeing her with Warren.

"The girls told him not to say anything," Jake said.

"You seemed to be doing well again," Frannie said, a hint of apology in her words. "We didn't want him to mess you about and hurt you all over again."

"Okay," Anna said slowly, not sure whether to be annoyed with them for interfering.

"But he spoke to you anyway, right?" Kylie asked, looking about as confused as Anna felt.

"Sort of. Maybe... do you mean at the party?"

"When you broke up," Jake said. "Ages ago."

Anna shook her head. "He didn't say anything."

"He *did,*" Jake insisted. "He told us he did."

"I think I'd remember." Anna also suspected she'd be back together with him if that conversation had taken place.

Jake stared at her. "He said you wouldn't entertain the idea of getting back together. That you told him he'd hurt you and you didn't even want to be friends with him. That you'd just be polite when we were all out for the sake of group dynamics."

A shiver ran down Anna's spine. "When is this conversation supposed to have taken place?"

Jake shrugged and looked at Frannie. "Eighteen months ago, right?"

"Probably," Frannie said. "It was about six months after you broke up. You'd just set up your online shop and seemed to be doing well. That's why we thought he should leave you alone."

Silence fell, and Anna took a large swig of her wine as she tried to get everything straight in her head.

"*Did* he try to get back with you?" Kylie asked as she watched Anna.

"I don't know," she said, rearranging a previous conversation in her head and trying to figure out if she could really have got it so wrong. "He invited me out for coffee one day," she said as that morning played out in her head. "He said he was sorry that he'd messed things up and that he hated how things were between us. And that he missed me."

"What did you say?" Frannie asked, a frown wrinkling her forehead.

"I thought he wanted us to be friends." Her voice sounded oddly hollow. "I thought he missed being friends with me and wanted us to still hang out as friends. That's what I said no to. I told him he'd hurt me and I didn't want to be around him. I was still so upset, and I couldn't stand the thought of spending time with him as friends. And I was devastated that he was so unaffected by the breakup that he thought we could continue being friends."

Kylie tilted her head. "He's been obsessed with you this whole time. We all thought you knew. *He* thought you knew."

"I can't believe this!" Jake threw his hands up and glared accusingly at Frannie. "I thought women were supposed to talk. Did it never occur to you to ask Anna if she still had feelings for Hayden?"

Frannie's gaze went to Anna. "You never really wanted to talk about it."

"Because I was so upset and humiliated," she said weakly.

Kylie's eyes widened dramatically. "Do you still have feelings for Hayden?"

With her thoughts all over the place, Anna closed her eyes to calm her racing thoughts. "I don't know," she murmured.

Chapter Twenty-One

After five minutes of pestering Anna with questions which she didn't know how to answer, Jake gave up and headed out to the pub. The sound of the front door closing behind him was followed by a momentary silence.

"He's gone," Frannie stated, sitting forward in the armchair. "Now we can talk properly. Do you still have feelings for Hayden?"

Anna sighed, sinking back into the couch cushions. "A week ago, I'd probably have said yes."

"And now?" Frannie pressed.

"Now I don't know."

"What's happened in the last week to make you so unsure." Kylie's eyes danced with mirth. "Can I take a guess?"

"It's Warren, isn't it?" Frannie said when Anna failed to answer.

Plucking the cushion from beside her, Anna held it over her face and let out a grunt of frustration. "I'm so confused."

"But you like Warren?" Kylie asked.

"Maybe." Anna put the pillow down again. "I always thought he was attractive, but I also found him intimidating. I tend to see him at the hotel when he's barking orders in the kitchen. Or when my sister's around and the two of them are bickering." She frowned. "When we were at the party, he was different. It was the first time in ages that I wasn't thinking about Hayden."

"I'm not surprised," Kylie said. "Warren was very attentive."

"It was all fake though," Anna said quickly.

Frannie's eyes swam with kindness. "*Was it?*"

"Yes. I helped him out with the thing with his parents, so he was repaying the favour."

"No way." Kylie shook her head. "I don't buy it."

"What do you mean you don't buy it? It's the truth."

"He was too convincing," Kylie said with a shrug. "He looked at you as though he was obsessed with you."

"I agree." Frannie's mouth pulled into a small smile. "It might have all been pretend, but he was clearly enjoying the pretence."

"That doesn't mean anything," Anna protested, while her stomach turned a cartwheel at the thought that he might feel something for her.

"He totally fancies you," Kylie said, in that cocksure way of hers that left no room for argument. "You should go for it."

"Hang on." Frannie raised her hands. "What about Hayden?"

"What *about* Hayden?" Kylie snapped. "He dumped Anna and then paraded a series of other women in front of her."

"I know," Frannie argued, "but it's Hayden... He might have messed up, but he isn't a terrible person."

"He's not," Anna agreed. "I don't think he wanted to hurt me. But..." She inhaled deeply, gathering her thoughts.

Kylie glared at her. "But what?"

Anna smiled sadly. "I'm concerned I'm one of those people who only want what they can't have. I spent the past two years desperate for Hayden to realise he'd made a mistake, but when he said that to me at the party, I just felt flat. And now I have a crush on Warren."

"And you think you can't have Warren?" Frannie ventured.

"I don't think he sees me that way." At least she wasn't willing to let herself hope he might. "Also, he's my brother's best friend."

Kylie curled her lip. "So?"

"So even if he liked me, I don't think he'd do anything about it."

"Well then, maybe *you* should do something about it," Kylie said, with a mischievous glint in her eyes.

"I think we all know I'm not forward enough to ask him out. Also..." She hesitated, unsure whether to share her other concern. When her friends looked at her eagerly, she released a breath. "I think Carla might have a thing for him."

"Woah!" Kylie's eyes lit up. "This conversation took an unexpected turn. Your sister likes Warren as well?"

"I don't know." Anna wrinkled her nose. "They always bicker, and it kind of feels like flirting."

"Isn't Carla a bit young for him?" Frannie said.

"She's younger than him." Anna paused, calculating. "By about six years, I guess. It's not that much."

"It's Carla," Kylie said, rolling her eyes. "If she fancied him, she'd have done something about it."

"Maybe she has..." Anna trailed off, wishing she'd kept that train of thought to herself.

Frannie lifted her eyebrows. "What does that mean?"

Anna bit down on her lip, thinking of Warren's story about the spider in Carla's flat. She'd been too amused by her sister's audacity to get the rest of the story. Had he gone over there? If he had, what had happened? Did he just remove the spider and leave? And had Carla really only wanted him to get rid of the spider, or was that just a ruse to get Warren to come over?

"Never mind," Anna said, not wanting to gossip about her

sister. "I'm just worried that maybe she likes him, but I'm probably overthinking things. She was the one who suggested I get him to pretend to be my boyfriend for the party."

"There you go then," Frannie said. "She wouldn't do that if she had feelings for him."

"Probably not," Anna agreed. Though perhaps it just wouldn't have occurred to Carla that there'd be more to it than just pretend.

Kylie beamed. "I think you should ask Warren out on a proper date."

Even the thought of it made Anna squirm. She looked to Frannie for her opinion.

"Maybe you can engineer ways to spend time with him," she suggested gently. "That should be pretty easy. Just conveniently be at the hotel bar when he's finishing work."

"That seems manageable," Anna said.

It would definitely be easier than finding the courage to ask him on a date.

Chapter Twenty-Two

Usually, Anna couldn't go for more than a few days without seeing her sister, but of course when she specifically wanted to speak to her, she seemed to be constantly busy. They'd exchanged a few messages over the week, but Anna was keen for a proper catch up.

On Thursday, she messaged Carla in the morning asking when she had time to meet. The response that came through was a list of her various jobs over the next three weeks.

Anna blinked slowly at her sister's hectic work schedule, which suddenly made her own calendar seem very relaxed. Carla always had multiple casual jobs, but the Christmas season was busy for her. As well as her usual jobs – working at a local dog shelter and some pet sitting work – she'd also be playing the role of a Christmas elf at a couple of local attractions.

From the schedule she'd sent over, she'd mostly be at a local educational farm, donning her elf outfit at the Santa's grotto.

You could always call in and visit Santa, Carla wrote. *I'll be there all day today, and it shouldn't be too busy. I can take a coffee break, and you can tell me about the party. Say you're my sister and they'll let you in the farm for free.*

I have work to do this morning, she replied, *but maybe this afternoon.*

It turned out that she struggled to concentrate anyway, so she gave up on packaging her soaps and candles after lunch and set off for the fifteen-minute drive to the farm.

Too embarrassed to talk her way in for free, she paid the entrance fee and accepted the map of the farm with its special Christmas events, including the Santa's Grotto, a light trail, and a festive train ride.

Carla's eyes lit up at the sight of Anna. "You made it!"

"I fancied visiting Santa," she said, tipping her head towards the cabin behind Carla.

Her sister tilted her head, making the bell on her hat jangle. "Have you been good this year?"

"Very good," Anna said, smothered by her sister's hug. "But I actually just wanted to see you since I don't think I'll see you until Christmas Eve at this rate."

"I took on too much work," she said, stepping back and setting her hands on her shiny belt buckle. "Not that this really feels like work. It's way too much fun."

"Do you get coffee breaks?"

"Yes. But I'll need to wait for the other elf to get back from his lunch break."

"There's a male elf?" Anna asked, lifting an eyebrow. "Is he cute?"

"All elves are cute," Carla said. "It's a requirement of the job. He's not my type, though." She smiled at the children in the line, then brought her attention back to Anna. "Why don't you have a look around the farm, and I'll come and find you soon."

With the decorations and a smattering of snowflakes in the air, the atmosphere on the farm was wonderfully festive. She'd visited the sheep and horses and was just walking out of the cowshed when Carla approached her with two takeaway cups in her hands. A big black puffer coat covered most of her elf outfit.

Only her striped red and green tights and polished black shoes stuck out of the bottom of the long coat.

"I've got fifteen minutes," she said, handing over a coffee. "Come with me."

Anna walked briskly with Carla around the stables to a few empty picnic benches. "It's always quiet round here," Carla said, straddling the bench. "How's everything with you?"

"Good. I thought I was busy until you sent me your schedule. Now I think I have a lot of time on my hands."

Carla grinned. "I love this time of year."

"I can see that," Anna said, flicking the top of her hat to make the bell tinkle.

"How was the party?" Carla asked. "You didn't say much in your messages."

"It was great."

"Yeah? How was it having Warren there?"

"Really good," she said and felt her cheeks flush.

Carla leaned forward, resting her elbows on the table. "Can you please be more descriptive in your answers! Remember, I only have fifteen minutes. Tell me the juicy details already. What did Hayden think of you having a date with you?"

"Warren reckons Hayden was jealous, but I'm not sure." She wrapped her hands around the mug for warmth. "For once, Hayden didn't have a date with him. He split up with Nicola."

"I bet he really hated that you had a date then."

"Who knows what goes through his head." Anna pressed her lips together. "He said something weird though..."

"What?" Carla asked eagerly.

"That he wished we'd never broken up."

Carla's eyes went comically large. "Seriously?"

She nodded. "I thought it was just because he'd been drinking and was a bit jealous of seeing me with Warren, but I spoke to Frannie and Kylie, and they seem to think he's had a thing for me this entire time."

"Why has he spent the last two years serial dating if he still has a thing for you?"

"Apparently, he tried to get back together with me, and I turned him down."

"What?" Carla curled her lip. "When?"

"Ages ago. Remember, I met up with him, and he wanted us to be friends?" She paused long enough for Carla to nod. "It seems he was actually asking if we could get back together, but I misunderstood."

"How could you possibly misunderstand that?"

"He said he missed me and wanted to fix things between us, but I thought he meant as friends. So I told him I didn't want to even be friends with him." She blew out a breath. "It was so long ago that I barely remember the conversation, but from what I can gather, we got our wires more than a little crossed."

"It sounds like it." She threw her hands up. "So what does this mean? Are you going to get back together with him?"

"I don't think so."

"Why not? You've been desperate to get back together with him ever since you two broke up."

"Yes. But now I'm not sure. Also, I've heard nothing from him since the party on Saturday, so I don't even know if he wants to get back together."

"He thinks you're together with Warren, though, doesn't he? Are you going to correct him on that matter?"

Slowly, she shook her head.

"I'm confused," Carla said. "I thought you'd be excited about the possibility of working things out with Hayden."

"Me too. But I'm not. I think I might finally be over him."

"Right." Carla's brow was all rumpled. "I don't really understand."

Anna stared down at her coffee. "I had a really good time at the party, and for the first time in ages, I wasn't missing Hayden or wishing we were still together."

"I guess that's good."

"Yeah. Having Warren there was great... and I had a good time with his parents the weekend before as well."

"You said so in your messages. I hate to always take the credit, but wasn't it my idea for you to take Warren to the party? I knew it would make Hayden jealous."

"You can take the credit," Anna said, smiling over her coffee. "It was a good idea to take him."

Carla sipped her drink, apparently not reading between the lines.

"I had a really great time with him," Anna said pointedly.

"You already said that." Carla rolled her eyes. "Should I be worried about you repeating yourself?"

"No. I just wasn't sure you heard."

"I heard." She slipped her fingers under her hat to scratch at her hairline, then her gaze whipped back to Anna. "Wait... what's going on? Am I missing something..."

"Maybe. It was just really lovely pretending Warren was my boyfriend."

Carla closed her eyes and shook her head in a way that made her look like a cartoon character. "Yes, because it made Hayden jealous, and you didn't have to worry about your friends thinking you were still pining for him."

"Partly because of that, but mostly just because it was fun... he was really sweet."

"*Sweet* seems an odd choice of word to describe Warren."

"He *was.*"

"Okay, I'm glad you had a good time."

"I think maybe that's why I feel suddenly so indifferent about Hayden."

"How do you mean?"

Anna rolled her eyes. "I mean, I'm not thinking about Hayden because I'm thinking about Warren... I *like* Warren."

It seemed to take a moment for the words to sink in. "You *like* Warren?"

"Yes."

"In the sense that you'd like him to be your actual boyfriend and not just a pretend one?"

"Exactly."

For a second, her features remained void of emotion, then she snorted a laugh and slapped a hand over her face.

"What's so funny?" Anna asked.

"The idea of you and Warren together is funny, that's what."

"Why is it?" Anna asked, irritation sharpening her tone. "And why do you seem so surprised – you used to tease me for having a crush on Warren."

"I teased you because it annoyed you. I didn't actually think you liked him."

"I *didn't.* Not really. But I've seen a different side of him recently."

"And now you have a thing for him?" Carla asked, her laughter dissolving into a confused smile.

"Maybe."

"That's ridiculous."

"Why is it?"

"Because..." She grimaced and bit down on her lip. "Sorry. You and Warren just seem like a very unlikely couple."

"Why do we?"

"Because he's so sure of himself – and grumpy. He growls at people. And you don't like people who growl. You get nervous around people like Warren."

"He's not really grumpy." She dipped her head towards her shoulder. "Not properly grumpy anyway. Not deep down."

"So you suddenly know him on a deeper level?" Carla asked.

Anna gritted her teeth. "He's not grumpy with me. Maybe that's a side of him you bring out."

Carla's smile fell away completely. "Sorry," she said. "I wasn't trying to be negative. I just would never have put you and Warren together." She rubbed her hands together to warm them. "*Are* you together? What's going on?"

"No, we're not together. Nothing happened outside of us pretending to be together."

"What did that entail?"

"How do you mean?"

"Did you kiss him?"

Anna's stomach fluttered with butterflies. "Yes."

"Oh." Her hat moved down when she wrinkled her forehead. "I didn't imagine you taking the pretend thing that far."

"Do you have a problem with that?" Anna asked hesitantly.

She pulled her hat off and smoothed down her brown hair, a few shades lighter than Anna's. "Why would I have a problem with it?"

"You just seem uncomfortable with the idea of me having feelings for Warren."

"I'm surprised, that's all. Do you think he likes you?"

"I don't know. Frannie and Kylie think so. They said he was doing too good of a job of pretending. But I'm not so sure." She paused. "You don't have a crush on him, do you?"

"Oh, my god!" She stuck her tongue out. "Don't be gross. Of course I don't. He's completely grumpy and annoying. Why would you even ask that?"

"I don't know... I just..." She gave a jerky shake of her head. "Did you really call him one night to ask him to remove a spider from your flat?"

"Yes. Why?"

"Why did you call *him?*"

"Because Lewis was away, Dad was already in bed, and Mum told me not to be so pathetic. You would have been next on my list, but I assumed you'd be asleep, what with it being ten o'clock at night." She grinned cheekily. Then her eyes widened. "Oh my gosh, why did you think I called him? As some weird booty call? That's not what he thought, is it?"

"No. He didn't think that. He was only laughing about how scared you are of spiders. It just sounded odd that you'd called him, but it makes more sense if you tried other people first."

"Warren definitely wasn't my first choice of exterminator," she said, plucking her hat from the table as she stood abruptly. "Let's walk while we finish our drinks. I said I wouldn't be long."

Anna smiled as she fell into step beside her. "You know it's really pathetic that you had to call someone because of a daddy longlegs in your flat."

"It wasn't a daddy longlegs!" she insisted, slightly high-pitched. "It was a massive thing. Like maybe someone's pet tarantula escaped."

"Really?" Anna asked sceptically.

"No. Not really." Carla gave her arm a shove. "But it was a nasty, black, hairy thing, and I was worried it might attack me in my sleep like that massive spider from The Hobbit. I didn't want to end up cocooned in its web."

"You're ridiculous, you know that?" Anna beamed, partly at her sister's tendency to make a drama out of everything and partly because she was no longer concerned that Carla would have a problem with her pursuing Warren.

Now, all she was concerned about was when she'd see him next.

Chapter Twenty-Three

The festive decorations in Chipping Campden kept a smile on Anna's face – and her nerves at bay – as she ambled along the main street later that day. Sadly, spotting Warren approaching his car outside the hotel wiped out her Christmas cheer.

When his gaze snagged on her, he paused with one foot in the car. "I'm not sure you could look less pleased to see me," he said lightly.

"Sorry." She shook her head, pulling herself together. "I was upset to see you *leaving*. I was hoping I might catch you."

"Me specifically?" he asked with a grin. "Or someone to cook for you?"

"Specifically, you to cook for me." She'd also been hoping to coax him into having a drink at the hotel bar with her after his shift, but apparently she hadn't timed it well. "I assumed the restaurant would still be open."

"It is, but it's quiet, so I thought I'd head out early. Liam's still there and will no doubt rustle you something up."

"I didn't think you trusted Liam to leave him in charge of the kitchen unless absolutely necessary," she teased.

Warren rolled his eyes. "He might not be as useless as I made out. But I can't imagine there will be much for him to do anyway."

Anna looked at the hotel, rubbing her hands together against the cold as she contemplated whether she still wanted to hang around, or give up and go home. "Is Lewis here?"

"No. He's still in London."

"Ivy?"

He shook his head. "She left an hour ago."

Disappointment tugged at Anna's belly. "I'll probably just find food at home then."

"Want a lift?" he asked, tipping his head at the car.

She hesitated for a moment, then nodded her acceptance and moved to get in the passenger seat.

Once the engine was on, Anna held her hands in front of the air vent to warm her chilly fingers.

She inhaled deeply. "Why does your car heater smell so delicious?"

He chuckled as he put the car into gear. "It's not the heating. It's my dinner." He indicated the back seat, and she turned to see a shopping bag. "I take dinner from the hotel sometimes so I don't have to cook at home."

"That smells amazing," she said, inhaling the delicious aroma. "What is it?"

"Beef stew and dumplings."

She groaned. "Heaven."

He laughed properly now. "Now, you're making me feel as though I should offer to share."

"Oh, no," she said automatically. "I wasn't hinting at that." Though maybe she should. If she wanted to spend time with him, it wouldn't hurt to be more proactive.

"Can you stop drooling all over my car, please?"

"I'm not..." She trailed off when she caught the playful glint in his eyes. "Don't tease me."

He concentrated on the road for a moment. "There's enough for two if you want to eat with me."

"Really?"

"Yes."

"I can provide drinks and possibly rustle up dessert," she offered.

He turned onto the side road. "Sounds good."

Apparently, her timing hadn't been bad after all. Warren had just stopped the car outside Anna's flat when he swore under his breath.

"What's wrong?" she asked.

"Nothing." He looked thoughtful. "I just remembered I have dinner for my neighbour too. I messaged to tell her I was bringing food, so she'll be waiting for it."

Anna's smile felt insincere. "If you need to go, it's fine..."

A muscle twitched in his jaw. "Sorry."

"It doesn't matter. I can grab myself a sandwich." Swallowing her disappointment, she reached for the door handle.

"Hang on," he blurted. "I could drop her food off and come back..."

"I don't want to put you out."

"It's not a problem."

"We could also eat at your place," she suggested. "But you'd still need to drop me home again later. Let's just leave it, shall we?"

"You could come to my place," he said slowly.

Her lips stretched into a full smile. "That was an extremely half-hearted invitation."

"I was just trying to think what state I left it in this morning."

"I've never been to your place," she said. She also couldn't recall Lewis ever mentioning hanging out there. "Has Lewis ever been?"

"No."

"He's your best friend, and he's never been to your home?"

He pursed his lips. "We tend to hang out at the hotel. Maybe the pub if we're feeling adventurous."

"I'd actually like to come to your place. I'm intrigued now."

"It's nothing impressive."

"I want to see," she said.

He lifted one shoulder in a shrug. "Okay."

Once they were on their way again, Anna took in the serious set of his features and could have sworn he was nervous. Which only made her more curious.

"Do you often take dinner for your neighbour?" she asked eventually.

"A couple of times a week." His eyes snapped to her. "Lewis knows about it. He said it was fine."

"I wasn't suggesting you were stealing or anything. I only wondered."

"She lives on her own. I know how annoying it is to cook for one person, so I bring her food sometimes. She cooks for me on Mondays when it's my day off."

"Every Monday?"

"Yeah."

"So you eat together as well as bringing her food?"

"Most of the time. I can just drop it off today, though. She won't care."

Anna smiled weakly, surprised once again at how little she knew about him. And by how much she disliked the thought of him regularly sharing meals with his single female neighbour.

Chapter Twenty-Four

The cul-de-sac lined with large, detached houses came as yet another surprise. Previously, Anna had had a vague notion of where Warren lived, but this wasn't at all what she'd had in mind.

"I thought you said your place was small," she remarked when he parked in the driveway of the furthest house.

"It is," he replied, pulling the handbrake on. "This is my neighbour's house."

"Which one's yours?" She looked at the houses on either side. "They all look pretty impressive to me."

He didn't reply but reached for the bag on the back seat, then stepped out of the car. "Come on."

Curiously, she followed him up the drive to the front door, which opened when he got close.

"I thought I heard your car," the elderly lady said. Her eyes flicked behind Warren and landed on Anna. "Oh, hello."

"This is Anna," he said. "Lewis's sister."

"Hello, dear." She offered her hand, then clasped Anna's hand in both of hers. "I'm Edith, but call me Edie."

"Hi," Anna said. "Lovely to meet you."

"I'm going to have dinner with Anna," Warren told her. "So I'll just drop yours off when I've warmed it up. I'd have called and let you know, but it was a last-minute plan."

"Don't worry about me. I can rustle something up for myself."

"It's no problem," he said. "I'll bring it over in a bit."

"If you're sure."

"Of course. I can't have you fading away. If you pop your clogs, I'll end up homeless."

Her eyes brightened as she beamed. "He likes to tease me," she said to Anna. "But I can't complain because he looks after me."

"I'll bring dinner over in ten minutes," he said with a grin. "You can do one of your brain training exercises while you wait. Got to keep that mind sharp!"

Edie swatted a hand at him, but he dodged out of the way. "See what I mean about the teasing," she said to Anna, but looked entirely amused.

Warren beckoned to Anna with a flick of his chin, and she followed him around the side of the house.

"Edie is my landlady and my neighbour," he said, moving the shopping bag to his other hand and pulling a set of keys from his pocket.

When he stopped at the door on the side of the garage, Anna failed to hide her confusion. "Where are we going?"

"My place." Turning, he gave her a sheepish grin. "I told you it's nothing impressive."

Taken aback, she remained quiet as she stepped into the converted garage. Her eyes darted around the compact space. In front of her, bright white kitchen units formed an L-shape around a wooden table and chairs. To the left was a simple living space, and to the right, the bedroom door stood slightly ajar. Presumably, the closed door beside that was the bathroom.

"It's small," Warren said, tossing his keys on the table.

Anna stepped further into the cosy space. "It's cute."

"It works for me."

"Doesn't the tiny kitchen drive you crazy?" she asked as he set his shopping bag on the sideboard.

"I never cook here. If I'm cooking on my day off, I do it at Edie's place. She's always happy to have me pottering around her kitchen."

"She seems very sweet." Anna smiled to herself, thinking of her earlier trepidation over the idea of Warren being so close to his neighbour.

"She's great." He retrieved a Tupperware container from the bag and pulled out a pan from a cupboard.

"Have you lived here the entire time you've worked at the hotel?"

"Yeah. To start with, it was appealing because the rent was so cheap, but then it worked out well."

"How did you find it?" she asked, taking a seat at the table.

If it weren't for his slight grimace, she'd have suspected he hadn't heard her, given how long it took him to reply.

"It's a long and slightly odd story," he finally said.

"Now I definitely need to know." She propped her elbows on the table and rested her chin on her interlocked fingers as she looked at him eagerly.

He pulled a face at her, then got to work transferring the stew into the pan. "Edie's husband, John, was quite an entrepreneur. He converted the garage himself and jumped on the Airbnb bandwagon right from the start."

He scraped the remnants of the stew out with a spatula, then gave the pot a stir before turning and leaning against the sideboard. "I booked in for one night when I had my interview at the hotel. I didn't know how long it would take, and I didn't want to worry about getting back to London if it ended up being a long day. In the end it would have been fine, but I'd booked and couldn't cancel at the last minute, so I stayed anyway."

Glancing at the stew, he folded his arms across his chest. "I was just about to fall asleep when I heard someone shouting for help. I ran over to the house to find John collapsed and Edie hysterical. I waited for the ambulance with them, then drove Edie to the hospital. It turned out John had had a stroke. I ended up staying at the hospital with Edie all night. We hardly spoke, but it bonded us."

A lump thickened Anna's throat, and she struggled to speak. "He died?"

"Not that night. He survived the stroke, but never left the hospital. He had a second stroke a week later that killed him."

Tears pricked at the back of Anna's eyes, and she couldn't think of anything to say.

"I kept in touch with Edie. We were talking on the phone every couple of days. When I told her I'd got the job and was moving to the area, she offered for me to live here. She wasn't keen to continue renting it to strangers without John around." He inhaled deeply. "I think we both expected it to be more of a short-term thing, but it just works. For both of us."

Anna touched the corners of her eyes to catch tears. "How come I've never heard that story before?"

He turned to stir the stew. "I never told Lewis."

"Why not?"

"We weren't friends when I first came here. It felt like a weird thing to say to my new boss... like maybe he'd think I was a bad omen or something."

It occurred to her once again that Warren really had kept his head down for the first year that he'd worked at the hotel. Maybe it was because she was caught up in her relationship with Hayden, but she really hadn't known Warren at all back then. He'd only started socialising with them in the last couple of years, when he and Lewis had become closer.

"You could have told him later," she said gently.

"I could have, but it still feels like a weird story to tell."

"I think it's a nice story."

He arched an eyebrow. "Weirdo!"

"I mean, apart from the fact that Edie's husband died. That's not nice, but it seemed like good timing that you were here to help her, and it's sweet how attached to you Edie is."

"It's mutual," he said flatly as he took bowls from the cupboard.

After putting one portion into a bowl, he gave Anna a stern look. "Make sure the rest doesn't burn while I take this to Edie."

"I think I can manage that." She beamed. "I promise not to get distracted by my phone. I don't want you shouting at me."

At the door, he turned back and poked his tongue out. The sparkle in his eyes made her stomach flutter riotously.

Left alone, she inhaled a full breath and fought to calm her swirling emotions.

Chapter Twenty-Five

Having something to do kept Anna's nerves at bay, and she stirred the thick stew while inhaling the hearty aroma. When it bubbled, she turned the hob off and moved the pan to the back ring. With no sign of Warren returning, her eyes roamed the humble kitchen, then she moved to nosey at the bathroom. It was small – with a toilet, sink, and a cubicle shower. Everything was neat and tidy, but presumably in such a small space you'd need to keep everything well organised.

Closing the bathroom door again, she wandered to the living room and ran her hand along the back of the two-seater couch, which faced the TV unit. The far wall contained floor to ceiling bookshelves, and she angled her head to read the titles. The mix of crime and action novels made her smile. She'd never imagined Warren to be a big reader.

After taking a few steps, she paused at the section of the bookcase dedicated to cookbooks. She supposed it shouldn't be a surprise given his profession, but there were just so many – from the familiar celebrity chefs, to names she'd never heard of, and books dedicated to speciality cuisine.

The only window in the room looked out onto the neighbouring garden, and she watched a robin hop along the branch of a small bush. Turning towards the door, she listened for Warren, but with everything quiet, her eyes drifted to his bedroom before she wandered back there.

She'd just stuck her head around the door when the sound of Warren's voice startled her.

"Snooping?" he asked casually.

"Sorry," she said, backing out of the bedroom.

"It's fine. You're welcome to look around. Did I make the bed this morning?"

"Yes. It's all very neat. It's a really nice place."

"Thanks." He made for the stove. "You left dinner unattended."

"I switched it off. I'm sure it's fine." She grimaced. "I hope so anyway."

"I was only winding you up about burning it," he said while filling the bowls.

Anna sat back at the table. "Was Edie okay with eating alone?"

"Yeah. It just took a while to get away because she felt the need to give me a lecture on safe sex."

The way he deadpanned the words made Anna laugh loudly. "She did not!"

"No." He put a steaming bowl of stew in front of Anna. "She didn't. But she had a few questions about my visitor."

"What was she asking?" Anna dragged her spoon through the stew, smiling at the thought of Warren having to answer questions about her.

He sat opposite her and took a mouthful of his stew before answering. "She wanted to know if you're my girlfriend."

"What did you say?"

"I told her you were just my friend, but sometimes you like to pretend you're my girlfriend."

Anna shook her head when she caught the mischievous

twinkle in his eyes. "Edie's right about you and your teasing. You didn't really say that did you?"

"No. I said you're just my friend, but she didn't seem to believe me."

"I take it you don't often bring women back here?" Anna asked, hoping she sounded casual.

"All the time. But I usually sneak them in to avoid getting lectures from Edie."

Anna rolled her eyes. "Are you going to say anything serious this evening?"

He stared into his stew. "Okay, fine. I don't bring a lot of women back here."

The ensuing silence was uncomfortable. Mostly because she realised she hadn't been at all subtle in delving into his love life. Since she was probably already bright red, there didn't seem to be any reason not to blunder on.

"Have you been in a relationship since you moved here?"

He shook his head. "Nothing serious. A few dates here and there, but I've been focused on my job."

"You work really hard," she remarked, then blew on a spoonful of piping-hot stew.

"It's easy to work hard when you do something you love."

"I guess there's also a bit of pressure now you have a Michelin star in your sights."

Her words had been jokey, but she didn't miss the way Warren's shoulders bunched up as he became suddenly fascinated by his stew.

"Sorry," she said, a whisper of panic rolling through her that she'd said the wrong thing.

"It's fine." He gave a quick shake of his head and seemed to relax again.

"So you *do* feel some pressure over that?" she asked quietly.

"It won't happen," he said. "So, no, I don't feel any pressure over it. I just feel awkward that other people think it will happen.

Your brother seems to have his hopes up, and I think he'll be disappointed."

"I guess Lewis just has more faith in your cooking than you do."

He looked suddenly weary. "That's probably true."

When he tucked into his dinner, Anna had the feeling she'd said the wrong thing – not only because of his sudden silence, but because the mood had shifted.

And not in a good way.

Chapter Twenty-Six

Despite the slightly tense atmosphere, dinner was over far too quickly. Anna pushed her bowl away and leaned back in her chair, considering how to get Warren to relax again, and how to draw the evening out. If they were at her place, it would be easier – she could offer dessert and suggest a drink, but here she should probably just follow Warren's lead. He'd been working all day, so maybe he was tired and wanted his space. That might be why he'd clammed up on her.

"That was delicious, thank you," she said when he took the empty bowls to the sink.

"You're welcome." He turned the tap on and reached for the washing-up liquid. When his phone buzzed on the counter a moment later, he craned his neck to check the display, then muttered a curse.

"Everything okay?" Anna asked.

"It's just my mum. I can call her back later."

"I can help..." Hopping out of the chair, she picked up the phone and swiped to answer it before moving it to his ear.

The look on his face made her flinch. So much for lifting his mood.

"What did you do?" he grumbled, pulling away from the phone.

"Answered for you," she whispered. "Since your hands are wet."

"That wasn't–" He cut himself off as a quiet voice emanated from the phone. "Hang on a sec, Mum." He sighed as he wiped his hands on a tea towel, then took the phone from Anna and said hello into the phone. "We're just eating dinner. I'll call you back later."

Whatever his mum said made Warren frown and rub at his temple. "Yeah, I'm with Anna. I'll tell her you said hi." He sat back down at the table, giving Anna a weary look while he listened to his mum. "Fine," he finally said, then moved the phone from his ear and tapped the screen before setting it on the table. "You're on speaker."

"Hi, Anna!" his mum said cheerfully.

"Hello." Anna sank onto the chair opposite Warren and leaned towards the phone. "How are you?"

"I'm fine, thank you. Sorry to disturb your dinner..."

Anna flashed Warren a look, and he threw his hands up, then jabbed a finger at her in a gesture that she couldn't decipher but which made her want to laugh.

"I just wanted to say again how lovely it was to meet you," Jen went on. "Also, I don't know if Warren mentioned our upcoming trip to Bath. I told him to invite you."

"I didn't invite her," Warren said impatiently. "I already told you I can't make it, so why would I invite Anna?"

"I thought you might change your mind. It'd be lovely if you came with us. You haven't joined a family trip in forever."

Warren rubbed the back of his neck. "I have to work."

"Can't you take a couple of days off? We'll be there for the week, but you could just come for as long as you can manage. Selena would like to see you, and it'd be good for you to spend some time with Joshie."

"It's a busy time at work," he said. "I'll visit in the new year as usual."

"Just think about it. Maybe Anna would like a nice festive break in Bath. It's lovely at this time of year. You could do some Christmas shopping."

"I haven't been to Bath in ages," Anna said, then stifled a laugh at Warren's menacing glare.

"It's beautiful," Jen said. "The house is just outside of Bath. In the countryside – lovely and peaceful. We always go for a little break before Christmas. It's a family tradition. Warren hasn't joined us there for years, though. Have you even been since the hot tub was installed?"

"No," he muttered, then gave Anna a gentle kick when she widened her eyes and mouthed 'hot tub' with mock excitement.

"Just say you'll think about it," his mum said.

"Okay. Sure. Well, we'll discuss it, and I'll get back to you. We're going to finish our dinner now."

"Yes, get back to it before it's cold. I'll talk to you soon."

There was a chorus of goodbyes before Warren jabbed at the phone to end the call.

"I can't believe you just outright lied to your mum," Anna said.

He threw his hands up. "And I can't believe you answered my phone. Why would you do that?"

"Sorry." She giggled at his look of outrage. "I thought you were annoyed about not being able to answer it because your hands were wet."

"No. I was annoyed by the call. I had no intention of answering it, even if I wasn't washing the dishes."

"Sorry," she said again. "I'd never dare to ignore a call from my mum, so I kind of assume other people are the same."

Warren smiled. "To be honest, I'd never dare ignore a call from *your* mum, either."

"How often does my mum call you?" Anna asked, assuming he was being hypothetical.

"Far too often!" He grinned. "It's not as much since Erin moved in with Lewis. I guess she gets the brunt of it now. It used to be that if Lewis didn't answer the phone, Fiona would call me as though I was his personal secretary. Sometimes I suspected she didn't even bother trying to call Lewis and just called me first. She'd ask me to pass on a message if she knew it was something Lewis would say no to."

Anna chuckled. "She's a nightmare sometimes."

"I far prefer phone calls from your mum to my own." His eyes glazed over, and he looked momentarily lost in thought before he stood abruptly. "Do you want a drink? There's tea or coffee... or possibly beer..." He opened the fridge, then nodded decisively. "There's beer."

"I'd love a tea," she told him, happy that he didn't seem to be in a hurry to get rid of her. "Do you have a variety of flavours?"

He rolled his eyes. "This isn't a hotel."

"Do you, though? Because I can absolutely imagine you having a quaint wooden tea box with different flavour tea bags."

"I don't," he said, taking two mugs from the cupboard. "I feel as though it's a luxury best saved for hotel stays." He filled the kettle, then got back to work on the dishes.

When the water had boiled, Anna moved to make herself useful.

"This mug is beautiful," she said, eyeing the unique ceramic mug with the words 'world's best chef' etched neatly on one side.

"Lewis got it for me," he said idly.

"Cute." She poured water over the tea bags and got milk from the fridge. Once he'd finished the dishes, she handed him a mug and wandered over to the living room with her own. Lowering herself onto the couch, she looked up at Warren and caught the troubled look on his face. "Sorry. I'm making myself at home. Did you want to sit at the table?"

"No." He sat beside her, looking momentarily unsure of himself before he reached for Anna's mug.

She watched in confusion while he set it on the coffee table in front of him and put his mug close to her.

It took a moment for her to figure out what was going on, and when she did, she bit down on her lip to smother a laugh.

"Did I take the wrong mug?" she asked, then pressed her lips together as the laughter crept up her throat.

"It's my favourite," he said sulkily. "And you're not even a chef, so it's inappropriate for you to take that one."

"You're kind of surprising, you know?" She relaxed back onto the couch and flicked her gaze to him as he picked up the mug, which he was apparently so attached to. "By the way, what family trip did your mum just invite me on?"

Ripples erupted on the surface of his tea as he snorted a laugh. "It's a trip to Bath. They always go before Christmas."

"And they stay in the same place?"

He nodded.

"And it has a hot tub?"

"Apparently it does now. It didn't when I was a kid."

"How long have you been going there?"

"As long as I can remember."

"It must be quite nostalgic, then?"

"I suppose so."

"But you're not going?"

He sipped his tea and shook his head. "No."

"I'm sure you could get an extra day or two off if you speak to Lewis."

"I could," he said. "But time off isn't the reason I'm not going."

"So that entire conversation with your mum was basically lies?"

"It's either lie, or tell her I can't stand the thought of spending more than a few hours with my family."

"Is it really that bad? I know you argued with your dad, and I can see how they might not be the most relaxed people to spend time with, but they also seemed perfectly nice when I met them."

His eyebrows drew together. "It turns out they're much more bearable when there's someone else around. I may need to recruit you for every family visit in the future."

Warmth spread through her stomach, which had nothing to do with the tea. "Does that mean I get to go to Bath to do my Christmas shopping?"

"No! Even you would get sick of my family after more than a few hours. I wouldn't subject you to entire days and nights with them."

Anna smiled. "Your sister's going?" she asked gently.

"Yeah."

"Do you get on with her?"

He swayed his head from shoulder to shoulder. "We used to get on well when we were kids. These days I don't see much of her."

"And who is Joshie?"

"My nephew." His eyes lit up. "He's four, and he's the only one who makes it at all tempting to go."

"Maybe you should go," she suggested. "Surely a couple of days with your family can't be that bad. And it might be worth it to spend time with your nephew."

He curled his lips in a frown, considering it.

"It's almost Christmas. You're supposed to spend time with your family."

He lifted a solitary eyebrow. "Are you supposed to *dread* spending time with your family?"

"I think it's pretty normal," she told him. "When is the trip to Bath?"

"The week after next."

"You have Mondays off, don't you?"

"Yep."

"So why not take the Tuesday off and go for a couple of days. You could drive back on Wednesday morning and be back to work in the afternoon."

"In theory, I could."

"I think you should go. It obviously means a lot to your mum."

"I'd regret it an hour after I arrived. Also, thanks to you, I'd be bombarded with questions about my girlfriend."

"You can explain that I'm just your friend."

"That's not really the issue. The problem is it will be stressful."

"I'm sure it won't be as bad as you think."

"Easy for you to say. You won't be there."

It was on the tip of her tongue to suggest she could join him, but a flood of nerves held her back. She could hardly invite herself on a family trip, no matter how appealing it was.

"I think you should go," she murmured weakly.

He grinned at her over his tea. "And *I* think you should stop pestering me to go. It seems neither of us is getting what we want." His eyes danced with amusement. "Unless..."

"Unless what?"

He set his mug on the table and looked thoughtful. "I'll go if you come and pretend to be my girlfriend."

The look he gave her was full of challenge. If she was reading him correctly, he didn't expect her to agree – it was his way of getting her to drop the subject.

"Okay," she said idly.

His smile slipped, and his eyebrows drew swiftly together. "*Okay, what?*"

A buzz of excitement replaced her earlier nerves. "I'll come with you and pretend to be your girlfriend."

Chapter Twenty-Seven

Warren was on dangerous ground. Taking Anna along for his family getaway was madness. If he'd thought for a moment she'd agree to it, he'd never have suggested it. But he *had* suggested it – albeit jokingly – and she'd agreed so quickly she'd left him speechless.

She'd only offered to come along for moral support, though. They were friends who'd been helping each other out recently, that was all. It wasn't a big deal.

It was hard to say whether he was relieved or frustrated that Lewis hadn't come into work at all over the weekend. Maybe it would be good to get the conversation out of the way, but putting it off wasn't so bad either. Especially as he kept thinking Anna might call and say she'd changed her mind about joining his family trip.

On Tuesday, when Lewis wandered into the hotel kitchen, Warren felt his guts twist at the sight of his best friend.

"Was everything okay here over the weekend?" Lewis asked.

"All good." Warren wiped his hands on a cloth. "Got time for a chat?"

"Yeah. I was actually going to ask if you fancy grabbing a drink when you've finished here?"

"Great. I shouldn't be too much longer."

"Come and find me in the office when you're ready."

An hour later they were making idle conversation in the pub down the road, while Lewis's border collie, Molly, snoozed by the fire in front of them.

"By the way, how did it go with Anna and her party?" Lewis asked when they were halfway down their second beers. "If my family's reports are correct, it went well, but I haven't spoken to Anna."

"It was good," Warren said.

"Did you actually pretend to be her boyfriend?"

"Yes." He fought a smile as he recalled the evening at the hotel.

"Was Hayden there?"

"Yeah. And I don't think he was overly impressed by my presence."

"Did he say something?"

"No, but I definitely got jealous vibes."

"Sounds like a successful evening."

"Yep." Warren sank back in his chair and pulled his chin to his chest. "I ended up staying over, by the way."

From the flicker of amusement in Lewis's eyes, Warren would swear he was enjoying watching Warren squirm.

"Stayed over at the hotel with my sister?" he asked.

"I slept on the floor," Warren said quickly. It didn't feel necessary to disclose that that was only the beginning of the night.

"Glad to hear it."

Irritatingly, Warren couldn't make out if Lewis's words were serious or mocking. He scratched his forehead. "I also wanted to mention something else… it's a bit weird…"

"Weirder than you spending the night in a hotel room with my little sister?"

"A bit, yeah." He hesitated. "Anna's going to come on a family trip with me."

The way Lewis's eyes bulged was comical. "You're going to need to explain that one."

"Anna found out I was avoiding a family trip and she was pestering me to go, so I jokingly said she'd need to come with me."

"Where is this trip?" Lewis asked.

"Just near Bath. And only two nights. I think Anna was keen on a shopping trip, and my mum was enticing her by telling her how nice the house is."

Lewis responded with a slow nod.

"Anyway," Warren said. "It's next week, but just at the beginning of the week, so it won't be a problem with the kitchen. Liam already agreed to work the Tuesday for me." He sat up straighter. "That's okay, right? You said the rest of the kitchen staff should be able to take on more responsibility when I'm not here..."

"Yeah. Of course." His lips twitched as though he wanted to say more and was trying to figure out how to word it. "Is there something going on between you and Anna?" he finally asked.

"No." It was a good thing he wasn't hooked up to a lie detector because his heart rate went wild. He shook his head and wondered if the action was a little too forceful. "No," he said again.

"Really?"

"Yeah. We're just friends."

"It's kind of strange that she agreed to go away with your family."

Warren shifted in his seat. "It was her idea. I didn't want to go at all. I'd already told my mum I wasn't going, but Anna insisted I should spend more time with my family. It is a bit of an odd situation."

"I didn't mean it was weird for her to go with you… I meant it's strange that she wants to."

"Tell me about it," Warren said, rolling his eyes. "If you'd met my family, you'd realise *just* how strange it is."

"No." Lewis chuckled. "I was commenting on the fact that Anna doesn't enjoy doing stuff like that. When she was with Hayden, she'd get nervous about going to his family gatherings, so I'm surprised she's volunteering to go with you. You should be careful…"

"How do you mean?"

"Maybe on your side it's just a friendship thing, but it might not be for her."

Warren's heart rate sped up even more. "I don't think so, but if it's an issue, I can cancel the trip. It's not a big deal."

"I wasn't saying it's an issue. It's fine. I just don't want things to get awkward for either of you, but it's also nothing to do with me. Don't tell her I said anything."

"I won't, but I also don't think you have anything to worry about."

"I'm not worried." He reached down to stroke Molly, then finished his beer. "Shall I get another round?"

"Okay." Warren checked his watch as Lewis headed to the bar, surprised by him suggesting more drinks. "It's a late night for you, isn't it?" he remarked jokily when Lewis returned.

Lewis chuckled, but otherwise didn't reply.

"How's everything with you and Erin?" Warren asked.

"Good." He shrugged. "Yeah. Fine. Why?"

"No reason, just asking. But your reply has me concerned. You didn't sound too sure there. Are you avoiding going home, by any chance?"

"Kind of." He blew out a breath. "But not because there's any big problem."

"What then?"

He scratched the bridge of his nose. "I think I might be a bit of a clingy boyfriend."

Warren couldn't help but smile. When Lewis glared at him he raised his hands and schooled his features back to a more serious expression. "Explain," he prompted.

"It's just that Erin's always busy. When she moved here she made a real effort to meet people and make friends. She joined different clubs and classes – yoga and art stuff and whatever else took her fancy."

"So she has a hectic social life and you sit at home waiting for her to have time for you?"

"No." He shook his head but didn't look convincing. "Well, it's not quite like that. But her being busy draws attention to the fact that I'm not. I used to spend all my time at the hotel. Now that I'm not there so much, I'm not always sure what to do with myself. I walk Molly, and I spend more time with my dad these days, which is nice."

He looked thoughtful. "When the weather was better I was doing some fishing trips with old school friends, but sometimes I feel as though I should have more of a social life."

"So you're just hanging out with me this evening to tick a box?"

"No!" Lewis grinned. "But we also don't hang out much these days. We should go for drinks more often."

"It's because we always used to hang out at work and now you're never around."

"Exactly. We need to get into new habits. Go for a drink once a week or something."

"I'd love to," Warren said, a mischievous smile pulling at his lips. "The problem is I work long hours for my demanding boss."

Stretching out his leg, Lewis kicked him, causing Molly's ears to prick up as she lifted her head to check what was going on. She sank back onto her paws when she decided they weren't about to get into a fight.

"I hope he at least pays you well," Lewis joked.

"I can't complain."

"We'll hang out more," Lewis said, then took a sip of his pint. "It's good that you're taking the time off next week, too. It'll be nice for you to spend more time with your family."

"I'm not sure about that," Warren replied, but wasn't dreading the family get together like he usually would.

In fact, he was looking forward to it.

Which was worrying, since his anticipation for the trip had absolutely nothing to do with spending time with his family.

And everything to do with Anna.

Chapter Twenty-Eight

When Warren called on Wednesday evening, Anna's heart thundered. Sure he was going to cancel their trip, she contemplated not answering, but in the end her desire to talk to him won out. As she answered, she told herself she could talk him into it again if he tried to back out.

But he only asked if she was sure she was okay with joining him, and warned her again that his family could be difficult to spend time with. When she insisted she was happy to go, they chatted about the details of when they'd set off.

He also asked how her workshop had gone that afternoon. Touched that he remembered, she told him all about her chilled-out session at the care home and how much she enjoyed spending time with the elderly.

"They don't make you nervous, then?" he asked, while she relaxed back on the couch.

"Not really. I had a few nerves before I arrived, but not like the other workshops I do. In my experience, old people are easy to please."

"That's true." He paused, and the conversation felt like it

was winding down. "What have you got planned for the rest of the week?"

"I have a craft fair on Saturday, so I need to make sure I have enough stock. And I might do some Christmas shopping on Friday."

"I thought you wanted to go shopping in Bath?"

"I do, but I doubt I can get everything in one shopping trip."

He made a hum of acknowledgement. "I suppose you also can't buy my gift when I'm with you."

She spluttered a laugh. "What makes you think I'm getting you a gift?"

"I think it's the least I deserve after you keep insisting on me pretending to be your boyfriend."

"You're the one who wanted me to pretend to be your girlfriend for your family holiday."

"Because you answered the phone to my mum!"

Her smile lingered. "If you're expecting a gift from me, does that mean you're getting me one?"

"If you want. Just send me a link with what you want. Maximum twenty quid."

"That's not how gift giving works."

"It is in my family. But without the spending limit."

"You're supposed to put some thought into it. Get something special."

He groaned. "Who has time for that?"

"I see you have no Christmas spirit. You realise it will be embarrassing when I give you a thoughtful gift and you have nothing for me in return."

"I don't really do embarrassment. I find it a waste of time."

"Lucky you."

"Hang on," he said, at a noise in the background. She listened to half of a muffled conversation before his voice came clear again. "I have to get back to work."

"Okay." She felt a rush of disappointment over ending the call.

"I'll see you on Monday, if not before."

"Yes." Her stomach did a flip at the thought of it. "See you Monday."

❄

Arriving in Evesham for her shopping trip on Friday afternoon, Anna fired off a message to Frannie, suggesting they meet for a coffee when Frannie finished work. The primary school she taught at was nearby, so it wasn't unusual for Anna to message her if she was in the area.

Not expecting an immediate reply, she set off wandering around the shops, trying to tick off items from her shopping list and looking for inspiration for a couple of gifts.

With less than two weeks until Christmas, the shopping left Anna feeling slightly frantic. The familiar Christmas music had a somewhat calming effect as she strolled from shop to shop. It slightly counteracted the discomfort of being inside heated buildings while dressed for the freezing weather outside. That and the stress of shopping on a deadline.

At least she wasn't under too much pressure. She still had time for more shopping trips. Including when she was in Bath with Warren. The thought made her stomach flutter, and she stopped outside Boots and checked her phone.

A message had come through from Frannie to say she'd love to meet, and asked Anna for a location. Realising the message had come through half an hour ago, she hit dial and they had a quick discussion about which coffee shop to meet in.

Half an hour later, they were tucked in the corner of a quaint little cafe with a pot of tea on the table between them. Here, the Christmas soundtrack was purely instrumental, and she barely noticed it as Frannie regaled her with tales of the rehearsals for the Christmas concert at her school.

"Christmas must be the best time to be a teacher," Anna remarked when she could get a word in. "It sounds like so much fun."

"It's crazy at this time of year. I love it though. Plus, there's the big payoff on the horizon." She grinned wickedly. "Thirty-two Christmas presents – most of which will be wine or chocolates!"

Anna grinned.

"Speaking of Christmas presents." Frannie's gaze went to the selection of shopping bags beside Anna's chair. "You look as though you were successful."

"I was." Since it was playing on her mind, she reached into the brown paper bag and pulled out the ornately carved wooden tea box she'd found in the independent home decor shop. "What do you think of this?"

"It's so cute." Frannie took it and opened the glass lid to peer in at the many compartments. "This would be a perfect gift for my gran. Where did you get it?"

"The shop a couple of doors down."

"Is it for your mum?" She frowned. "Does your mum like different teas? I imagine Fiona to be a PG Tips kind of woman. Probably stored in a tin she inherited from her grandmother."

"That's exactly right," Anna said, chuckling as she took the gift back. "It's for Warren. And I'm not sure if I should panic now, since you clearly think it's a gift for an old woman!"

"Oh! I'm sure it's a great gift for a twenty-something year old man, too." She grimaced, making her scepticism clear.

"When we stayed at the hotel after the party, he got all excited about the tea selection. So I joked about him having something like this." She stared at it in her hands. "It's a stupid gift, isn't it?"

"No. It's a nice gift. Especially with the story behind it." She reached for the teapot and poured them each another cup. "Do you think he'll give you a gift? Or is it just a case of getting something because you joked about it?"

"I don't think he'll get me anything. The other day he was joking about getting each other gifts. But he was joking..." Nerves crawled up her spine. "Maybe it'll be awkward if I give him a gift. I might not give it to him after all."

"I'm sure he'll like it." Her smile wasn't exactly reassuring. "Have you managed to engineer ways to spend time with him?"

"Yeah." Anna returned the box to the bag. "I had dinner at his place."

"That's great."

Her stomach stirred with amusement in anticipation of Frannie's reaction to the bigger news.

"I'm also going away with him and his family next week," she said nonchalantly.

Frannie stopped with her teacup before her lips. "What?"

"Just for a couple of nights. His family is having a pre-Christmas break in a house near Bath. He asked me to go along and pretend to be his girlfriend."

Returning the cup to the saucer, Frannie set her elbow on the table and propped her chin on her hand. "You're *good.* Very good."

"It's ridiculous, isn't it?" Anna laughed. "When he asked me, I think he was joking. There's no way he expected me to agree, but I had a burst of courage."

"He must want you to go, though. And if he's keen for you to go away with his family, he must really like you. I bet you'll get together with him while you're there."

"Stop it! I'm nervous enough without you saying things like that."

"Don't be nervous. It's exciting." She went to pick her cup up again, but paused. "What are the sleeping arrangements? If his family thinks you're a couple, I assume that means you'll be sharing a room."

"I wondered the same, but he called me earlier in the week to check I hadn't changed my mind. He said not to worry about the sleeping arrangements because he always takes a room up in the attic."

"How do you mean, *always?*"

"They stay in the same holiday house every year. Apparently, they've been going since he was a kid."

"That's nice."

"Yeah. Anyway, there are two bedrooms up in the attic, so he said we won't need to share, but everyone will assume we're sharing. No one else goes up in the attic."

"That's annoying."

"Yeah," Anna agreed before the two of them burst into laughter.

"I assume you haven't heard from Hayden?" Frannie asked when they calmed down again.

"No. Nothing. Which is a good thing, I think."

"He thinks you're with someone else, so it would be shady of him to make a move now."

"Yeah." Her shoulders sagged. "It's so good to finally feel I'm moving on."

"I still can't believe you were pining for him for all that time. I honestly had no idea."

"I should probably have talked to you about it, but with hindsight, I'm glad I didn't. I think things work out as they should. Hayden and I weren't right for each other."

"And you think Warren is right for you?"

"It feels different. When I'm with him, I can be myself."

"And you couldn't with Hayden?"

"I'm not sure I could, no." She dragged a hand through her hair. "I hope I'm not getting ahead of myself. Maybe Warren only sees me as a friend."

"A couple of nights away with him should make things clearer. When do you go?"

"Monday morning. And I have a stall at a Christmas market tomorrow, so I won't have too much time to think about it over the weekend."

"You're looking forward to it, though?"

"Yeah. I am."

She wasn't entirely sure what to expect.

But she was definitely excited about spending more time with Warren.

Chapter Twenty-Nine

Warren was saying something, but Anna didn't register the words as she stepped out of the car at the end of the sprawling driveway and gazed up at the stylish Georgian house, built from the distinct golden-coloured Bath stone. Having expected a quaint cottage, the building – which was more of a small manor house – was slightly intimidating.

Two rows of miniature fir trees, tastefully decorated with soft orange fairy lights, were lined up like soldiers to lead the way to the front door.

"This is where you came on childhood holidays?" Anna asked, glancing at Warren as he lifted their bags from the boot.

"Yes." Gravel crunched underfoot as they moved towards the front door. "You heard what I said, right? You got yourself into this? If you have a terrible time, you only have yourself to blame."

"I'm not worried," she said. "I think it'll be fun."

"I wish I had your confidence."

"I think that's the first time anyone's ever said that to me," she replied, amused.

"You know what I mean," he said with a hint of an eye roll.

He insisted on carrying her bag as they ascended the few steps to the front door. Weirdly, she felt pretty confident while they waited in silence after the extended melodic chime of the doorbell.

"They probably forgot we're coming," Warren said, giving up on waiting and trying the handle to find the door open. He walked into the spacious entranceway, at the centre of which was a tall Christmas tree, decked out with stylish blue and silver baubles.

"Hello!" Warren called, depositing their bags at the foot of the wide staircase. "Anybody home?"

Anna's eyes flittered over the selection of abstract paintings on the white walls. She was no art aficionado, but she'd guess they weren't cheap.

"Where is everyone?" she whispered, feeling suddenly like an intruder.

"They'll be around here somewhere." He tipped his head and set off along the hall.

"It's huge," Anna remarked when he opened the second door they came to and revealed a large but cosy living room with three walls lined with glass-fronted bookcases and the other wall containing a huge wall-mounted TV.

"It's *too* big," Warren said. "You can't find people. Let's try the kitchen."

They hadn't got much further along the hall when a voice reached them – loud and assertive and seemingly mid-argument.

"That's my sister," Warren said flatly.

He knocked on the doorframe of the open doorway at the end of the hall as he stepped through it. Anna followed him into the large open-plan kitchen/dining room. At the marble top island, a young woman sat perched on a high stool with a laptop and a bunch of papers spread in front of her. She glanced up, her eyes landing on Warren and Anna before darting back to the laptop screen to continue her video call.

"I have to go," she said. "My brother and his girlfriend just arrived. But make the changes to the contract. If we have to redo it later, so be it. And if Peter Fisher gets back to you, I want to know about it straightaway." Her lips pulled to what might have been a smile, but was so fleeting it was hard to say for sure. Then she closed the lid of her laptop and slid off her stool.

Even if it weren't for the logos on her crisp white shirt and the buckle of her belt, the perfect tailoring of her jeans and shirt made it clear the outfit was all designer labels. Together with her neatly styled blonde hair, perfectly made-up face and subtle but striking jewellery, she looked as though she'd just stepped out of a high-class magazine as she strode over to them.

"It's so great you could make it," she said, leaning into Warren and greeting him with an air kiss beside his cheek. "I said to Mum, I'd believe it when I saw you, but here you are."

"Here I am," Warren parroted, then gestured beside him. "Selena, this is Anna."

"Lovely to meet you." She smiled, but made no move for physical contact. "Mum's been telling me all about you."

"It's good to meet you too," Anna said. "This house is gorgeous."

"Yes, I love it. Sometimes I just need to get out of the city. It's the perfect escape."

"Where are Mum and Dad?" Warren asked.

"In the study." Selena grimaced. "Mum said to tell you something came up with the deal they're working on. They'll probably be on video calls all afternoon, but she said you should make yourselves at home."

Her phone rang, and she backtracked to her makeshift desk. "That's my assistant, Patricia. I should probably take it." She cast Anna an apologetic smile. "It's a little chaotic today, but we'll all have dinner together later." She swiped her finger across the phone screen. "Hang on one second, Patricia." Setting her phone on the worktop, she collected up her papers and lifted them into the crook of her arm with her laptop.

"Where's Josh?" Warren asked.

"With Tamara. I think she was taking him to some play centre in Bath. They'll be back for dinner. We'll eat at seven." With her phone at her ear, she waltzed past them, then stopped in the doorway and turned back. "You're in the back bedroom. The one that used to be the playroom."

"I thought we'd be up in the attic," Warren said.

She wrinkled her nose. "Why would you be up there?"

"Because that was always my room."

"You must have been a teenager the last time you slept in that room. Of course you wouldn't sleep up there. Besides, Josh sleeps up there with Tamara."

"Right," Warren said wearily.

Selena looked as though she was about to speak into her phone, but shifted it to her shoulder at the last minute. "I can recommend afternoon drinks in the hot tub. There's plenty of champagne in the fridge out there. See you later." As she turned, she pressed her phone to her ear. "Patricia, are you still there? What's the latest from Peter?"

"She seems nice," Anna said as Selena's voice receded along the hall.

Warren snorted a laugh. "It looks as though we're entertaining ourselves for the afternoon. Do you want a drink?"

"Champagne in the hot tub, please," she said dryly, then grinned when she caught Warren's eye. "Or a cup of tea would be fine, too."

While he filled the kettle, Anna drifted to the console table at the end of the dining room, which was loaded with framed family photos – all of which appeared to have been taken professionally. She frowned as she got closer.

"These are all of your family," she said, picking up one of the four of them, where Warren looked to be a young teenager.

"Yes," he said, coming over to stand beside her.

Anna's jaw slackened, and she turned to look at him. "I thought this was a place they rent out for one week a year, but... is this...?"

"My parents own it."

"They own it and rent it out?" Anna asked, confused. "Or they just have a second home?"

"Second home."

Anna's eyes felt huge. "Wow."

"Yeah."

"So you've spent a lot of time here?"

He nodded. "Most school holidays when we were growing up."

"I didn't realise," Anna whispered, then turned to look at the place with fresh eyes. It was stylish in a minimalistic way, but it didn't have much warmth to the decor, which was all white and chrome and glass.

"I haven't been here for years." Warren drifted back to the kitchen and opened a few cupboards before finding mugs.

"Why not?" Anna asked, leaning against the island.

A muscle in his jaw twitched, and he seemed to avoid looking at her as he focused on making drinks. "I don't really know," he said eventually, but it felt like a lie. Anna suspected he knew exactly why and just didn't want to say. "I'm usually busy with work when they're here."

"That's a shame," she said, taking the elegant white mug with the gold rim.

His hum of response was ambiguous as he sat on a stool at the island.

"Let's drink these and see what the playroom looks like these days," he said after a moment.

Anna supposed they wouldn't be in separate rooms after all. She lifted her mug to hide the smile that crept over her face.

Chapter Thirty

"I can sleep on the floor," Warren said, looking around the guest bedroom with a wrinkled brow.

Anna wandered to the large bay window. "For half the night, maybe."

"I can also just ask Mum if there's another room," he replied, not reacting to her joke. "I've never actually told them you're my girlfriend, and there's no reason they need to think that."

"It's fine." Anna glanced at the bed. "The bed is enormous, and I don't want to put your mum to any trouble." Her eyes darted to Warren. "Unless it's an issue for you," she said, her stomach tightening at the thought that he'd rather they have separate rooms. "If you're not comfortable sharing, then ask your mum if there's another option."

He hesitated for long enough that Anna felt a pang of disappointment.

"I'm not sure what your brother would think about us sharing a bed," he finally said.

Her eyebrows twitched together. "Why does it matter what my brother would think?"

"Normally it wouldn't matter, but your brother is my best friend, so his opinion about it matters."

"Call Lewis then and ask." Shaking her head, she turned away from him.

"Is that a joke?" he asked.

"I just think it's stupid that you think it matters what Lewis thinks."

"I'll sleep in a different room," he said firmly.

Disappointment hit her in a wave, but she didn't have time to dwell on it as Warren continued speaking.

"I don't even know how you talked me into this," he grumbled. "I didn't want to come. I think that was quite clear. Why the heck did *you* want to come?"

Her heart was going crazy. Any hint of confrontation put her on edge. For the life of her she couldn't remember why she'd agreed to come. And especially not why she'd *wanted* to come.

"I don't know," she replied so quietly she wasn't sure her words were even audible.

Part of her expected him to apologise for snapping at her, but when she turned, he was perched on the end of the bed, hunched over, with his elbows resting on his knees. Suddenly, she suspected his bad mood wasn't anything to do with her and the sleeping arrangements.

When they'd arrived, it hadn't struck her as particularly odd that his parents hadn't appeared to say hello, but now it seemed rude. She tried to imagine how she'd feel if it were her parents, but couldn't quite manage it. Even after a few days of not seeing them, her parents greeted her as though it had been years.

"So this used to be a playroom?" she asked, breaking the silence after a few minutes.

He massaged the back of his neck, looking for a moment as though he might ignore her. "It's completely different now."

She nodded slowly, wishing her heart would calm down

since she was starting to feel queasy. "I guess a lack of toys changes the vibe a little."

A shadow of a smile played on his lips. "It was bigger," he said, then pointed across the room. "They added a bathroom."

Gathering her courage, she moved to sit beside him on the bed. "What's your favourite memory from this house?"

"I don't know."

"You must have some good memories. I bet this was an amazing place to play hide and seek."

"It's not as good as you'd think," he said. "We could only play on one floor at a time. If we could hide anywhere in the house, it was too difficult."

"I didn't think of that," she mused.

He stayed silent for a moment. "The garden was my favourite."

"Yeah?"

"Not even the garden." He stood and went to the window. "The fields beyond the garden. I used to love jumping over the wall and taking off into the fields. There are woods down in the valley with a stream running through. I'd go off with a net and a bucket and I could spend all day out there seeing what creatures I could find in the stream."

"That sounds very wholesome."

He stared out of the window. "It was my favourite thing about my childhood. I had my favourite trees to climb too."

"Show me," she said, staring at his profile.

"What?"

"Let's go for a walk. You can show me all your favourite places."

He pulled his sleeve back to check his watch. "We have time to drive into Bath and do some shopping if you want."

"I'd rather go for a walk."

"It's freezing."

"What do you want to do, then?" she asked impatiently. She

was trying to make things easier for him, and he seemed determined to hinder her attempts.

He smiled properly then.

"What's so funny?"

"It's just surprising when you get annoyed."

"I get annoyed a lot."

"You don't show it a lot."

She shook her head. "What do you want to do this afternoon?"

"We can go for a walk," he said in a way that sounded as though he was doing her a favour. "Just don't complain that you're freezing and have inappropriate footwear."

"I wouldn't dare," she said mockingly.

❄

It took about ten minutes of walking for Warren's anger to dissipate. Annoyingly, it wasn't just his family who'd got under his skin. His irritation had spilled over to Anna too, since it was her who'd encouraged him to come.

Because of *her,* he'd even looked forward to it.

Now, crunching over the frosty grass, he cast a discreet glance at Anna with her rosy cheeks and her dark hair poking out from beneath her grey bobble hat.

His family would never change, and there was really no point in being frustrated that they'd put work first yet again. What he should do was make sure Anna had a good time.

"Sorry for being grumpy before," he said, as they tramped steadily down into the valley.

"You're forgiven," she said without missing a beat.

Amusement took the last of his bad mood. "That's big of you."

"I don't tend to hold grudges."

"I was expecting you to question what I was talking about, or say you hadn't noticed me being grumpy."

Her eyes sparkled as she cast him a sidelong glance. "It would have been pretty difficult not to notice."

"I wasn't that bad."

"You were pretty bad, but you apologised, so let's forget it." She pulled a strand of hair that had flicked into her mouth. "Show me which trees we're climbing."

A laugh escaped him. "We're climbing trees?"

"Yes." She beamed. "We're reliving your childhood. Unless you think you're not up to it?"

His eyes trailed over her, taking in her skin-tight jeans and sturdy knee-high boots. "I think *I'll* manage," he said, pushing a branch out of the way at the edge of the woods.

The scent of pine hit him as they followed the familiar path through the trees. A few minutes later, they reached the dried-up stream.

"It's more fun in summer," he said, hopping over the gulley where the water babbled in the warmer months. Anna kept up easily as he picked his way through the rocks and shrubs until he reached a small clearing with a large tree in the middle. "This is the best climbing tree," he said, putting a hand against the rough bark of the old oak tree.

"It looks like a good one." Anna walked around to the other side and disappeared from view. A moment later, she peeked around the trunk, looming a foot above him. "Race you to the top," she said, mischief flashing in her eyes.

"Who *are* you?" he muttered as he pulled himself up onto a low branch.

Near the base of the tree, the abundant branches were so close together that it was more like climbing an uneven ladder and required little effort. As soon as the branches thinned out, Anna stopped and sat on a solid branch, with an arm on the tree trunk to steady herself.

"You took your time," she said when he stood on the branch below hers, so he was at eye level with her.

He opened his mouth to reply, but all that came out was laughter.

"I prefer it when you're not being grumpy," she said, smiling softly.

"Me too." Instinct had him reaching to push the stray lock of hair from her face, but he withdrew his hand, remembering what he'd said to Lewis about only seeing her as a friend.

"Did your sister used to come here with you?" Anna asked.

He nodded and shifted his weight to lean against the trunk of the tree. "We were close when we were young. Probably until we were teenagers, and then we couldn't stand the sight of each other. Were you the same with Lewis and Carla?"

She shook her head. "We've always been close. They annoy me from time to time, but I never really had the feeling that I didn't want to be around them. They've always been the easiest people for me to hang out with."

"You're lucky." He thought of all the family dinners and get-togethers he'd been to with her family and couldn't help but compare them to his own family. Feeling his mood shift, he pushed the thought away. "What was your favourite thing to do when you were a kid?"

"Ice skating," she said immediately. "I wanted to be a figure skater."

It wasn't difficult to imagine – she had the grace and poise of a figure skater. "What happened?"

"I wasn't very good."

"Really?"

"I'm not being modest. I was *good* at skating, just not *good enough.*" She paused. "I used to make Lewis skate with me. I'd make up elaborate routines."

"I'll bet he loved that."

"I think he secretly did. He was really good. It was annoying."

"We should go skating in Bath tomorrow," he said, liking the idea of gliding round the rink with her.

"Can you skate?"

"Yeah. I played hockey as a kid – so I have speed, but not a lot of finesse."

Her eyes sparkled with mischief. "That's probably not something to brag about!"

"I'll be honest," he said, chuckling. "When you dragged me out here, I didn't imagine sexual innuendo in a tree."

Her smile was glorious. "No, you expected me to complain that I was cold and my feet hurt."

"Exactly."

She bunched her shoulders up. "I'm freezing."

"Let's head back," he said cheerfully. "I have an idea of how to warm up."

If he really thought about it, he'd probably conclude that he should avoid spending time in the hot tub with his best friend's sister.

So he decided *not* to think about it.

Chapter Thirty-One

The walk altered Warren's mood dramatically. Reclined in the hot tub with his head resting back and his eyes closed, he looked utterly content. Anna's breath fogged in front of her face. The contrast of the cold air on her cheeks and the warmth of the water enveloping her body was wonderful.

Darkness had descended on the garden, but the patio was gently lit around the hot tub and adjacent seating area. Gurgling water sloshed up to Anna's chin when Warren pulled himself up to take a swig from his glass of champagne.

She kept her eyes on him as he set the glass back beside hers on the edge of the hot tub.

"You're staring," he said as he sank back into the water.

"When did you get your tattoos?" she asked, eyeing the black ink on his chest.

"When I was at university," he said, lips twitching to a smile. "It was my way of rebelling."

"Why did you feel the need to rebel?"

"Because I hated my course. Spending so much of my time doing something I wasn't particularly interested in was stifling.

Getting tattoos felt like blowing off steam. With the bonus that it pissed off my parents. Especially my dad."

Beneath the water, Anna found his hand and raised his arm to examine the inked skin.

"They don't mean anything much," he said, twisting his arm for her to get a better look. "I really liked going into the shop and leafing through books and just choosing whatever I felt like at the moment."

"There seems to be a nautical theme," she said, her finger trailing over the old-fashioned sailing ship and then a compass and an anchor. Between them were twining vines and flowers, with a decent amount of natural skin still showing in between. "I like them."

"Have you ever thought of getting one?"

"Yes." Her hand fell away from his arm and sank beneath the bubbling water again.

"And?"

"And then I got one." She fought to keep a straight face at the way his forehead wrinkled.

"Where?"

"Somewhere hidden."

He lifted his eyebrows as he stared at her. "I don't believe you."

"Why not?"

"Because you don't seem like someone who'd get a tattoo."

"Well, maybe you don't know me very well."

"Show me it," he demanded.

"No." Her cheeks ached with the effort of containing her grin.

"You won't show me because you don't have one."

She shook her head. "I won't show you because my brother wouldn't approve of me showing you."

His slow blink was extremely satisfying. "Earlier you said Lewis wouldn't care about us sharing a bed."

"He wouldn't, because that could be totally innocent."

"And seeing your tattoo couldn't?"

"Not really, no." Calmly, she closed her eyes and sank lower into the water.

"I know you're only messing with me."

For a moment, she considered standing up and shifting aside her bikini bottoms to reveal the delicate feather along her bikini line.

That was the champagne squashing her inhibitions.

"It's at my bikini line," she said, not quite brave enough. "I can't show you, but I promise it's there."

He cleared his throat and sat up again. "Here," he said, holding her glass out. "You better finish this."

"You can give me as much alcohol as you want," she said, taking it from him. "I'm still not showing you." It wasn't actually true. She suspected it wouldn't take much more alcohol at all, but she was enjoying teasing him.

"That's not the reason I think you should drink more." He drained the contents of his own glass. "We're having dinner with my family soon. I find it's best not to be too sober for that."

❄

As she got dressed after a shower, Anna wondered what the sleeping plans were now. Warren hadn't mentioned moving rooms again, and his stuff was still in the same room.

It wasn't just that Anna wanted to share with him – she also wanted *him* to want them to share.

And it wasn't as though she was thinking anything would happen between them. She just liked the idea of sleeping beside him, and of him being there when she fell asleep and when she woke up. As far as getting to know people went, it seemed like a fast track.

When she came out of the bathroom, he went straight in

there to get changed. Sinking onto the edge of the bed, she checked her phone and found a message from Frannie asking how things were going.

Great, she typed in reply. *The more time I spend with him, the more I like him.*

Her stomach erupted with butterflies. She didn't just *like* him, she realised. She was falling for him – fast.

After spending so long pining after Hayden, having feelings for someone new felt wonderful. Especially since they were interwoven with hope, whereas her feelings for Hayden had been twisted with desperation.

Glad you're having a good time, Frannie replied. *Keep me updated.*

After dragging her fingers through her damp hair, she got her hairdryer from her bag and moved to sit at the dressing table. Five minutes later, she turned the hairdryer off and tilted her head at the sound of voices. So far, the house had been silent. Now the signs of life felt overly pronounced.

"Are you hungry?" Warren asked, rubbing a towel over his hair as he walked out of the bathroom.

"Yes." Anna caught his eye in the mirror. "Does someone speak Spanish?"

"Yeah." His eyes twinkled. "Tamara. She's funny."

"Who's Tamara?"

"Josh's nanny. She only speaks Spanish. Or so she claims. But she's been his nanny for a couple of years now, so I'm sure it can't be true that she doesn't understand a word of English. I think she just likes being able to ignore my sister when it suits her."

"So she only speaks Spanish with Josh?"

"Yes. Which seems to work fine."

"It's pretty cool, actually. Kids pick up languages easily."

"He seems to understand her. I'm not sure how much

Spanish he speaks yet, but from what I've seen, they communicate fine. It's her and my sister who have issues communicating – it's hilarious to watch." He tipped his chin. "Are you ready?"

She ran the brush through her hair one more time. "As I'll ever be."

Chapter Thirty-Two

At the top of the stairs, Anna looked over the banister at the commotion around the Christmas tree in the entrance hall.

"They get dressed up for dinner," she murmured, her eyes darting from Warren's mum in a body-hugging black dress to his dad, who wore a three-piece suit. Selena looked as though she might be off to some high-end nightclub in her silver, floor-length cocktail dress. "I am so underdressed," she said to Warren out of the corner of her mouth. "Why didn't you tell me jeans were inappropriate?"

"You're not underdressed," he replied. "It's definitely them who are inappropriately dressed."

"Are we going out?" Anna asked in a panic. "I thought we were just having dinner at home."

"That's what I thought too. I'm fairly sure that's what's happening."

"Do they usually get so dressed up for dinner at home?"

He shook his head. "No, this is over the top, even for them."

"I feel like a street urchin," she hissed. It was ridiculous though – five minutes ago she'd been happy with her jeans and soft cashmere sweater.

"Don't worry about it," Warren said, placing a hand at the small of her back to encourage her on.

"There you are," Jen said when she spotted them. "I've got you an early Christmas present, Warren." She sashayed across the room and plucked a suit bag from the back of a cupboard door.

"A suit?" Warren said flatly.

"I hope it fits." His mum handed it over. "Go and try it on quickly."

He curled his lip. "Why are you all so dressed up?"

"I thought we'd get a family photo since we're all here. Go and pop that on."

Warren opened his mouth, then glanced at Anna and closed it again with a tight smile. He moved to a chair at the side of the room and laid the bag over it before undoing the zip.

"Don't get dressed here," Selena said, rolling her eyes. "Go to your room like a normal person."

Amusement flashed in his eyes as he pulled his hoodie over his head, his T-shirt briefly rising with it. "To save us from arguing, I'll wear the shirt." He pulled it from the bag and ripped off the tag.

"It's an expensive suit," Jen said. "Please put it on."

"No," Warren said, slipping his arms into the shirt.

His dad stood beside a shiny mahogany console table with a glass of whisky in his hand. "For once in your life, can you not be so stubborn and just do as your mother asks?"

"No," Warren replied calmly. "I'm a grown man. You don't get to dress me up so you can pretend to your friends that we're some normal, happy family. I'll wear the shirt, or I won't be in your photo at all. Your call."

With her eyes darting between family members, irritation had Anna's heart rate increasing. "*Hi,*" she said pointedly, since they seemed to have forgotten about greetings.

"Hello." Jen swept over and gave Anna a brief hug. "How are you?" she asked, as though this entire situation was normal.

"Fine." Anna tried to catch Warren's eye, but he was buttoning up his shirt and didn't seem at all bothered that his parents hadn't even said hello to him.

"Can you at least put the jacket on over the shirt?" Jen said.

The noisy arrival of a small boy thundering down the stairs saved him from answering. A lithe young woman with curly brown hair followed him, yammering away in Spanish.

"Uncle Warren!" the boy shouted, launching himself at Warren from the third step. He caught him effortlessly and pretended to choke when the kid hugged him tightly around his neck.

"How are you, Joshie?" he asked.

"Good. Can you throw me?"

"No!" Selena snapped. "He's not going to...No! Warren! Don't even–" She cut herself off with a gasp as Warren put his hands under Josh's armpits and launched him straight up in the air.

It wasn't only Selena who gasped, but everyone in the entranceway. Seeing how high he'd thrown him, Anna slapped a hand over her face, covering her eyes. She opened them again at the sound of a high-pitched giggle.

"Do it again?" Josh demanded in Warren's arms.

"Don't you dare!" Selena said, marching over to them. "How many times have I told you he's not a rag doll? You can't just throw him."

"I didn't just throw him," Warren said, making a face at Josh as he set him down. "I also caught him. He loves it."

"It's fun!" Josh said, tipping his head back to grin at Warren.

"It's messed your hair up," Selena said. "Tamara, have you got a comb?"

The nanny produced one from her back pocket and got to

work on his gelled hair, which still looked perfectly styled to Anna.

Bemused by the whole scene, she was taken aback when Jen put a hand on her arm.

"We won't be long with the photo. If you want to wait in the kitchen, Rachel will pour you a drink." Without waiting for a response, she waltzed over to a camera on a tripod facing the Christmas tree. "Warren, will you *please* put the jacket on?"

Ignoring her completely, he flashed Anna a reassuring smile. "Told you it was best not to be totally sober."

"Is it always like this?" Anna whispered.

"Yeah. Some version of this madness, anyway."

"Who's Rachel?"

"The cook." He glanced behind him as his mum told him to move and stand beside his dad. "Go get a drink," Warren said, backing away. "At least one of us can escape this circus."

For a moment, Anna watched Jen direct them all into position, while also giving Tamara directions about the camera. Since Tamara only responded in Spanish, it was hard to know what she made of it all, but she seemed to take it in her stride.

Leaving the noise behind, Anna strolled along the hall to the kitchen.

"It smells amazing in here," she said to the tall woman with her hair tied back in a French twist.

"Thank you." She turned from whatever she was stirring on the hob. "Veal with creamed cauliflower, roasted vegetables and mushroom sauce."

"That sounds delicious."

"I hope so. You must be Warren's girlfriend." She wiped her hand on her apron before extending it to Anna. "I'm Rachel."

"Anna," she replied, deciding not to comment on whether she was Warren's girlfriend.

"Can I pour you a drink?"

"Wine would be lovely, please."

"Red or white?" She went to the table, set with a white tablecloth and gleaming silver cutlery. Decanters of red and white wine sat in the table's centre, and every place setting had wine and water glasses.

Anna opted for white and was a little gobsmacked when Rachel poured her a taster glass.

"If it's not dry enough for you, I can open another," she remarked while Anna swilled the wine in her mouth and wondered who in their right mind would ask for something different when they were a guest in someone's house.

"It's lovely," she said, handing the glass back to be topped up.

When Rachel drifted back to the kitchen, Anna moved to the window and spotted a flutter of snowflakes illuminated by the outdoor lights.

She was still there when Warren came to stand beside her five minutes later.

"It fits you well," Anna remarked, eyes raking over his new shirt while her lips curled to an appreciative smile.

"I like it," he said. "But don't tell my mum that."

"Your secret is safe with me. Did your mum get the photo she wanted?"

"I think so." He turned away when his dad asked him what wine he wanted, then the two of them launched into a surprisingly earnest conversation about the best wines to serve with veal.

"I forgot you have to do wine pairings for work," she remarked when they all moved to take their seats. "Are you secretly a bit of a connoisseur?"

"I don't think it's a secret," he said, taking the place beside her.

"Do you like it?"

"Wine?" He looked confused. "Yes."

"No, I mean, do you enjoy choosing the wines at the restaurant? Is it a part of your job that you enjoy?"

He looked thoughtful for a moment. "I love it. Wine is part of the experience for the guests. Choosing the perfect wine to complement the meal feels like a challenge."

"I want to sit next to Warren!" Josh shouted.

"Your seat is over here," Selena said, standing behind the chair with a booster seat on it. "Come and sit down."

"No! I want to sit next to Uncle Warren."

"Here," Jen said, giving up her chair for him. "He can sit here."

"Mum!" Selena hissed. "He needs to learn that he can't get his own way all the time."

"Maybe, but I'd also like to eat while the food is still hot and not have to listen to Josh scream the house down." Jen tipped her head at her daughter. "Choose your battles."

"Fine." She took the booster seat to him and helped him onto it. When her phone rang, she pulled it from her back pocket. "I'll just be a minute," she said before striding from the room with the phone at her ear.

Rachel discreetly set bowls of soup in front of them, and there was no mention of waiting for Selena to return – they all tucked in.

"How's work?" Dennis asked, eyes on Anna. "Have you done any more markets?"

"Yes. There was one on Saturday." She ran her spoon through her soup, waiting for it to cool. "It went well. And I did a private wreath-making workshop, which ended up bringing in a lot of sales to my online shop, so I've been busy fulfilling those orders."

He nodded, but his attention was on his phone, which lit up beside his bowl. While tapping on the screen, his brow wrinkled. "Carl thinks we should accept five percent less," he said to Jen.

"Of course he does." Jen replied, her tone clipped. "Carl always prefers to play it safe, but I guarantee if we sit tight, they'll come around to our terms in the end."

With no idea what they were talking about, Anna looked at Warren.

"The soup's good," he said, nodding at her bowl and subtly reminding her to eat. Then he turned to his nephew. "How's school going, Joshie?"

"Good."

"What's your teacher's name?"

"Mrs Clarke. She's the bestest teacher in the whole world."

"Wow. You got very lucky then. Have you got lots of friends?"

"Yes." He excitedly listed them and then happily chatted away while his grandparents continued their conversation about business at the other end of the table.

Selena returned when they were in the middle of the main course and took the seat on the other side of Josh.

"Eat the vegetables," she said to him. "Not just the meat."

"I don't have to," he replied with his mouth full.

"You do if you want dessert," she said, reaching for her wine.

Josh shook his head. "I have to eat one piece of everything, and I already ate one piece of carrot and one piece of potato."

"You have to eat it all," Selena said, the muscles in her jaw tightening.

"No, I don't. Tamara says I only have to eat one piece of something if I don't like it."

"Eat your vegetables," Selena said. "And don't argue."

His eyes flashed with defiance, and he opened his mouth, but Warren leaned close to him and spoke quietly.

"Do you know what I do if I don't like something?" he said. "I eat that first, and I eat it quickly. Then it's over and done with and you can enjoy the rest of your food."

Josh looked thoughtful for a moment, then began stuffing vegetables into his mouth.

"Not so fast," Selena admonished before releasing a sigh and making a start on her own dinner.

Since his parents had paused their conversation to eat, Anna smiled over at them. "I'm surprised you didn't get Warren to cook."

Jen frowned. "It's good for him to have a break."

"Yes, but you must also enjoy taking advantage of his culinary talents from time to time."

Warren pushed his empty plate away and shifted in his seat. "It's always good to have someone cook for me for a change. And Rachel's an excellent cook."

Anna glanced around, but the cook was nowhere to be seen.

The shrill ring of Dennis's phone filled the air. "That's Carl," he said, then took another mouthful of food before pushing his chair back and answering the phone as he left the room.

"Carl thinks we should accept the offer," Jen said to Selena.

Selena choked. "We absolutely should not."

"That's what I said."

Shaking her head, Selena set her napkin beside her plate and stood. "Dad better not be considering it."

"I already told him we should hold firm." She smiled across the table as she stood. "This deal was supposed to be tied up last week," she said and rolled her eyes before following her daughter out of the room.

A moment later, Tamara scuttled in as though she'd been loitering while she waited for the family to leave. Taking a seat, her eyes sparkled as she spoke to Josh in rapid Spanish. Whatever she said made him giggle before he continued eating his meat.

Anna's gaze went to Warren. "Don't you ever cook for your family?"

"No."

Her eyes widened, but she didn't have a chance to say any more before he stood and went to retrieve the desserts, which Rachel was dishing up.

"Apple pie and custard," he said, setting the steaming bowls in front of Anna and Josh before going back for his own.

"Is Tamara not allowed to eat with the family?" Anna asked quietly.

"I'm fairly sure she's allowed to," Warren said, plunging his spoon into his bowl. "I think she chooses not to."

Tamara said something to Josh, who then looked up at Anna. "She likes to eat later."

"I don't blame her," Anna said dryly, and assumed from the amused twitch of Tamara's lips that she could understand everything they said.

Tamara continued chatting to Josh while he ate – her speaking Spanish and him responding in English.

"I have to go for a bath now," he announced when Tamara flicked the crumbs from his mouth with a napkin. "Then it's story time. We're in the middle of a pirate story, and there's a very funny parrot who can talk."

"What book is it?" Anna asked as he climbed down from the chair.

"It's not a book. Tamara makes up stories. They're the best stories in the world." He grinned at them as Tamara led him away by the hand. "Goodnight!"

"Night," they responded in unison.

"Are your parents coming back?" Anna asked, looking at the plates which still had food on them.

"I doubt it," he said, taking their dishes to the kitchen and loading them into the dishwasher.

"Leave it," Rachel growled when he went back for the rest of the dishes at the table. He raised his hands and exchanged an amused look with Anna. "Thanks for dinner," he called across the room. "It was delicious."

"You're welcome," Rachel replied.

Warren picked up the decanter of wine from the table and tipped his head along the hall. "It's comfier in the library."

Chapter Thirty-Three

The library turned out to be the room they'd looked into earlier, which Anna had assumed was the living room.

"What's the deal with Rachel?" she asked, sinking into the plush, dark green couch. "Does she always cook for your family?"

"Yes. She's worked for my parents for years."

"Does she live-in?"

"When they're here, she does. In London, she has her own place and comes in every day."

"Wow."

Warren topped up her wine and relaxed back into the couch cushions. He didn't flinch when she pried more into his childhood and his upbringing. He chatted away as though growing up with staff and multiple homes was all completely normal. Apparently, to him, it was.

"It must be weird for you when you spend time with my family," she remarked as she neared the bottom of her wine.

"No." He stretched his legs out and rested his head back. "Not at all."

"But it's very different," she said.

His lips twitched upwards. "A different kind of crazy. But I prefer your family's crazy to mine. Your family cares about people."

"I'm sure yours do too," she said, setting her glass aside and pulling her legs under her as she turned sideways.

"Maybe," he mused. "They're definitely not good at showing it."

"No." The food and wine were making her sleepy, and it crossed her mind to bring up the sleeping arrangements again, before thinking better of it. She didn't want to remind him of his insistence on finding another bedroom.

In the silence, her mind drifted back to her conversation with Carla.

"I have a question," she said, feeling brave.

"Why does that sound ominous?"

"It's not." She smiled. "What happened the night my sister wanted you to remove the spider from her flat?"

His features scrunched up. "What do you mean?"

"Did you just go over there and remove it, or...?"

"Or what?" His eyebrows lifted slightly.

Her stomach lurched, and she wondered whether the conversation was a good idea. "It just seems a little odd that she'd call you late in the evening to get a spider out of her flat."

When he didn't answer, Anna's stomach plummeted even further.

"I don't understand this conversation," he finally said.

"I asked her about it. And she said she only called you because Lewis didn't answer his phone and Dad was already in bed. But it didn't quite ring true."

"You think she only called me?"

"Maybe."

"And you think it was actually some bizarre excuse for a booty call?"

"It was just a thought. You two flirt a lot."

"No, we don't."

"I only asked what happened," she said testily. "If nothing happened, you could just say that."

"Of course nothing happened! I didn't even go over there. I told her she was being ridiculous and there was no way I was going over to deal with a spider."

"Okay," Anna said, wishing she hadn't brought it up. "There was no need to bite my head off."

"Sorry." He turned his head on the cushions. "I'm just shocked you thought something had happened between me and your sister. Apart from the fact that she's really annoying, she's also way too young for me."

"She's not that young."

"She's immature and annoying."

Instinctively, Anna gripped the nearest cushion and swung it so it smacked him in the face.

"What was that for?" he asked, laughing as he pushed the cushion away.

"Don't be mean about my sister!"

He grinned. "I meant it affectionately."

"How would you like it if I was mean about your sister?"

"I wouldn't mind at all. We may be up all night though if we get onto that subject."

"Let's not then." She yawned. "I think I need to go to bed."

"I'll join you."

"Will you?" she asked. "I thought you were going to sleep elsewhere."

"There isn't actually another room free, so I'd be sleeping here." He patted the couch. "And you're right that the bed is massive. You just have to promise to stick to your own side."

Butterflies fluttered in her stomach. "I'll try my best."

Chapter Thirty-Four

Waking beside Anna stirred feelings in Warren that he refused to dwell on. It took a fair amount of willpower, but he didn't linger to watch her sleep. Quietly, he pulled on his clothes and left her snoozing. The house was blissfully still, but the fresh coffee in the pot told him Rachel wasn't far away.

Only after he'd poured himself a mug did he notice the weather. A foot of snow covered everything, and it was still falling fast.

Turning a dining chair, he sat looking out over the back garden, fascinated by the way the snow made the undulation of the ground more pronounced. Soft sunlight fought its way through the hazy clouds to make the snow on the boughs of the fir trees glisten majestically.

A robin fluttered onto the patio, landing on the back of a chair before taking off again a moment later.

He savoured the coffee and the quiet and stared out at the peaceful landscape until Anna appeared half an hour later.

"Morning," she murmured and the single word made his pulse react.

"Sleep well?" he asked.

"Yes. Did you?"

He nodded. "Do you want a coffee?"

She put a hand on his shoulder, stopping him when he went to get up. "I can get it. Do you want a refill?"

"Please."

She'd only just walked away when his mum arrived in the room.

"Morning!" she chimed.

Warren ignored the way the muscles in his jaw clenched. He wouldn't let them get to him, he reminded himself.

"I'm getting coffee if you want one," Anna said.

"No, thanks," his mum replied. "I've already had three cups this morning."

"Have you been working?" Anna asked.

"Of course she has," Warren replied. "There's no rest for the wicked."

His mum rolled her eyes. "I'll rest once this deal goes through."

"Sure you will," Warren muttered, but his animosity was drowned out by the joyful shouts of his nephew as he ran into the room.

"It's snowed!" He stopped in front of Warren and jumped up and down. "It snowed a lot. Did you see it?"

"I've seen it," Warren said, the excitement in Josh's eyes making him smile. "Are you going to go sledging?"

Josh looked around, eyes landing on Selena as she strode in.

"You haven't got a sledge here," she said. "But Tamara is going to take you out for a nice snowy walk."

"Aren't our old sledges in the garage?" Warren asked his mum.

"I think so, yes."

"He's not going to play on a twenty-year-old sledge," Selena said in her usual haughty tone.

"I want to go sledging!" Josh declared.

"The wood is probably rotten on those old things," Selena insisted. "But I suppose Tamara could take you out to buy a new one."

"It's thick snow," his mum pointed out. "Don't let her drive in this with Josh in the car. It's not safe."

Selena shook her head. "They'll just go for a walk then. Josh, go to Tamara, and she'll help you get your snow gear on."

Warren took the mug of coffee from Anna, noticing that Josh ignored his mum's instructions and stayed put.

"I don't see what the problem is with using the old sledges," Warren said to his sister.

"Yes," she said tersely. "But you also don't see the problem with throwing him into the air or hanging him upside down."

"True." Feeling mischievous, he directed his next words at Josh. "I'll get a sledge out for you."

"Warren!" Selena hissed. "It's nothing to do with you. Keep out of it."

He tilted his head as he looked at her gleefully. "Don't you have some work to do?"

She opened her mouth to argue, but her phone rang, and she only looked torn for a moment before answering it and striding from the room.

Josh looked at Warren. "Will you come sledging with me?"

"Tamara will go with you," his mum answered for him. "Warren would like to spend some time with Anna, I'm sure."

"Anna can come too," Josh said.

"They want to spend time just the two of them," his grandmother explained.

"Why?"

"Because that's what new couples do. But you'll have fun with Tamara."

Josh frowned. "Do you want to come sledging?" he asked Anna.

"I'd love to," she said, blowing on her coffee.

"Suit yourselves," his mum said, heading out of the room. She turned back at the doorway. "Help yourselves to breakfast. We'll all do our own thing for lunch, but Rachel will be around if you want her to make you something. We'll have dinner at seven again."

"Great," Warren said. "See you later."

❄

Warren seemed completely at ease as he made them toast for breakfast – and while he told Tamara to take the morning off, and got Josh into his snowsuit and boots. Anna watched him closely as the three of them set off walking through the back garden with the two wooden sledges, but there was no sign that he was in any way bothered that his family made no effort to spend time with him.

He was nothing but calm and cheerful when he showed Josh the best hill for sledging, and while they spent the next hour racing each other down the hill and marching back up it.

"It's your turn to race me," Josh said to Anna as he dragged his sledge back up the hill beside Warren and immediately sat down to go again.

Anna stamped her feet to ward off the cold. "At the risk of sounding pathetic, I don't think I can go again. I'm not sure I'd make it back up the hill."

"Totally pathetic," Warren said, exchanging a conspiratorial look with Josh. "Girls just aren't as good as boys, are they?"

"Hey!" Anna scooped up a ball of snow and threw it at the back of his head.

"They can't take the teasing either," Warren added, removing his hat to shake off the snow.

"Are you going to race me again, Uncle Warren?"

Anna caught the grimace which said he was just as tired as she was from trekking up the hill. "Why don't you go alone this time?" he suggested. "I want to watch and see how fast you go."

"I'm very fast!" Josh said, then immediately shuffled the sledge forward until it gathered momentum and sped off down the hill.

"Oh, you just want to watch, do you?" Anna said mockingly. "Nothing to do with you being too knackered to drag yourself back up that hill again?"

"Please don't make me look weak in front of my nephew." He straddled the sledge and took a seat. "I'm completely done in. I don't understand how he's still going."

His gaze drifted down the hill, and he waved at Josh, who'd come to a slow stop where the hill tapered off.

"Do you think we'll be able to coax him into leaving soon?" Anna moved around to perch on the front of the sledge. "I think I need to go and get warm. My toes are numb."

"Mine too," Warren said, stamping his feet. "I can't imagine he'll be happy about it, but I reckon with a bit of bribery, we could convince him it's time to leave."

"He's definitely looking a little tired." Anna waved at Josh, who had stopped partway up the hill.

He beamed back at them. "You two are too big to ride together!"

"No, we're not," Warren replied.

"You are!" Josh called out, giggling. "Two grown-ups can't ride on one sledge!"

"I think I'll take that as a challenge," Warren said.

"No, you won't," Anna argued, just as Warren's arms sneaked around her waist and pulled her back until she was flush against his chest.

"You better watch out," he called to Josh, "because this is going to be the fastest sledge you've ever seen."

"Probably," Anna said. "Due to all the weight!"

"You really shouldn't make such derogatory comments

about yourself," Warren said in her ear, earning himself an elbow to the ribs just before he pushed them off.

Laughter bubbled out of Anna as they gathered speed. She clutched at Warren's arms around her waist as a flurry of snow flicked up around her and they sped toward the tree line at an alarming pace.

"We're going to crash!" she shouted, not sure if Warren could hear her over the wind whipping around them.

"Maybe," he replied, but he didn't sound overly concerned.

The ground levelled out, slowing them enough that she was no longer worried about colliding with a tree. With that fear out of the way, she basked in the feeling of Warren's arms around her.

He didn't immediately get up once they came to a stop, but seemed to enjoy the closeness too.

"That was so fast!" Josh said, running over to them with wide eyes. "Can we all go down together on one sledge, so we're the fastest sledge ever?"

Warren stood up. "We can't all three fit on a sledge. And it's time for us to go home and get warm. We've been out here ages."

"I don't want to go home yet," Josh said. "Can we just go one more time, all three together?"

Anna stood. "I really need to go back to the house because I can't feel my toes anymore, and I'm worried they might fall off." She pulled a face at Josh. "And that would be quite disgusting, wouldn't it?"

"Your toes can't fall off, silly," Josh said.

"Do you know what I'm going to do when we get home?" Warren said, crouching to Josh's level. "I'm going to make hot chocolate – and it's the best hot chocolate you've ever tasted."

"Rachael makes the yummiest hot chocolate in the whole world," Josh said, deadly serious.

Warren shook his head. "Does she make it with real chocolate?"

Josh seemed to mull it over. "She makes it with chocolate powder."

"Then it's definitely not as good as mine," Warren told him. "But I'll need you to try it so you can decide for definite who makes the best hot chocolate in the entire world."

Distracted, Josh seemed to forget all about the three of them riding down the hill. Warren took his sledge from him and set off, pulling the two sledges up the hill while Josh and Anna followed slowly. They didn't get very far before Josh stopped dead and declared his legs wouldn't work anymore.

Warren backtracked a little. "Sit on the sledge and I'll pull you up."

With a radiant smile, Josh clambered onto the sledge.

"Hold on tight," Warren said before setting off again.

"Wait a minute!" Anna said, hurrying to catch up with them.

Warren turned and offered her the rope from the empty sledge.

"I wasn't offering to help," she said cheekily. "I was thinking I'd quite like a ride back up the hill, too." Her gaze was all challenge as she sat on the empty sledge.

Warren rolled his eyes. "Really? You actually think I'm going to pull you both back up this hill?"

"I *do* think so," she said teasingly. "Because I'm fairly sure you're going to take this as a masculine challenge, and you'll do it just to prove that you can."

Warren cocked his head. "I think you're overestimating my need to prove my masculinity."

Josh looked at Anna. "He can't pull both of us. He's not Superman."

Anna almost choked on her laughter – knowing she couldn't have come up with a more perfect line to stir Warren's ego.

"What did you say?" Warren demanded, glaring at his nephew.

"Superman could pull both of the sledges easily, but you're just a normal man, so you're not strong enough."

"That's a very good point." Anna got up from the sledge. "I didn't think of that, Josh, but you're absolutely right — he's definitely not strong enough."

"I can see what you're doing," Warren said, turning his glare on Anna now. For a moment, he was silent. Then he nodded at the sledge. "Sit back down."

"I just don't think you're strong enough," she said sweetly as she took a seat.

He shook his head at her teasing, then turned and pulled both sledges up the hill, seemingly without too much exertion. Josh exclaimed delightedly the whole way, pronouncing that Warren was Superman. At the top of the hill, he hopped off and bounced around, slapping Warren's hand when he reached out to high-five him.

"That was a very impressive display of masculinity," Anna said, getting off the sledge.

"Do me a favour..." Warren took her elbow and led her a little away from Josh. "If I collapse, can you distract Josh so I can keep up the pretence of being insanely strong in his eyes?"

She laughed. "You made it look like no effort at all."

"Because I'm a good actor!" He heaved in a breath and sank his head to her shoulder. "I may need to go to bed for the rest of the day."

Biting back a suggestive remark, Anna looked over at Josh.

"Come on," she called. "Superman says it's time to go home."

Chapter Thirty-Five

Warmth gradually seeped back into Anna's toes while she sat at the kitchen counter with Josh, sipping Warren's luxury hot chocolate. He stood beside the counter, smiling at his nephew's chocolate moustache, which grew bigger with every sip he took.

"I hope you're not messing the place up," Rachel muttered, giving Warren's arm an affectionate pat as she walked into the kitchen.

"Uncle Warren made hot chocolate with real chocolate," Josh said, then dragged his arm across his mouth, smearing chocolate milk all over his sleeve.

"Hopefully not with the chocolate I was about to use to bake biscuits," Rachel said, eyeing Warren with a mock-frown.

"I didn't use it all," he said. "There's plenty left."

"You're making biscuits," Josh said excitedly.

"And mince pies." Rachel opened a cupboard and began collecting ingredients.

"Can I help you?" Josh asked.

Her hesitation signalled she wasn't at all keen on the idea. "I suppose so," she said eventually. "If it's okay with Tamara. And as long as your uncle doesn't hang around telling me where I'm going wrong."

"Warren makes the most amazing mince pies," Anna said idly.

She tried to catch his eye, but he moved to help Josh bring a chair from the dining table into the kitchen. Parking it at the counter, Warren looked uncertainly at Rachel.

"Would you mind if I did the baking with Josh?"

Rachel turned to face him and set her hands on her hips. "Are you asking if I mind you taking over here while I go and read my book for an hour?" She shook her head. "I don't mind at all. Make enough mince pies and biscuits to last a couple of days. And make sure you tidy up afterwards!" She smiled warmly and wandered out of the kitchen.

Josh clambered up onto the chair and gazed up at Warren. "What do we need to do first?"

"First, we need to wash our hands." He lifted him from the chair and flew him over to the sink. "Then I'm going to teach you how to make pastry."

At the island, Anna watched the two of them chatter away. Warren was helping Josh sieve flour when he looked over at her.

"Once the mince pies are in the oven, I'll make sandwiches. Are you hungry?"

"I'm fine," she said contentedly.

"Uncle Warren." Josh tugged on his arm. "When we've finished making everything, can we watch TV?"

"Maybe. If it's okay with Tamara."

"She won't mind. Can we get all the cushions and make a bed on the floor like we did last time?"

Warren's eyebrows pinched together. "I'd forgotten about that. You have a very good memory."

"I remember everything. Can we do that again?"

"I think it sounds like a great idea. We can eat the mince pies and biscuits and watch Christmas films."

"Yes!" Josh cheered. "This is the best day ever."

Warren ruffled his hair, but his smile slipped away when he glanced at Anna. "Oh, wait. We were going to go into Bath."

"It's fine," she said, shaking her head.

"But you wanted to do your Christmas shopping. And ice skating..."

"I'd rather stay warm and cosy here." And there was no way in the world she'd take Warren away from spending time with Josh. "Mince pies and Christmas films sound like a great way to spend the afternoon."

Warren mouthed 'thank you' and held her gaze long enough for her stomach to turn a somersault.

Staying in wasn't exactly a hardship – she really was happy to go along with their plan for the afternoon. As she joined in with the baking, while Christmas music filled the kitchen, there was nowhere else she'd rather have been.

Snuggling up in a nest of cushions and blankets while snow continued to flutter outside the window of the library felt perfect, too. Anna felt a warm sense of joy as they watched the sweet, animated Christmas film about a young reindeer who wanted to join Santa's team. When Josh begged to watch the sequel straight after the first film ended, neither Warren nor Anna took a lot of persuading.

Josh barely moved as he stared at the screen, utterly transfixed. His concentration disappeared the moment the film ended. He jumped up, fleeing the room while announcing he had to tell Tamara about it.

"I think you're probably very popular today," Anna said, feeling so relaxed she was drowsy, and not keen to move from her snug spot on the cushions.

"He seemed to have a good time," Warren said, eyes on the door where Josh had run out.

"I didn't just mean with Josh," Anna said, turning her head on the cushions to look at Warren stretched out beside her. "I'm sure Tamara and Rachel are both happy about you taking over some of their work for the day."

"It was a good day," he said, looking just as relaxed as she felt. "Sorry you didn't get your trip to Bath."

She scrunched her nose. "This was much better. Except I feel so relaxed I'm not sure I can move."

With a flash of mischief in his eyes, he tugged a cushion out from under her so she rolled sideways.

"Hey!" She laughed and swatted at him as she lolled helplessly in the dip beside him. Then she pulled the cushion from under his elbow, so he dropped beside her. "Now we're both stuck," she declared, then wriggled madly as he tickled her.

"I want to play too!" Josh called, his footsteps thumping rapidly as he charged into the room.

Beaming, Warren pulled Josh down and tickled him until he was breathless.

It wasn't long before Tamara arrived in the doorway, babbling in Spanish and gesticulating wildly.

"Dinner's ready," Josh told them, jumping up and dashing from the room.

Warren hauled himself up and reached a hand to help Anna up. "I guess that means the fun is over," he quipped. "Let's see what drama the family dinner brings today."

There was a reassuring reply on the tip of Anna's tongue, but her attention was on her hand, which Warren hadn't released. Glancing up at him in the hallway, she caught the vulnerability in his eyes and tightened her grip on his fingers.

"It's only dinner," she murmured. "I'm sure you'll survive."

The skin around his eyes crinkled as he smiled. "That's about all I ever hope for with my family dinners."

Chapter Thirty-Six

Warren didn't release her hand until they reached the dining room, where quiches, pizzas, and salads were arranged in the centre of the table. His parents were chatting over wine and wearing far more casual attire than the previous evening, though still looking fairly smart for a family dinner.

"I had the best day ever!" Josh announced to his mum, who walked in while the rest of them were loading up their plates.

"That's good," she said, running a hand over his hair and settling herself on the chair beside him.

"Uncle Warren makes the best hot chocolate in the world. Even better than Rachel."

Warren winced and looked over at the kitchen. "Sorry, Rachel."

She smiled and waved her hand before continuing with tidying up the work surface.

"And he made chocolate chip cookies," Josh said excitedly. "I helped, and they're yummy. Do you want to try one after dinner, Mummy?"

"I'd love to," Selena replied.

"I have to give one to Tamara," Josh said. "But I think there's enough for you, too."

"There are plenty," Warren said quickly, not quite covering the fact that Josh seemed to hold the nanny in higher esteem than his mum.

Josh's childish chatter dominated the conversation over dinner, and Selena had to keep reminding him to eat. As soon as he was finished, he slid from his stool, insisting he needed to take Tamara a biscuit.

Warren had remained quiet while they ate, and there was a tension in the atmosphere which contrasted with their relaxed day with Josh.

When her phone vibrated in her pocket, Anna discreetly pulled it out under the table and checked the screen.

Why on earth was Hayden calling her?

Her heart rate sped up, and her mind flashed up an image of dancing with him at the Christmas party and him saying he wished they'd never split up.

"In case you haven't noticed," Warren said, leaning close to her. "My family doesn't care about people taking phone calls at the dinner table. You can answer it."

"No. It's fine." Quickly, she pressed the button to ignore the call. "It's not important."

He lifted an eyebrow, but didn't pry.

"I'm very surprised you never get Warren to cook for you," Anna remarked, fumbling to push the phone back into her pocket and shove thoughts of Hayden from her mind.

"We wouldn't want to do Rachel out of a job," his mum said lightly.

"I just meant a meal or two." Anna loaded her fork with quiche and salad. "It'd give Rachel a break too."

"I'm sure he wouldn't want to cook when he's taking time off," Selena said.

When Anna opened her mouth to continue, Warren caught

her eye and gave a small shake of his head, effectively telling her to drop the conversation.

She ignored his silent request. "You must be proud of him though," she pressed. "Of his career."

Selena shuffled her salad around her plate. "I don't know if you can really call working in the kitchen of some country pub a career."

"It's not a pub," Anna corrected her. "It's a hotel."

"Same difference," Selena said, setting her knife and fork down on her plate.

"No," Anna said, ignoring the warning look Warren gave her. "It's not the same at all."

His dad cleared his throat. "The problem is, he spends his days taking orders from someone else. Which is fine for some people, but he could do so much more. It'd be good to see him fulfil his potential."

"But... I..." Anna's brain struggled to comprehend the conversation.

"Don't bother," Warren said while he chewed. "It's really not worth it."

Anna stared at him as his eyes pleaded with her to drop the subject.

"But he's the head chef," she finally said, her voice coming out far louder than she'd intended. "You talk as though he has some lowly kitchen job, but he's the one in charge. He gives the orders."

"Really?" Selena said, a flicker of appreciation flashing in her features. "Is that true?"

Warren merely nodded.

"It'd be different if he owned the restaurant," his dad said, swilling his wine in the glass. "But as things are, he'll always have to answer to someone else. And he'll always be on a fixed wage."

"It's also not as though he's the head chef at an upmarket

restaurant," Selena added. "It's some tiny place in the middle of nowhere. Hardly high-class dining."

"It is, though!" Anna's heart was galloping, and her hands had gone all clammy. She knew her cheeks were bright red. "Michelin even published a review of his cooking."

"A good one?" Selena asked without a hint of mocking.

"Of course a good one!" Anna growled. "They don't give bad reviews."

His dad sat up straighter. "You got a Michelin star?"

"No." Warren rubbed at his forehead.

"He probably will get one," Anna argued.

"Restaurants get stars, not the chef," Warren said, frowning at her. "And we *won't* get one."

She tried to read his features. For the life of her, she couldn't figure out how he could stay so calm while his family made derogatory comments about his career, but got angry when she praised him.

"It doesn't even matter." Anna's eyes shifted between his sister and parents. "The restaurant gets booked up weeks in advance, thanks to Warren's cooking. Have you even looked at his reviews? People love his food."

"That's fine," his dad said, looking completely unfazed as he tucked into a slice of quiche. "But at some point he'll realise that he wants the freedom that money buys, instead of being tethered to a dead-end job and being constantly in debt."

"But it's not a dead-end job. He's the *head chef.*" She couldn't fathom the comment about debt, but the man seemed so far removed from reality that he probably assumed everyone who didn't own their own business ended up in debt.

"Anyway," Warren said cheerfully. "This quiche is lovely."

"It's delicious," his mum said. "Rachel really is a godsend."

"I don't understand," Anna murmured.

"Just drop it," Warren said. "It's not an issue."

"But it *is* an issue." She glared at Jen. "How can you be so complimentary about Rachel and so dismissive of Warren's talent?"

Jen smiled condescendingly. "If you have kids one day, you'll understand about wanting the best for them."

"I'd want them to be happy," she said, feeling suddenly choked up. "Do you even care about that?"

"Reaching his full potential would make him happy," his dad said.

"Wow!" Anna was gripping her cutlery far too tightly. "I can't believe this is an actual conversation."

Warren's hand on her leg got her to look at him. "Please, just drop it."

She might have done just that if she hadn't caught the vulnerability in his eyes.

"They're horrible people," she said, not taking her eyes off him and not lowering her voice at all. "They're *really* horrible people."

His sister made a noise that was somewhere between a screech and a burst of laughter. "How lovely of you to sit there and criticise us."

"Well, you have no problem criticising Warren. At least I'm being truthful. You are horrible. All of you." She plucked her napkin from her lap and threw it on the table as she stood. "I can't sit here. I can't even be in the same house as you."

Warren called her name as she stormed out, but she didn't stop. In the entrance hall, she pushed her feet into her boots and angrily pulled on her coat before striding outside.

The wind caught the door when she pulled it behind her, and it slammed so violently that she winced. It didn't break her from her anger though, and she stomped the entire way to the end of the drive before calming down enough to realise she didn't know where she was intending to go.

Chapter Thirty-Seven

Anna's biggest regret when she paced beside the gate was that she hadn't picked up her hat and gloves before storming out of the house. With her hands shoved into her pockets and her shoulders hunched up to her ears, she stayed where she was as Warren walked casually towards her.

"I didn't mean to slam the door," she said when he got near. "The wind caught it."

His smile was only a small curve of the lips, but his eyes sparkled. "That's what you're worried about? The door slamming?"

"I realise I shouldn't have told your family they're horrible people, but I just don't feel bad about that yet. It was true."

"I feel as though the dynamics are all off here. The way you explained it to me, I'm fairly sure I can say bad things about my family, but you can't. At least that was how it worked when I said something about Carla."

"But you didn't say anything to them!" she shot. "You just sat there and took it. They were being mean."

"They–"

"Please don't defend them," she cut in. "They were mean, and I'm furious."

"I can see that."

His eyes went pointedly to her hands, which were balled into fists at her sides. "There's a wall there if you need it." He tipped his head and smirked.

"Don't tempt me."

"Really? You're thinking of lying in the snow with your legs in the air?"

"No." She almost smiled at that. "I was thinking of punching it."

"Ah!" He pursed his lips. "That would hurt."

"It would." She rubbed the back of her hand across her forehead. "Could you please get my stuff?"

"What stuff?"

"My clothes and everything. I don't want to go back in there."

"Where are you planning to go?"

"You could drive me to a train station or something."

He glanced around. "How about we just walk to the pub?"

"I can't stay here tonight," she said, but followed when he set off along the road.

"Why not?"

"Because I just called them horrible people. *To their faces.* Multiple times."

"It's probably not as big of a deal as you think it is."

"Of course it's a big deal." She hurried to keep up with his long strides. "I'm going to feel terrible when my anger wears off."

"We'll have a drink at the pub. Everything will seem better then."

"But they won't want me in the house," she said. "There's no way I can stay there."

"Let's worry about that later."

"I'd rather worry about it now while I still have time to get a train home."

"It's too late to get a train anyway," he said.

"Can you drive me home, then? You didn't want to come in the first place. Not really. I convinced you it was a good idea. I've changed my mind. It wasn't a good idea, so we should leave."

"I'm not driving in the dark on icy roads. We'll go tomorrow morning as planned."

"Warren," she said with a sigh.

"Everything will be fine. I promise."

Sulkily, she kept quiet for the rest of the ten-minute walk to the village pub, and didn't speak again until they were settled in the corner of the warm room with drinks in front of them.

"Why didn't you defend yourself?" she asked as her nervous system gradually settled back into a relaxed state.

He hesitated before answering. "Because I know what they think, and I know nothing I say can make them think differently. I love my job, and that's enough for me. I don't need it to be enough for them."

"But it upsets you." She rested her elbows on the table. "When your parents came to visit and your dad spoke to you about it, you were upset. As I recall you were so upset that I had to order you out of the kitchen."

"That's true." He took a sip of his pint. "I guess it's easier to deal with my family when you sit there and shout at them and tell them they're horrible people."

"We're not joking about that yet. In fact, I don't think we'll ever joke about that."

"Sorry." His shoulders shook as he chuckled. "I can't help it. It was funny. I'm going to laugh about it often."

"You'll have to laugh about it alone," she huffed.

"I don't think so. Not once I tell Carla about this."

Fighting a smile, she threw a beer mat at him.

He caught it and threw it straight back, making her smile properly.

"I can't believe I shouted at them," she said, covering her face with her hands.

She relaxed back in the chair as the faint buzz of alcohol loosened her tight muscles.

"Was there any point in your life when you considered going into the family business?" she asked seriously.

"Yes. That was my plan for a long time."

"Really?" She shook her head. "What exactly is the family business, by the way?"

"Private equity. They essentially buy companies that aren't performing well, restructure them and sell them on."

"And you were going to do that?"

"It didn't feel as though I had much choice," he said with a shrug. "I grew up being told I'd join the family business and I didn't particularly question it."

"Until when?"

"Until I got a job in a restaurant when I was at university."

"You decided you wanted to be a chef?"

"Pretty much. Working in the kitchen interested me far more than my degree in economics, or my parents' business talk. Even when I was only doing food prep."

"What happened? Did you finish your degree, or switch to a catering course?"

He ran a finger up the side of his glass. "I continued with the economics degree until about halfway through the final year. Then I dropped out of the course."

He paused, looking thoughtful. "I'd known for a while that I wanted to become a chef. I didn't dare say anything, or do anything about it, but I knew that once I finished my degree, I'd have to go and work with my parents. That was the plan, anyway. The closer I got to that reality, the more I panicked. Eventually, I told them I wasn't going to work for them. Which wasn't actually the worst thing. If I had some other dream that they approved of, it would probably have been fine."

"But they didn't approve of you being a chef?"

He shook his head. "They thought it was beneath me."

"That's crazy."

"Maybe. But remember that they employ a full-time cook. To them, my job is on the same level as the household staff."

"I don't even see why that's a bad thing."

"Yeah, but you're not like them."

She wouldn't argue with that. "How come you didn't finish your degree if you were so close to the end of it?"

He rubbed his forehead. "Because my dad said that if I didn't finish it and do something worthwhile with my life, that he wouldn't pay off my student loan. That was the deal, you see… they wouldn't support us financially through university because they believed their kids shouldn't get used to having things handed to them. But when we graduated and joined the family business, they'd pay off any student debt."

"But if you were so close to the end of your course, why not just finish it and join the business for long enough for them to pay off your loan?"

He turned his glass on the mat. "Because I knew it would annoy my dad more if I didn't."

"You quit your degree out of spite?"

"Yeah. Admittedly, not the greatest idea I've ever had, but in my defence, I was young and angry."

She sighed as a thought occurred to her. "That's why your dad mentioned you being in debt."

"Yes."

Not an entirely random comment then.

"Which I'm not, by the way."

"You paid it off?"

"Yes." His eyebrows twitched. "The perks of living for cheap in someone's garage. I saved money."

"Does your dad know you paid it off?"

"I don't think so. I certainly never told him."

"Don't you feel like telling him?"

"No."

"Why not?"

He sucked in a breath. "Because nothing I do will be good enough for them so I gave up on trying to get their approval. Anything I achieve, I'll keep to myself rather than risk their opinions spoiling it for me."

"That's really sad."

"It is what it is. I don't agree with my parents, but I do think they want the best for me. We just have different ideas about what that is."

A heaviness weighed on Anna's chest. "I think you're a brilliant chef," she said eventually. "I'll just be proud of what you've achieved instead of your family."

She'd expected him to laugh at her, but he held her gaze and looked at her in earnest.

"Thank you," he said, then looked over his shoulder at the bar. "Should I see if they're still serving food? You probably didn't eat much since you were so busy shouting at my parents."

She rolled her eyes. "I'm actually surprisingly hungry."

They ordered chicken wings and chips to share, and stuck to lighter topics as they ate. Warren told her stories about the time he'd spent in the area as a kid and all his tricks for slipping away from the nanny to go off on adventures in the countryside.

By the time they set off back to the house, Anna's anger had dissipated and she looped her arm through Warren's, sticking close by his side to shelter from the freezing wind.

"I can't go back in there," she said when they reached the front door. "I'm too embarrassed."

"Don't worry about it. It'll be fine."

She screwed her face up. "I really don't want to go in."

"Remember the night I argued with my dad and I told you it would just get forgotten and never mentioned again..."

"I really don't think that in the last two hours they'll have forgotten me shouting at them over the dinner table."

"Maybe not forgotten, but I don't think they'll draw attention to it."

"The atmosphere will be terrible."

"If it is, you can go straight to bed, and we'll leave first thing in the morning."

"Okay," she said, while looking at the door with trepidation.

Following him inside, Anna held her breath and had just begun to take her coat off when Selena stalked into the entrance hall.

"You should probably keep your coats on," she called angrily.

Anna's stomach twisted. So much for them pretending nothing had happened.

Chapter Thirty-Eight

Anna's heart was beating uncomfortably fast as Warren looked at his sister with a puzzled expression.

"What's going on?" he asked, as Selena paced at the foot of the stairs with her phone pressed against her ear.

"I told you," Anna hissed at Warren. "They don't want me here when I was so awful to them."

"You weren't awful," he said, as though he genuinely believed that.

Pressing her phone to her shoulder, Selena lifted her chin to shout loudly as she walked towards the kitchen. "Mum! I think I'll just drive home. Tamara can wake Joshie and bundle him into the car."

"The roads are black ice!" Dennis's voice boomed in response. "You're not going anywhere."

"No one is answering the phone," Selena shouted to no one in particular. "Mum, did you get hold of anyone?"

"Your dad's trying to get through to someone now," Jen called from the direction of the kitchen.

"I wanted to have a bath!" Selena huffed, passing them to hurry upstairs.

Anna frowned at Warren as they headed for the kitchen. "What's going on?"

"Your guess is as good as mine."

"There you are!" Jen tilted her head and smiled at Anna. "You hardly ate anything at dinner, sweetie. I put a plate in the fridge for you. Help yourself, won't you?"

Anna stared in disbelief. "Thank you," she mumbled.

"Told you," Warren said, disguising his words by clearing his throat.

Jen propped her hands on her hips. "I'm afraid we have a slight problem."

"Selena's run out of bubble bath?" Warren suggested dryly.

Jen didn't acknowledge the joke. "The boiler has stopped working. We've got no heating or hot water."

"I can't find anyone who will come out and look at it tonight," Selena grumbled, reappearing but not looking up from her phone. "It doesn't matter how much money I offer, no one will come out until the morning. I really think I'll drive home. Or go to a hotel."

"Just put an extra jumper on," Dennis said, shaking his head as he swirled whisky in his glass at the table. "I think we can manage one night."

"I can't even shower," Selena complained. "And we'll probably all freeze to death in our sleep. Poor Joshie. His teeth will be chattering."

"I gave Tamara an extra blanket to put over him," Jen said. "There are plenty of extra blankets. No one will freeze to death. Don't be so dramatic."

"I spoke to a local company, and the guy said he'll come over tomorrow to look at it," Dennis said. "I can't find anyone who can come any sooner than that, so I'm afraid there's not a lot we can do."

"So much for a relaxing break," Selena muttered, then wandered away with a comment about calling her husband.

"Did you have a good walk?" Dennis asked, looking at Anna.

She nodded dumbly. "Lovely, thank you."

"Get Anna a hot drink," Jen said, patting Warren's arm. "She looks half frozen."

"There's food in the fridge, too," Dennis added.

"We ate at the pub," Anna told him, then followed Warren to the kitchen.

"Tea?" he asked as he filled the kettle.

"Please." She leaned against the counter and whispered. "I'm not sure what just happened."

"I mentioned that my family isn't like yours. A bit of screaming over the dinner table isn't unusual here, but when the heating has the audacity to break, it's the end of the world."

"It is a bit chilly," Anna said, wrapping her arms around herself. "Selena was quite dramatic, though." She paused and pressed her lips together. "I may not say that in the morning when I'm having a cold shower."

"I reckon we'll survive a night," he said. "I'd probably recommend waiting and showering at home if there's no hot water in the morning."

"Good plan."

❄

By the time Anna got changed into her pyjamas, the temperature had noticeably dropped. She rushed from the bathroom and shot under the covers, shivering as she snuggled down.

"It's cold," she said, stating the obvious.

Warren shrugged and threw an extra blanket on top of the duvet.

"Aren't you freezing?" she asked, the sight of him in a short-sleeved T-shirt making her shiver even more.

"Not really," he said. "You're just a bit pathetic, I reckon."

She averted her gaze as he removed his jeans.

"Here," he said, flinging one of his jumpers at her. "Put that on."

"Thank you." She sat up and pulled it on, getting a whiff of his scent as she did.

Feeling much cosier, she settled herself on the pillow and watched Warren get into bed.

"What are you so happy about?" he asked when she grinned at him.

"Your family," she said, then shook with laughter. "They're hilarious."

"You weren't so amused a few hours ago when you wanted to pack your bags and leave."

"True," she said as he switched the light off.

"You also might not find them particularly funny tomorrow when you wake to the sound of my sister squawking about not being able to have a hot shower."

"Maybe not." Gradually, her gaze adjusted to the darkness, and she could just make out the angles of Warren's face. "Do you wish we hadn't come?" she asked quietly.

He hesitated for long enough that she wasn't sure he was going to answer. "No. It's actually been okay."

"Really? This family trip has been better than others?"

"Yes." His laughter reverberated around the quiet room. "I realise how ridiculous that must seem."

She wouldn't call it ridiculous, just very sad. "Sorry," she whispered.

He sighed heavily. "Shut up and go to sleep. You're annoying me."

"I'd apologise, but it turns out I quite like annoying you."

"Go to sleep," he said again, but she could hear the smile in his voice.

❄

Warren woke with Anna fixed to his side like a limpet. Her right arm was draped over his chest, and her legs were entwined with his.

"Sorry," she said, apparently sensing him waking. "I was cold."

"You're wearing a hat in bed," he remarked, ignoring the way his body responded to hers and focusing on the fluffy bobble on top of her hat, which tickled his neck.

"My ears got cold in the night. I had to go and find it." She shifted her head on his chest to look up at him. "Sorry for using you as a hot water bottle."

"It's okay," he said, wishing she'd get off him, while also wishing they never had to move.

She was his best friend's sister, and he'd told Lewis there was nothing more than friendship between the two of them.

"I don't know if I'm brave enough to venture out of this bed," she said lightly. "It's very cold outside of these blankets."

"Central heating seems like the ultimate luxury at this moment," he remarked idly. Though if he were honest, the lack of heating in the house felt as though it was currently working in his favour.

She shifted and propped her chin on his chest, her eyes adorably sleepy and her dark hair tumbling out from beneath her bobble hat. "I think I'll make coffee," she said, her voice slightly hoarse with sleep.

"I can go." His hand moved automatically to tame a lock of her hair, which poked out of her hat at a funny angle. The softness had him twirling it over his finger. "Sorry," he muttered, catching himself. But when his eyes met hers, she didn't seem perturbed by him pawing at her. Then again, she was the one who'd initiated the physical contact.

She also wasn't moving away from him, and his heart beat steadily faster as her eyes roamed over his face.

He should move.

If he shifted a little, she'd move off him. Except he didn't quite have the willpower to put distance between them. The curves of her body fit perfectly against him, and the way she was gazing at him was intoxicating. His hand returned to that lock of her hair.

When he turned it over in his fingers, her eyes met his with an intensity that made his racing heart stop dead.

As she shifted her weight, he braced himself for her to break the contact between them, but she only moved along his body until her face was level with his.

After a momentary hesitation, she leaned closer and brushed her soft lips against his.

He should definitely put a stop to this. He should gently shift her off him and get the heck out of this bed.

He really should.

But he didn't.

Instead, he trailed his fingers down her neck. When she drew back and looked at him searchingly, he pulled her closer, then breathed in the scent and taste of her while tilting her chin to deepen the kiss.

He should put a stop to it.

Kissing his best friend's sister was a bad move.

Her nose pressed against his, and her hand caressed his cheek while her mouth devoured his.

With his hand on the tantalising curve of her spine, he closed his eyes and basked in the feeling of bliss that coursed through him.

A moment later, he forced his brain into gear.

He couldn't kiss his best friend's sister. His boss's sister. What was he playing at?

In a move so speedy he wasn't sure how he managed it, he put an end to their kiss, slid out from under Anna and exited the bed to scoop up his jeans on the way to the bathroom. He only breathed again once the door closed behind him.

In the mirror above the sink, he scowled at his reflection, then shook his head.

He was an idiot.

When he walked out of the bathroom with his jeans on, Anna was sitting up in bed, hugging her knees. He avoided eye contact as he pulled his hoodie over his head, but even from the corner of his eye, he could read her facial expression.

It was very similar to the way she'd looked at dinner the previous evening while announcing that his family were horrible people.

Which was probably fair enough. He felt pretty horrible.

But he'd feel more horrible when he had to face Lewis at work later.

"I'll get some coffee going," he said.

If she replied, he didn't hear her as he strode out of the room, closing the door behind him.

Chapter Thirty-Nine

Fuelled by anger, Anna muttered to herself as she dragged her clothes on. At least her annoyance distracted her from the cold. With extra layers on, she headed for the kitchen to find Selena speaking loudly on the phone – complaining about the lack of heating while a constant stream of Spanish poured out of Tamara, who was eating breakfast at the table with Josh.

Warren caught her eye from beside the coffee machine, but he looked away again quickly.

"It snowed even more," Josh said, his bright blue eyes boring into her.

"Did it?"

"Yes. I'm going to play in the snow later."

"That sounds like fun," she told him.

Selena ended her call and looked over at her son. "You can't play in the snow until the heating is fixed. You'll never warm up again."

"I don't care," he said. "I'll just be a snowman."

Anna smiled at his adorably cheeky grin.

"Do you want coffee?" Warren asked, clearly speaking to her, despite keeping his back to her.

"No," she replied curtly. She was actually dying for a cup, but didn't feel like accepting anything from him after his abrupt departure earlier.

"Tea?" he asked, finally turning.

This time it was her who refused to make eye contact.

"I think I'm going to go outside and have a look at the snow," she said, aiming the remark at Josh – the only person in the room she could bear to converse with.

His eyes lit up. "Can I come?"

"You'll have to ask your mum," she told him, then turned on her heel and left the kitchen to the sound of Selena arguing with Josh – and Tamara joining in too.

After pulling on her boots and coat, she headed for the back door and ignored Warren when he called out to her. This time the door slamming had nothing to do with the wind, and she didn't feel a smidge of remorse about it.

Alone in the winter wonderland that was the back garden, she inhaled the icy air and let her gaze linger on the fresh layer of glistening snow piled up on every surface. The tree branches were impossibly loaded, and there was a calmness about the scene, which she hoped she could absorb.

"Anna!" Warren called from the patio, making her stop and turn. The patio door stood open behind him, and he was pulling on his coat. At the sight of him, any calmness she'd achieved was washed away by a surge of anger.

Without a lot of thought, she scooped up snow and squished it into a ball between her hands. She threw it directly at him.

Surprise flashed in his eyes as he narrowly dodged the snowball. Taking advantage of him being off guard, she grabbed more snow and took aim again. This time, he raised an arm to block it, and it hit his forearm with a satisfying thwack.

"What's that for?"

"I think you know what it's for?" She gathered more snow. "And I think you know you deserve it."

This time when she threw, she got him on the shoulder, and he winced at the shower of snow that fluttered over his neck.

As she laughed, Anna felt immediately lighter.

"Don't you dare!" she shrieked when he bent to collect snow himself.

He made a show of pressing the snow into a compact ball, and Anna had no doubt about his aim. With a peal of laughter, she turned to run as he drew his arm back. Her boot refused to grip on the icy ground, and she felt herself slip about a second before the snowball hit her on the back of the head.

The ground came up to meet her in a blur, and the shock of the snow on her face made her gasp. Her brain seemed to shut down, and she lay face down in the snow with laughter bubbling inside her.

"Anna!" Warren's hand on her arm got her moving, and she rolled onto her back, blinking snow from her eyes to stare up at him.

"Are you okay?" he asked, kneeling beside her and brushing snow from her face.

"I'm fine," she said happily.

He continued wiping her face. "You just gave me a heart attack, but I'm glad you're amused."

She moved his hand from her face but kept hold of it as she looked him right in the eyes. "Why did you freak out?" she asked quietly.

"I thought I'd knocked you out with a snowball," he said, tilting his head.

"Not then. *Earlier.* Why did you freak out when I kissed you?"

His sigh was highlighted by the slump of his shoulders, and he only managed a small shake of the head before Josh's voice interrupted them.

"Anna!" he shouted. "Tamara said I can play in the snow, too."

"He's going to freeze," Selena complained to Tamara inside the patio doors. "There's no hot water for a bath to warm him up."

Tamara threw her arms up and released a frantic flow of Spanish while she helped Josh on with his hat and gloves.

As soon as he'd shoved his hand into his gloves, he shot outside while his mother and Tamara continued to argue in their different languages.

"Why are you lying in the snow?" Josh asked, ploughing through the snow to get to them.

"I'm making a snow angel," Anna replied, flopping onto her back again.

"How do you do that?" he asked eagerly.

"Just fall backwards in the snow and wave your arms and legs up and down."

Warren moved out of the way while Anna flailed in the soft snow. Josh fell beside her, giggling loudly.

"Joshua!" Selena shouted. "You haven't got snow trousers on! Get up out of the snow!"

Before she'd finished her sentence, Tamara joined in with shouting instructions.

"What's Tamara saying?" Warren asked Josh.

"She told me to have fun. And to ignore my mum."

"Does she often tell you to ignore your mum?" Warren asked.

"Yes." His cheeks were bright red from the cold. "But Mummy tells me to always listen to Tamara and do what she says. That means I get to play in the snow."

"Warren!" Selena shouted. "Bring Josh back here, please. It's far too cold, and he's not dressed properly."

"He's fine," Warren shot back. "He's got a massive coat on."

"But he doesn't have his snow trousers! Josh, come back inside right now!"

Anna sat upright. "Do you want to make a snowman?" she asked Josh.

"Yes! Can we make a really big one?"

"I don't see why not."

"Joshua!" Selena screamed. "I said get back here!"

Warren moved to crouch beside Josh, who was still flapping his arms and legs. "I think we might need to shut your mum up before we make a snowman." His eyes sparkled as he scooped up snow.

"She'll go crazy," Anna said, grinning as Warren carefully smoothed his snowball.

"She's already crazy," Warren said, catching Anna's eye and beaming. "Watch this," he said to Josh as he straightened up.

"I mean it, Josh!" Selena bellowed as she pulled her boots on in the doorway. "Now I have to come out to get you, and you've made me very cross."

"She's going to be even more cross when she's got a face full of snow," Warren muttered, pulling his arm back. He waited until Selena stepped outside to launch his freezing weapon.

Focused on Josh, Selena didn't even see the snowball coming. It struck her on the side of the head, making her stop dead and gasp loudly.

Anna held her breath as she waited for Selena's reaction. Behind her, Tamara had her hand over her mouth to hide her glee, while Josh's amusement came out in peals of childish laughter.

"I can't believe you just did that!" Selena said, her icy glare aimed at Warren.

"And I can't believe you won't let your kid play in the snow."

Selena seemed to consider her next move before she reached down and gathered a snowball of her own.

"How do you feel about being a human shield?" Warren asked Josh.

"What's that?" he asked, sitting up.

"It's where you help your uncle out!" He picked Josh up and held him at his chest as he took steps backwards and away from Selena.

"You wouldn't seriously use your nephew as a shield," Selena called, ready and armed with a perfect ball of snow.

"I won't need to," Warren said. "Because I don't think you'll really throw snow at your child."

Anna hopped up and moved out of the firing line while Josh continued to giggle at the fun.

"You're so annoying!" Selena grumbled, then fired the snowball straight at Warren and Josh.

At the last moment, Warren swung around so it missed Josh and hit him squarely on the back.

"You threw a snowball directly at your child's face!" Warren said, laughing as he set Josh down.

"I knew you'd move," Selena said, a smile cracking over her face.

"Can I build a snowman with Anna?" Josh asked, skipping over to his mum.

"Let the kid have some fun," Warren said, dusting snow from his jeans.

"You can't stay out for too long," she told Josh. "And I'm going to get Tamara to bring your snow trousers. You need to put them on."

"I need a carrot for the nose," Josh said, ignoring her instructions. "Can you bring us one, Mummy?"

She huffed out a sigh and cast Warren a mock scowl before retreating inside.

"We need to make one big ball of snow," Josh said, looking at Anna. "And one small one. Do you know how to do that?"

"I do," Anna told him. "Warren can make the big one, and we'll make the small one."

Apparently, the conversation about their kiss was being put on hold.

But they were definitely coming back to it later.

❄

Warren's fingers had gone numb inside his gloves, and he wanted to suggest going inside, but Anna and Josh were having such a good time building a family of snowmen that he didn't feel he could suggest it. Since the three icy figures of varying sizes had all their facial features in place, they were now foraging for sticks to use as arms.

Warren stamped his feet on the patio and blew into his cupped hands to warm his fingers. The door opened behind him, and his sister stepped out. He only cast her a quick glance, then shifted his gaze back to Anna and Josh, who were tramping in the snow by the garden wall.

"I like her," Selena said, taking him by surprise when she stood close beside him.

"What?"

"Anna. She's nice."

He kept his expression blank. "I think your seal of approval makes me like her less."

Selena bumped her shoulder against his, then remained glued to his side. Not used to any kind of physical contact from his sister, his instinct was to move away, but he overrode it and stayed still.

"I especially liked it when she shouted at us all over dinner last night."

Warren snorted a laugh. "It was definitely the highlight of the trip for me."

Selena rested her head on his shoulder. "I looked up your restaurant online."

"Yeah?"

"It's got great reviews."

"That's because I'm a brilliant chef," he said, a jokey tone to his words.

"Apparently so."

The earnestness in her words made him turn to search her features while he waited for the joke or the put down, but nothing came.

"Josh needs to come in soon," she said eventually. "Maybe you can convince him, since he never listens to me."

He paused, taken aback by the entire conversation. "It might be the nanny," he ventured uncertainly. "The reason Josh doesn't listen to you."

"I know, but he adores her." She moved towards the door. "I'll make hot chocolate. You must all be frozen."

"Thanks," Warren called, stunned by the civilised conversation.

Chapter Forty

Sitting around drinking hot chocolate and eating mince pies with Warren's family after playing in the snow was wonderfully relaxed. There were hugs and handshakes before they left and shouts of happy Christmas as they bundled into the car.

After the cheerful atmosphere, Anna wasn't keen to bring the mood down by raising the subject of their kiss. Besides, Warren not wanting to talk about it – and the speed at which he'd put a stop to it – should probably indicate how things stood between them.

Except that it wasn't at all clear.

It wasn't clear from the way he looked at her, or the ease of their conversations, or even in the comfortable silences between them. Nothing felt very clear.

Nothing except for how much she enjoyed his company, and how their kiss had made things very clear for her.

She wanted a lot more than a fake relationship.

On the drive home, the silence between them no longer felt comfortable, and the conversation was increasingly stilted too.

By the time Warren pulled the car over in front of her flat, Anna's irritation had returned with full force.

"Are we going to talk about this morning?" she asked.

He looked pained. "I'm not sure what to say."

"I would just like to know how things stand between us..."

His jaw clenched. "I don't know."

"Well, are we just friends and the kiss was a mistake, or did it actually mean something?"

"I don't know."

She nodded. "This feels like a really pointless conversation."

"I'm sorry." He squeezed his eyes closed, and she waited for him to say more, but he stayed quiet.

"Do you know what's funny?" she said, unclipping her seatbelt and shifting to face him. "When I first met your family, you seemed nothing like them, but now the similarities are showing."

She caught his puzzled look, but didn't wait for him to question her before she continued. "If something makes them uncomfortable, they ignore it and avoid talking about it. Apparently, you do the same."

She reached for the door handle and stepped out of the car. After grabbing her bag from the back seat, she returned to the open passenger door. "In case you're wondering, it meant something to me. But I take it from your unwillingness to even have a conversation about it that the feeling isn't mutual." Tears stung her eyes, and a lump rose in her throat. "I'll see you around."

She closed the door with too much force.

Apparently, over the last twenty-four hours, she'd become someone who slammed doors.

A tear slipped down her cheek as she fumbled with her keys. Warren called out to her, but she ignored him and pushed through the door into the stairwell. It didn't click behind her, so she wasn't surprised when he called out to her again.

Continuing up to the first floor, she hastily wiped at her cheeks and dropped her bag on the doormat. Footsteps sounded on the stairs, and she'd just got the key in the lock when Warren took her elbow and turned her to face him.

"I'm sorry. I'm an idiot, okay." Brushing his thumbs over her cheeks, he pushed her tears away. "I'm terrible at this stuff, but of course it meant something to me."

"Then why did you jump out of bed as though you were being attacked? And why wouldn't you talk about it?"

His hands remained cupping her face. "Because you're my best friend's sister, and a few days ago, I swore to Lewis that I only saw you as a friend."

"Was it the truth?"

His chest expanded as he inhaled. "I don't know if I was lying to him or lying to myself. In my head, I thought we could keep things platonic. I didn't even let myself imagine you'd want anything else."

"Do you want things to stay platonic?"

He tilted his head. "No. But it's complicated. I need to speak to Lewis."

"You could have said that before." She pressed her lips together and tasted the salt from her tears.

"I could, but I freaked out, and obviously I'm not great at communicating."

"Obviously," she said, managing a smile. "I can talk to Lewis. He won't care, though."

Warren shook his head. "I need to talk to him."

"Okay." She leaned her head, pressing her cheek into his hand. "Why don't you speak to Lewis, and when he tells you he doesn't have an issue with you dating his sister, you can call me and ask me out on a date?"

"Yeah." His thumb grazed her jaw. "I like that plan."

"Good."

"Good," he repeated, but didn't make any move to leave.

"Are you going to kiss me again? Or do you need permission from my brother first?"

He shot her a mock scowl, then leaned in and kissed her softly.

Chapter Forty-One

When her phone rang on Thursday afternoon, Anna jumped for it – fully expecting it to be Warren. Disappointment squeezed at her chest when it wasn't his name on the screen.

She contemplated not answering, but she'd already ignored one call from Hayden. She may as well find out what he wanted.

"Hi," she said, thinking that if he was calling to talk about what he'd said to her at the party about wishing they hadn't split up, he had exceptionally bad timing.

"Hi," he said brightly. "How are you?"

"Fine." She sat rigidly on the couch.

"I tried calling you the other day. I wasn't sure if you were ignoring me." The jokey edge to his words was unconvincing, and she could have sworn he sounded nervous.

"I've had a busy few days," she said, fighting the urge to apologise.

"Everything okay with you?"

"Yes. Everything's fine." Her mind flashed to Warren kissing her goodbye, and she felt a rush of butterflies in her stomach. When she thought about that, things felt way better than fine.

"Listen..." His tone was suddenly serious. "I was wondering if we could meet up sometime?"

"Oh." She grimaced, torn between saying no and also curious as to why he suddenly wanted to meet.

"I've been wanting to speak to you, and it will be easier in person." He paused. "And it's been ages since we properly caught up."

She refrained from stating that it was difficult to have a proper conversation with him when he insisted on always bringing a date whenever they saw each other.

"How about I buy you dinner?" he asked in a rush. "Are you free tonight? I could book a table at The Bakers Arms."

Part of her wanted to curse him and hang up. For so long, she'd wished he'd call and ask to spend time with her. It seemed unfair that he'd waited until she was finally moving on.

"If you can't make it tonight, just let me know when," he added eagerly.

"Tonight is good for me." If she turned him down, she'd always wonder why he'd wanted to speak to her. Better to get it over with so she could finally put that part of her life behind her.

Maybe they could be friends now. She couldn't face it after they broke up, but now she could imagine them having a platonic relationship.

"Do you want me to pick you up?"

She told him she'd meet him there. That way, she could leave whenever she wanted and wouldn't feel trapped.

Ending the call, she flopped back on the couch and reflected on the phone call. After what he'd said to her at the party, and what she now knew from her friends about their crossed wires after they broke up, she was fairly sure he wanted to talk about them patching things up.

Maybe she should have insisted they have the conversation over the phone. It wasn't as though anything he said would convince her they should give it another go. Finally, she'd moved on, and even though things with Warren felt a little uncertain, she knew it was something she wanted to pursue.

But if she was about to start a relationship with Warren, she really wanted to get proper closure on her relationship with Hayden.

In the end, she was glad she had dinner plans to focus on. It saved her from dwelling on the fact that Warren hadn't called. She'd really thought he'd have been in touch by now, though she supposed it was only yesterday that they'd spoken. He was no doubt busy with work, too.

She was all ready to head out and meet Hayden when her phone rang again. Disappointment hit when it wasn't Warren calling. She checked the time, debating whether to answer or just message Carla and say she'd call her back later.

In the end, she swiped her finger across the screen, then put her on speaker so she could chat while she got her coat and boots on.

"I haven't got long," she said. "I'm about to go out. Is everything okay?"

"Fine," Carla replied. "I just wanted to hear how it went with Warren's family."

"All good." She dragged the zip of one boot and then the other. "Apart from when I told his parents and sister they were horrible people and stormed out of dinner."

"You didn't!"

"I did." She smiled thinking of it. "I even slammed the door behind me."

"Why?" Carla asked, through gentle laughter.

"Long story. I'll tell you next time I see you, but I really have to dash now."

"Where are you going?"

She grabbed her coat from the rack and pushed an arm in. "I'm meeting Hayden for dinner."

"What?" Carla's voice was high-pitched. "Like a date?"

"No." She struggled with the other arm of her coat. "He just wanted to catch up."

"Where are you having dinner?"

"The Bakers Arms."

"That's totally a date place."

"It's not a date. We're just meeting as friends to catch up."

"No way. He wants to get back together with you. And he's taking you to a country pub where couples go on dates."

Anna rolled her eyes and picked up her bag. "It's also just a place where people go to eat. The food is great. Hayden and I used to go there all the time."

"Yeah, when you were dating. Because it's a date place."

"It's really not a date," Anna insisted.

"I'll bet he thinks it is. Call me later and tell me how your date went!"

With another eye roll, Anna said goodbye to her sister and ended the call. Then she checked her reflection in the mirror and took a deep breath before heading out of the door.

Chapter Forty-Two

Walking into the Bakers Arms, Anna swept her gaze over the festive decorations while Michael Buble's rendition of *White Christmas* hit her ears. She pulled her hat off and looked at the booth in the back corner – their preferred table. Hayden raised a hand to wave and stood when she walked over.

"Hi," she said curtly as he kissed her cheek.

"It's good to see you."

She slid onto the bench seat. "How are you?" she asked, unwinding her scarf and shrugging her coat off.

"Good." He sank back onto his seat opposite her. "Busy with work as usual."

"How's that going?" After university, he and a friend had set up their own software development company and, from what she'd gathered, it was going well.

"It's great. I work crazy hours, but it pays off."

"I'm glad."

"How about you? It seems you're never short of work either?"

"No. I'm pretty busy most of the time, but I love it, so it doesn't feel like work."

"My mum said she saw you at a Christmas market recently."

"Yeah." Anna brightened. "It was nice to see her. She bought a wreath and some Christmas cards."

"The wreath has pride of place on her front door."

They paused as the waitress came to take their order – they both opted for fish and chips like they'd done on their previous visits.

Hayden asked about her parents and Carla and Lewis, the neutral conversation feeling easy and safe.

"Do you really think you might open your own flower shop?" he asked once the food arrived. "At the Christmas party, I got the impression you were thinking about it seriously."

"I don't know. It's something I think about from time to time. But more like a pipe dream, I suppose." She took a bite of fish – tasty, but the batter wasn't as good as Warren's. "I've been thinking about it a bit more seriously, but I still don't know. It feels like a risk."

"What would you do, take a loan from Lewis?"

"If I were serious, I'd make a business plan and see if I could get a bank loan."

Hayden took a swig of his Coke. "I guess it might feel weird to borrow from your brother," he said with a questioning lilt.

"Lewis would give me the money regardless of whether he thought it was a good business idea or not. That would feel weird. And if it turned out not to be a good financial decision and I couldn't pay him back, I'd feel terrible."

Hayden nodded. "I suppose that could be uncomfortable."

"Anyway, I'm fine as I am for now. It can stay a pipe dream until I get fed up with working for someone else."

They finished their food in silence, and Hayden waited for the waitress to clear their plates before he gave her that look that Anna knew too well. The look he had when he wanted to say something serious. He'd had the same look when he'd told her he didn't want to be with her any more.

"It's good to catch up with you," he said, then exhaled a sigh. "I really missed this."

Anna fixed him with her gaze, and any apprehension she'd had about having this conversation completely left her. "Why did you want to meet up? It wasn't just to catch up on each other's lives, was it?"

"No." He leaned forward, resting his forearms on the table. "What I said to you at the party the other week..." As he trailed off, Anna found herself amused that he was the uncomfortable one for a change.

"When you said you wished we'd never split up?"

"Yeah. I know this is unfair of me, but you said things weren't serious yet with Warren... so I thought I should say something before it got serious."

"Say something about what?" Anna's emotions were all over the place as she waited for him to say the thing she'd wanted him to say for the last two years.

That he missed her, and he loved her, and that he wanted them to get back together.

"I miss you," he said, reaching to take her hand.

"Do you?" she asked, anger seeping through her.

"I missed you almost as soon as I broke things off." With his free hand, he wiped at his brow. "I thought I wanted something else, but I was such an idiot."

Anna nodded, agreeing with him on that.

"But you didn't want something else," she said, not bothering to remove her hand from his, partly because she was intrigued that the contact meant nothing to her. "You wanted some*one* else."

"I didn't cheat on you," he said quickly. "I know it probably seemed as though I started dating other people really quickly, but I swear there was no one else when we were together."

"That's not what I meant." She pulled her hand away and clasped it in her lap. "I meant you didn't want to be with me."

He tugged at his earlobe. "I don't understand?"

"You said you didn't want to be with me because I was too shy and quiet, and that when we were out together, you had to look after me, and it annoyed you."

He had the decency to look remorseful as he shook his head. "I'm sorry."

"It was true, though," she said through a lump in her throat.

"I *thought* it was true. But I was wrong. I don't care that you're not as sociable as I am. It doesn't matter. We always made it work somehow."

"We made it work because one of us always compromised," she pointed out. "I forced myself to go to parties that I had no interest in, and you forced yourself to have more quiet nights at home than you really wanted to."

"I liked it when we just hung out at home, too."

"I haven't changed. I'm still not outgoing, and I think it's safe to say I'll never be the life of the party."

"I don't care," he said, a brittleness to his voice. "I really don't."

"You didn't want to be with me because of my personality," she said, unable to hide her bitterness. "And to make that point even clearer, you then dated a bunch of women who were everything I'm not..."

"Anna," he pleaded, but she didn't let him speak.

"And you paraded them in front of me as though hurting me once wasn't enough. You had to keep twisting the knife." Tears filled her eyes, and she hated them.

"None of them could even come close to comparing to you." He reached across the table, but she didn't want his comfort. Not now. "Maybe to start with, I brought a date to annoy you. I thought if you got jealous, maybe we could figure things out. Which I realise is pathetic. But it was even more pathetic because it seemed as though you didn't care. After that, I felt I had to bring someone so no one would notice what a mess I was without you."

"Apparently they all noticed, anyway. Everyone but me, who genuinely thought you were having the time of your life."

"You always seemed fine with it."

"I wasn't," she admitted sadly.

"I'm sorry."

She wiped a tear that slipped from the corner of her eye. "It doesn't matter any more."

"It does," he said. "I hate that I hurt you."

She huffed out a humourless laugh. "So what are you thinking – that we'll call it water under the bridge and get back together?"

"I'm not saying it would be as easy as that."

"But you want to get back together?"

"I'll do whatever it takes to fix things with us."

The desire to laugh was almost overwhelming. It was only the earnestness of Hayden's gaze that prevented her.

"You broke things off because of my personality," she said again.

"That's not..." He closed his eyes briefly, apparently searching for an answer when they both knew there wasn't one.

"How could we make that work?" she asked, reaching for his hand and covering it with her own as all her anger disappeared. "I'd just be waiting for you to get bored with me again."

He shook his head, but clearly thought better of arguing.

"If it's an option, I think we could be friends." She squeezed his knuckles. "Properly friends, not just because we have mutual friends."

"I don't know if I can do that. Not now, at least. Not when you're seeing someone." He paused. "You are still seeing Warren?"

"Yeah," she said hesitantly.

He raised an eyebrow, and she realised it would be cruel to leave him with a spark of hope.

"Things are a little complicated..."

"Complicated like you might ditch him and sort things out with your ex?"

The joke only narrowly covered his vulnerability.

"No. Things are complicated, but..." Her stomach fluttered wildly. "I'm excited to see where it goes."

It took Hayden a moment to speak. "It would have been better if you'd chosen someone easier for me to hate."

Her lips pulled into a small smile. "Sorry I fell for a nice guy."

Chapter Forty-Three

It was hard for Warren to decide whether Lewis not being at the hotel on Wednesday and Thursday was a blessing or a curse. On the one hand, putting off speaking to him about Anna felt like a relief. At the same time, it meant he hadn't seen Anna since they got back from Bath.

He'd almost called her the night before, but with only a few days until Christmas, the restaurant had been extra busy and it had been late by the time things had calmed down at work. Plus, he was keen to have a conversation with Lewis first.

And that felt as though it should be a face-to-face conversation.

Thankfully, Lewis was in the office when Warren arrived at work on Friday morning. Otherwise, he'd probably have gone and tracked him down at home.

"Come in," Lewis said, glancing up from the computer screen but not pausing in typing. "I just need to send this email, but I'll only be a minute."

Warren sat opposite him and waited for him to finish what he was doing.

"How are you doing?" Lewis asked when he switched his focus from the computer and pushed his keyboard aside.

"Fine."

"How was the family trip?"

"It was okay. Easier having Anna there."

Lewis merely nodded. "I guess you want to go over the menu for the next couple of weeks?"

Warren scratched his forehead. "We can go through it if you want." It wasn't as though Lewis ever gave much input – he was more of a sounding board. "I talked it through with Liam and Sam. They had some good ideas." He supposed it shouldn't have been too surprising that chatting it through with the kitchen staff was more helpful than chatting everything over with Lewis, but they'd got used to doing things a certain way and had stuck with it.

"Right," Lewis said, his eyebrows pulling together.

"I thought you wanted me to give the rest of the kitchen staff more responsibility and whatnot."

"I did." He tapped on the desk. "I *do.* It's good. So you don't need to go through it with me?"

"Not unless you want me to."

Lewis shrugged. "I guess we don't need to."

"The kitchen and restaurant seemed to run smoothly while I was away," Warren added. "I can't say for sure if the staff agree, but I think we have a more harmonious atmosphere in the kitchen. I've been trying to make some changes anyway."

"That's great."

"It's all pretty calm for now. Let's see if it stays that way. The restaurant is booked out every evening until the new year, and we have a lot of lunch reservations too."

"You'll need a break in January."

"Yeah." He'd also be in need of some time with Anna. At this rate, she'd have to visit him at work for them to get any time together. With thoughts of Anna swirling in his mind, he sat up straighter and gathered his courage. "There's something I wanted to ask you. Not about work."

"Okay."

"I was wondering if you'd have any objection to me asking Anna out." He shifted his weight and rubbed the stubble along his jaw. "On a date, I mean."

Lewis stared at him as they fell into an uncomfortable silence. "You want to ask Anna out?"

"Yes."

"I thought you were just friends."

"We were. I mean, we are... but we've been spending a lot of time together and things kind of changed."

"Oh." The way he winced wasn't a brilliant sign.

"I wanted to run it by you because I don't want things to be weird between us."

"Right," Lewis said. "Yeah."

Warren waited for him to say more, but he seemed lost for words.

"It feels as though I've already made things weird," Warren commented eventually.

Lewis released a heavy breath and covered his face with his hands. "This is awkward," he muttered.

"You're not okay with it?"

"It's not really anything to do with me. Anna can date whoever she wants."

"I get that, but you're my best mate. If you have an issue with it, I'd like to know now." It occurred to him that he wasn't sure what he'd do if Lewis was against it. He hadn't thought that far ahead.

"Here's the problem–" Lewis's phone rang, cutting him off. Looking at the phone screen, he swore softly. "I have to take this..."

"Seriously? You need to take a phone call now? You couldn't just call them back?"

His thumb hovered over the screen. "I've been waiting for this guy at the bank to call me back. It shouldn't take long. I'll come and find you in a bit."

Warren stared at him impatiently, but Lewis swiped the screen and switched to a much more formal tone when he answered the call.

Irritated, Warren left the office. He hadn't really thought it would be an issue for Lewis.

Back in the kitchen, he struggled to concentrate and didn't make it ten minutes before snapping at someone. At least Liam looked surprised when Warren bit his head off – maybe that meant his attempts at creating a calmer working environment had been working.

With Liam fumbling to lower the heat on the sauce he was stirring, Warren caught sight of Ivy in the doorway, disappointment clear in her gaze.

"Sorry," he said to Liam, not even sure what he'd shouted at him for. "I'm not having a great day. I didn't mean to take it out on you."

"Okay," Liam mumbled, returning to his task.

"What's up?" Warren called to Ivy across the room.

"Nothing. I wanted to ask you something, but it can wait."

"It's fine." He beckoned for her to come in and she joined him at the back of the room.

"How was your time off?" she asked.

"Pretty good."

"I heard you took Anna to meet your parents?"

"Yeah."

"Are the two of you still just friends?"

He pushed his hip against the countertop. "I don't know," he said honestly.

Ivy smiled. "I think I'll get the gossip from Anna instead."

"Probably better. Is that what you came in here to ask me about?"

"No, but you seem busy, so I'll leave you to it."

He stopped her with a hand on her arm. "What's going on?"

"Nothing. It's only that Poppy was asking..."

He grimaced as he realised what she was going to say. "About baking Christmas cookies with me?"

"Yes. And I told her you're busy at this time of year but she said you promised..."

"I *did* promise." He rubbed the back of his neck. "I should have arranged it with you before. My head has been all over the place."

"It's fine."

"How about tomorrow morning? I'll be here to set out a buffet for Anna's wreath-making class, but there won't be the usual lunch service, so things should be relatively quiet. I can definitely squeeze in cookie-making with my favourite sous-chef."

"Thank you," she said, then pressed her lips together. "I also wanted to ask you something else... but you can absolutely say no if it's a problem... it's only that I still have some Christmas shopping to do and usually I'd ask my mum to look after Poppy but she's been stressed..."

"Go when Poppy is here with me," he said, struggling to see what the problem was.

"Really? Are you sure you don't mind?"

"Why would I mind?"

"I just hate asking for help when it comes to Poppy."

"When it comes to *anything,*" he corrected. "It's kind of rude though, because I enjoy hanging out with your daughter. I don't know why you think she's such a burden to put on people."

"Thank you." She gave him a kiss on the cheek and left looking slightly emotional.

Five minutes later, Lewis strode in. "Sorry," he said, tipping his head towards the food storage.

They lingered outside it, far enough from the rest of the staff not to be overheard.

"Do you really have a problem with me dating Anna?" Warren asked, folding his arms over his chest.

"No. That's not my issue."

"What's the problem, then?"

He grimaced. "I'd really rather not get involved, but it feels weird not to say something."

"Get to the point," Warren grumbled.

"Anna went on a date with Hayden last night. I only heard it from Carla, so I don't really know the situation, but I felt as though I should mention it."

"Oh." He hadn't been expecting that, and he wasn't sure how to respond.

"I'm not saying you shouldn't ask her out – but maybe you shouldn't get your hopes up. From what Carla tells me, Anna never really got over Hayden."

"Right." Warren rubbed his eyebrow, dumbstruck.

"Sorry."

"It's fine," Warren said, mostly because he didn't really believe there was anything going on with Anna and her ex.

She wasn't someone who played games, and she'd been very open about her feelings for Warren. If she *had* gone out with Hayden, he was sure there was some explanation – one which didn't involve her getting back together with him. "Thanks for the warning. But just to get everything out in the open, you have no other objections to me making a move on your sister."

"I don't particularly like it when you put it like that." Amusement flashed in Lewis's eyes. "But no, of course I don't have a problem with it."

"Good."

Lewis glanced around the kitchen before lowering his voice.

"Not to freak you out, but there's a couple in the restaurant eyeing everything with scrutiny."

Warren frowned. "What?"

"It's probably nothing. These days, whenever I'm here in the evenings, I can't help but loiter in the restaurant and speculate over whether any of the guests might be a Michelin reviewer, but I guess there's nothing to say they wouldn't come for lunch. It also seems likely they'd send someone out over Christmas, don't you think?"

"I have no idea," Warren said, his tone clipped. "It's not something I think about."

"Yeah, right." Lewis gave his arm a friendly punch. "I don't believe that for a second."

"It's true," Warren muttered. "Do you honestly think there's a real chance we'll get a Michelin star for this place?"

"I don't see why not."

"We *won't.*" Warren shook his head. "If that's your goal, you may want to rethink it." Lewis opened his mouth, but Warren spoke over him. "What does it even matter? The restaurant is doing well, and we get great reviews from the customers. That's what you should be bothered about."

"That *is* what I'm bothered about," Lewis said, tilting his head. "A Michelin star wouldn't hurt, though. And after the review they gave you, I don't know why you think it's not a possibility."

"They didn't review *me,*" Warren said. "They reviewed the restaurant."

"Yes, but you're the head chef." He frowned deeply. "What's your problem?"

"I don't have a problem. I just don't think you should get your hopes up about the Michelin star."

"Okay." He lifted his shoulders in a shrug. "I didn't realise it was such a sensitive topic."

"It's not," he lied, then looked around the kitchen. "I have work to do."

"I'll leave you to it, but let's get together for a drink sometime soon." Lewis gave him an uncertain look and left the kitchen without another word.

Feeling the need to get his thoughts in order, Warren grabbed his coat and stepped out of the back door into the freezing cold air. A thin layer of snow covered the small car park behind the hotel, and Warren's breath fogged in front of his face as he stood on the steps.

He got his phone out, acutely aware that he owed Anna a phone call.

His gaze lingered on the screen for a minute before he decided he had no clue what he'd say. While he really didn't think he had anything to worry about regarding her and Hayden, there was a spark of doubt in his mind, which quickly ignited.

She'd probably be better off with someone like Hayden, anyway. He seemed like a straightforward guy.

He was probably honest too.

Which was something Warren definitely hadn't been.

Chapter Forty-Four

When Warren hadn't called by Friday afternoon, Anna caved and sent him a message asking how he was. She supposed she should have been pleased that he replied so quickly, but the message didn't exactly fill her with joy. He said he was fine, but was busy with work.

Did you speak to Lewis? she typed, wondering whether the conversation would be better as a call.

Yeah. I'll tell you about it when I see you.

When will that be? she asked, hating that she sounded desperate when his messages were definitely on the cool side.

I don't think I'll have a night off until the New Year. Sorry.

She waited, but that was all she got, and she wasn't at all sure how to respond.

Briefly, she contemplated calling Lewis to ask exactly how the conversation had gone between the two of them. She really didn't want to bring Lewis into it though, especially since she knew what he'd have said – that he was fine with it.

There was no way he'd say otherwise.

To distract herself, she nipped out to finish her Christmas shopping, then took an inventory of her stock to make sure she had everything she needed for the wreath-making workshop at the hotel the following day. That would involve seeing Warren and given his messages she wasn't at all sure how to feel about that.

She focused on the workshop itself. But that got her thinking about speaking in front of a room full of people, which sent her anxiety levels through the roof.

To calm her nerves, she mentally rehearsed her talk about the history of wreaths. Not that she needed to practice it – she knew it by heart. If anything, going over it only intensified her nerves.

By the time she got into bed, she was too worked up about it to fall asleep.

Tiredness had her moving on autopilot the following morning. The stress of the workshop combined with Warren's sudden coolness felt like too much.

By the time she walked into the hotel carrying a box of supplies, she was on high alert for any sign of him. Her eyes darted all around the reception and lounge area, then she scanned the dining room when she set the box down on one of the tables, which had already been arranged in a U-shape.

"I'm supposed to help you carry stuff," Kate, one of the waitresses, said as she approached Anna. "Have you got much more to bring in?"

"Quite a bit." Anna's gaze flicked to the kitchen doors, wondering if he'd come out and say hello or if he'd stay out of the way while she was there.

"Should I get someone else to help us?" Kate asked, leading the way back through the hotel.

"I think we'll manage," Anna replied. "Is Lewis here?"

"Yes. In the office. He said he had a few things to deal with but would come and see you when he's finished."

"Right." She supposed it was good that her brother had got

better at delegating tasks around the hotel, but she'd have felt better if he'd been there to help her unload and get everything set up.

There was still no sign of him when they'd carried everything inside. Warren hadn't appeared either. It frustrated her to think that there was only a wall between them and he hadn't even bothered to come out and say hello.

Stopping to take a breath, she cursed herself. Because she also hadn't made any effort to say hello to him. She had the excuse of being stressed about the workshop, at least.

"Hello!" A well-dressed middle-aged woman appeared in front of Anna. Her perfume pervaded the air and made Anna's nose twitch.

"Hi," Anna said nervously. "Are you here for the wreath-making?"

"Yes." She plucked a fir twig from the table, holding it under her nose and inhaling deeply. "I'm very excited. I've never made a wreath before."

"I'm just finishing setting up," Anna said. "We'll get started in about ten minutes. You're welcome to get a drink while you wait."

"I'll do that," the woman said before wandering over to the bar.

Steadily, the room filled up. Anna's nerves intensified at a rate that correlated with the increase of people in the room.

"It looks as though I'm in the right place for wreath-making," an elderly lady remarked, hovering in front of Anna and eyeing the selection of fir twigs, holly leaves and baubles on the table.

"Yes," Anna mumbled, feeling suddenly breathless. "If you could just excuse me for a minute. I just need to do something..."

With an insincere smile, she backed away and crossed the room while carefully avoiding making eye contact with anyone. Her lungs felt as though they weren't taking in enough oxygen as she walked along the corridor to Lewis's office.

She didn't bother knocking, but flung the door open. "You're going to have to say I'm ill or something," she announced, then tried not to react when her eyes landed on Warren, sitting on the couch at the side of the room, leaning back with one ankle propped on the opposite knee.

"What's wrong?" Lewis asked, leaning forward onto his desk.

"I can't do it. I don't know why I let you talk me into it again. Last year I didn't want to do it, and you just bullied me into it. I shouldn't have agreed to do it again this year."

"I don't understand." Lewis tucked his chin. "You said you were happy to do it since it went so well last year."

"Well I shouldn't have!" She could hear just how irrational she sounded, but her heart was beating irregularly, and she felt lightheaded. "I'm terrible at this stuff, and I should have known better than to agree to it. Tell them I'm ill or something."

Lewis rose slowly out of his chair, raising his hands as though dealing with a wild animal. "It's supposed to start in a few minutes. Everyone will be waiting."

"You're just going to have to deal with that."

Out of the corner of her eye, she spotted Warren shifting in his seat.

"Maybe you just need a few minutes," he said.

"And maybe you should keep out of it," she shouted without looking at him. "I'm sorry," she said to Lewis, before turning on her heel and making a dash for it.

On the street outside the front door, she dragged a hand over her face, then wrapped her arms around herself and rubbed at her upper arms as she inhaled the freezing air.

"Anna." Warren's voice was quiet but firm behind her.

"I can't do it," she said, spinning around and casting him a frosty glare. "And I really can't deal with *you* at the moment."

"I'm sorry you're annoyed with me."

She pressed her lips together. "I just said I can't deal with you now."

"Forget about me then. Let's talk about the people waiting for you to teach them how to make wreaths."

"I can't," she repeated, pacing the pavement in front of the hotel. "I should never have agreed to it."

"The other workshops you did went fine, remember?"

"I remember." She stopped and stretched her neck, gazing up at the hazy clouds, which threatened snow. "But that doesn't mean I'm suddenly cured of my nerves. This stuff will always make me nervous. I don't think that's ever going to change, so I should accept that and stop agreeing to do these events."

He stepped in front of her, close enough that his scent filled her nostrils. "You don't need to stop being nervous about these things. Being nervous is probably what makes you so good at it."

"I don't want to do it. I feel sick."

"Once you get in there, you won't feel sick any more. As soon as you stand in front of those people, you'll be fine. Because they're not there to listen to some over-confident person talk about wreaths. They want to listen to someone who knows what they're talking about and who's passionate about it." He tilted his head. "And mostly they want to have a fun morning making wreaths. You're the perfect person for this job – nerves and all."

She sucked in a deep breath, not sure whether it was his proximity or his words that were having the calming effect.

"Maybe I can do it," she said.

"You definitely can."

"You're pretty good at pep talks."

"Yeah?" He smiled shyly. "Do you feel better?"

"A bit."

"Maybe we can improve on that." He dipped his head and

caught her lips in a kiss that sent her stomach free falling. "Better?" he asked, his breath sweeping tantalisingly over her lips.

"I think you could have skipped the pep talk and just done that," she said, as her nerves faded into the background.

"Anna?" Lewis called from the hotel doorway.

"I'm coming."

"Are you okay?" Lewis asked, concern etched on his features as Anna strode past him.

"Yeah. I'm fine. I just freaked out a bit." She was vaguely aware of him following her as she hurried through the hotel and into the restaurant, where the guests were waiting for her. Without stopping to think about it, she moved to the centre of the room and called *hello* to get everyone's attention. Then she welcomed them and launched into an overview of what the morning would entail.

She was partway through her spiel about the history of wreaths when she glanced towards the bar and spotted Warren perched on a stool. His slow smile made her stomach flutter.

Knowing that her cheeks had just flared bright red, she stumbled over her words for a moment, then took a deep breath and found her stride again.

The next two hours flew by. At the end of it, she was completely embarrassed by her earlier outburst. With hindsight, the nerves made no sense, and she couldn't understand why she'd freaked out so much. She supposed her turmoil over Warren had also added to her frazzled state.

He'd disappeared after the introduction of the workshop, and she hadn't seen him since. Presumably, he was in the kitchen since the wait staff had been busy taking trays of food to the lounge for the guests to enjoy after the workshop.

After packing everything up and saying farewell to the stragglers of the group, she ventured over to peer in the window of the kitchen door. She frowned at the sight of Warren at the back of the kitchen, working with Ivy's little girl beside him.

After making it all the way across the kitchen without them noticing, she was right beside them and listening to them chatter about the ingredients when Warren whipped his head to her.

"Don't sneak up on us. We're already panicking about the health inspector catching us. I was just telling Poppy that if someone official looking comes in, she has to lie about her age and pretend that she's officially employed here."

"I have to say I'm sixteen," Poppy said, giggling. "And my name is Sue the chef."

"Not Sue the chef!" Warren's eyes lit with delight. "*The sous chef.* It's a type of chef. I'm the head chef and you're my sous chef."

Poppy looked confused, and Warren ruffled her hair in amusement. "Never mind. From now on you'll be Sue the chef."

Anna smiled lightly. "I'm not sure you'll pass for sixteen."

"We have a backup plan," Warren said.

Poppy cracked another egg into the bowl. "We'll give them lots of cookies and ask them not to tell anyone."

"Bribery seems like a more realistic plan." Anna eyed the mixture as Warren nudged Poppy to turn on the mixer.

"How was the workshop?" he asked over the noise of it.

"It went really well."

He nodded. "It seemed like it from what I saw."

"Thank you for the pep talk."

"You're welcome. I think you'd have been fine without the pep talk, though."

Her stomach fluttered as she thought of the way he'd kissed her. After spending the last few days wondering where the heck she stood with him, the kiss had been reassuring.

"Do you have time to grab lunch with me once you've finished your baking?" she asked quietly.

The uncertainty in his eyes quashed any reassurance she'd previously felt.

"I said I'd take Poppy out to the shops quickly when we're done here. She wants to choose a Christmas present for Ivy."

"I'm going to surprise Mummy with it," Poppy said.

"She'll love that." It crossed Anna's mind to say she could tag along with them, but hesitated, hoping Warren might suggest it.

"After that, I'll be busy here again," he said.

"Okay." If that hadn't felt like enough of a brush off, he then turned his back on her to help Poppy move the cookie dough onto the work surface.

"Warren?" Anna said when it seemed he was intent on pretending she wasn't there.

"Yeah?"

"I'm confused. I don't know what's going on in your head."

The twitch of his cheek told her he didn't want to have this conversation.

"Can you roll it out?" he said to Poppy before taking a few steps away with Anna. "I'm just busy with work at the moment. Next week should be quieter."

"And when work is quieter, will you want to spend time with me? It's hard to tell."

"Yes," he said with a weariness that made her feel as though she was some kind of nuisance.

"Why do you sound as though you'd rather not? No one is forcing you – I only want to know if you'd like to."

"I want to see you, but I need to speak to you properly, and things are going to be crazy here over the next few days."

"And you can't even find an hour to grab a coffee?" She glanced pointedly at Ivy. "It seems as though if there's something you really want to do, you'll find time for it."

He squeezed the bridge of his nose. "I promised Poppy ages ago."

"And that's really nice of you," she said, but the bitterness was clear in her tone. "Why don't we just leave things for now, and when you figure out if you want to make time for me, we can talk again. For now, I won't hold my breath for that date you said you were going to take me on."

Ignoring the lump that formed in her throat, she gave Poppy a quick squeeze while she continued to roll out the dough. "I hope Santa brings you everything you want," she told her, then gritted her teeth as she wished Warren a Happy Christmas.

"Anna!" he called, but sounded half-hearted, as though he didn't have anything more to say even if she turned back.

Which she had no intention of doing.

Chapter Forty-Five

With the workshop at the hotel out of the way, and all her Christmas orders for her online shop sent out, Anna had little to keep her occupied over the following two days. She expected Warren to get in touch and apologise, but there was no word from him, and the more she thought about it, the more annoyed she was with him.

On Christmas Eve, she dutifully went along to the Midnight Mass with her family. Squeezed between her mum and her sister on the pew, the service didn't fill her with Christmas cheer as it usually did. Even the carols – and Carla's out of tune and overly loud voice – did little to lift her spirits.

Waking on Christmas Day, her first instinct was to check her phone. Disappointment at the lack of contact from Warren made her pull the duvet over her head, and it was an effort to drag herself out of bed and get ready for the day. When she got in the car to drive over to her parents' house, she had the fleeting idea of calling in at the hotel.

The desire to see Warren was an ache in her chest, and she was desperate to know what was really going on with him.

She didn't believe his excuse about being busy with work.

He couldn't possibly be so busy that he couldn't send her a message or call her. Putting the car into gear, she swallowed her emotions.

The truth, as far as she could tell, was that he just didn't want to be with her.

She let herself dwell on that for the fifteen-minute drive to Bourton-on-the-Water. That was all the self-pity she'd allowed herself, though. She wouldn't let him ruin Christmas Day for her.

With that sentiment ringing in her head as she pulled up in front of her parents' house, she lifted her bag of gifts from the back seat and forced a smile. She didn't have to fake it for long – the sight of her parents stepping out of the house to greet her in their matching Christmas jumpers – complete with flashing lights – made her laugh out loud.

"You're the last to arrive," her mum said, burying her in a hug. "Lewis was just threatening to start lunch without you."

Molly, Lewis's border collie, came rushing out of the house to bounce around Anna, and she felt herself relax as she patted her down.

"Come in," her dad said, waving her through the doorway. "Let's get the party started."

"Finally!" Lewis chimed when she walked into the kitchen. "We're starving!"

She gave him a hug, then moved to greet Erin and Carla.

"It's only just midday," Anna said. "I'm not even late."

"Lewis is just overly excited about Christmas dinner," Erin said. "He's been talking about it for a week."

"It's the best meal of the year," he said happily as he took a seat, then waved a blue Christmas cracker at Anna.

She pulled it and made a show of teasing him when she got the bigger half.

The usual round of Christmas cracker jokes ensued, and ten

minutes later they were all tucking into the turkey dinner with colourful party hats on their heads.

"When do you leave for London?" Anna asked, knowing that Lewis and Erin had plans with her family between Christmas and New Year.

"Tomorrow," Erin replied. "We'll have a big family dinner tomorrow evening with my sister and lots of extended family. After that, it should be very chilled out."

"It's good that you'll both have a break," their mum said. "Employing a general manager for the hotel was the best thing you ever did."

"Is he working out okay?" Anna asked.

"He's perfectly competent," Lewis said with a shrug. "He's not particularly charismatic, but he gets the job done."

"Ivy doesn't like him," Carla remarked.

Lewis rolled his eyes. "Ivy's problem is he's doing the job she should be doing, but there's not a lot I can do about that since she refused to take the job."

"You can see why she'd be reluctant," their dad said. "She has a lot on her plate."

"It would have been perfect for her," Lewis argued. "But she declined, so now she has to put up with the strait-laced general manager. It's not really an issue."

"It's Warren who's currently causing issues," Erin muttered.

Lewis narrowed his eyes as he pinned her with a look. "Let's not talk about work. You're ruining Christmas dinner for me."

"Is there an issue with Warren?" their dad asked, ignoring Lewis's plea.

"Lewis is concerned he's looking for another job," Erin said casually.

Their mum sat up straighter. "Surely not?"

"Why would you think that?" Anna asked, unease churning in her stomach.

Lewis sighed heavily, apparently resigning himself to the conversation. "Recently, I had a word with him about the way he runs the kitchen. The atmosphere between us has been tense since then."

"You're his boss," Erin pointed out. "It's normal that sometimes you have to say things he doesn't like."

"But he's a great chef. I probably shouldn't have said anything."

"He's always run the kitchen in his own aggressive style." Carla spoke with her mouth full. "Why did you have a word with him now?"

"It seemed as though things got worse." Lewis flicked his eyes to Anna. "I heard you had to intervene to stop him from firing the entire kitchen staff on the spot."

"That seems like a slightly exaggerated tale," Anna said weakly.

"It wasn't as though I really planned on having a word with him," Lewis went on. "But it came up, so I told him I thought the kitchen could be run more efficiently."

Carla reached for her wine. "Sounds a bit harsh."

"I think it was fair," Erin said. "The week before that, I'd heard him shouting when I was in the dining room. It doesn't make it a very comfortable meal when the guests can hear the chef screaming in the kitchen."

"To be fair, it's unusual for him to be that loud." Lewis shrugged. "I think he was probably just stressed about some stuff in his personal life."

"Do you really think he's looking for a new job?" their mum asked.

"I know he's been headhunted by other restaurants, so he wouldn't have a problem finding another job if he wanted to leave."

"I can't imagine he'd be petty enough to leave just because you said something he didn't like," Carla said.

Silently, Anna agreed with her, but didn't want to get too involved in the conversation.

"I don't think it's only because of what I said." Lewis had his eyes on his plate as he loaded his fork with turkey and roast potato. "I suspect it's also to do with the Michelin review."

"How so?" Anna asked.

Lewis chewed his food before answering. "I wonder if he thinks the Michelin *review* is as much as he's going to get if he stays at the hotel. And I guess he's secretly desperate to get a star."

"Why can't he get one at the hotel?" Carla asked.

"Because the Michelin stars aren't given purely based on the chef and how well they can cook. It's the whole dining experience."

"So they only give them to snobby, obnoxious restaurants?" Carla asked.

"No, but I guess Warren thinks the hotel isn't the right vibe for them. He's convinced there's no way we can get one."

"He was funny about that when I mentioned it too," Anna mused. "When we were away with his parents, I made a remark about it being on the cards and he got really grumpy about it."

"I don't know what's going on with him." Lewis reached down to stroke Molly, who lay contentedly beside his chair. "But he's been in a weird mood recently."

"You said the kitchen is a lot calmer though," Erin put in.

"Yeah. He seems to have stopped throwing his weight around quite so much."

"That's good, isn't it?" their mum asked.

"In theory. As long as it's not just that he doesn't care enough to get angry with anyone because he's planning on leaving."

"He's your best friend!" Carla threw her hands up. "Just ask him what's going on. I can ask him if you want."

Lewis shook his head. "I'm hoping things will settle down

again. And if he's thinking of leaving, I don't want to know about it yet. Not when we're going to London tomorrow. I won't be able to enjoy the time away if I know I have to find a new chef when I get back."

"It doesn't sound like Warren," their dad said. "I always thought he was as loyal as they come."

"He is," Lewis said. "Hopefully, I'm wrong about him leaving."

Anna's mind was going crazy, churning everything over. She had no clue what was going on with Warren, but she had the unshakeable feeling that his odd behaviour at work was related to her. Or maybe the other way around... perhaps him going cold on her was something to do with his job. Maybe he *was* thinking of leaving.

If he'd got a job somewhere far away, that could explain his aloofness. Maybe he didn't think it was worth starting a relationship if he was moving.

The thought made her stomach tighten, and she pushed her plate away, claiming she was full.

As the conversation shifted, Anna's mind remained stuck on Warren. Several times over the afternoon, she looked at her phone, hopeful that he might get in touch. There was no contact though, and she did her best to focus on her family as they exchanged gifts, then let Carla coax them into playing a card game she'd bought for Lewis, which involved throwing beanbags at each other when a certain card was drawn.

As usual, the day ended with Anna feeling that she'd eaten far too much. Mostly too much sugar, since her mum had plied them with a seemingly endless supply of treats over the afternoon.

With the sky completely dark outside, Anna declared she

was leaving fifteen minutes before she made it out of the door. The farewells felt as endless as the sweets.

"I can help," Lewis said, picking up a bag of presents for her since she was carrying a stack of Tupperware with leftovers and even more treats.

"Everything okay with you?" he asked when she opened the boot of the car. "You seemed quiet today."

"I'm fine," she lied, then paused and watched her brother load her gifts into the car. "Actually, I have a question." She hesitated long enough for him to stare at her expectantly. "I don't want to put you in an awkward position, but it's about Warren."

"What about him?" Lewis asked, pushing his hands into his pockets.

"Did he have a conversation with you about me?"

"Yeah." He frowned. "I'm not sure I'm supposed to tell you about it, though."

She pressed her lips together, not wanting to push him into breaking a confidence, but thinking he ought to show some sibling solidarity. "I understand, but can you just tell me if you gave him any reason to think you'd have an issue with me having a relationship with him?"

"No."

"No, you can't tell me, or no, you didn't say that."

"I told him I didn't have a problem with it."

"So he did ask?"

"Yeah. I'm confused. You like Warren?"

She stared at him. "Yes."

"Ah, okay."

"Are you sure you didn't say something to make him think you weren't okay with it? Because he said he wanted to talk it through with you and then he'd ask me on a date. Except he didn't ask me on a date, and I don't know why. He was vague when I spoke to him. He said he was busy with work, but I think that's just an excuse."

"I didn't realise you were interested in Warren."

She frowned. "You used to tease me because you thought I fancied him!"

"Yes, but that was ages ago. And it was before Carla told me you weren't over Hayden."

"I am over Hayden."

"Really? So you didn't go on a date with him recently?"

"I went out with him. It wasn't a date..."

Lewis grimaced and took a defensive step away from her.

Anna slapped a hand across her mouth as she gasped. "You *didn't?*" she growled. "Please tell me you didn't tell Warren I went on a date with Hayden."

He held up his palms. "He asked if I was okay with him asking you out. I told him it was none of my business, but I didn't think you were interested because you'd been on a date with your ex."

Anna growled.

"Sorry," Lewis said.

"I'm not angry with you. Well, I am. But mostly I'm angry with Warren. Why the heck wouldn't he just tell me what you'd said and check the facts?"

"Maybe because he's a guy and was worried about his ego."

"He should probably worry about more than his ego now." She shook her head, then kissed Lewis's cheek. "Have a good time in London. I'll see you on New Year's Eve."

"Are you going to see Warren?"

"Yes." She rushed around the car and opened the door.

"Remember, it's Christmas! Go easy on him."

"I can't promise that," she said, smiling as she hopped into the car.

One way or another, she was determined to get some answers. It was the most positive she'd felt all day.

Chapter Forty-Six

Drinks were clearly flowing in the hotel lounge. The cheerful chatter of the guests mixed pleasantly with the Christmas music and the pine scent from the Christmas tree, which permeated the air. At the back of the building, the restaurant was empty except for a middle-aged couple sitting at the bar.

Through the small windows into the kitchen, Anna spotted Warren hunched over the bench at the back of the room, perched on a stool. A couple of the younger kitchen staff stood chatting in the centre of the room. About to push at the door, Anna stopped as she felt her phone vibrate. Pulling it from her pocket, her pulse skittered at the notification of a message from Warren.

Quickly, she clicked into it, then rolled her eyes at the message, which simply wished her a happy Christmas. She supposed it was at least comforting to know he'd been thinking of her. Definitely a bit lacking, though.

Another message came through.

I'm sorry.

She waited while dots skittered along the screen, indicating he was writing another message.

I miss you.

That was a bit more like it.

"Happy Christmas to you," she said as she crossed the kitchen.

Swivelling on his stool, surprise flooded Warren's features. His eyes darted from her to his phone as though he might somehow have magically summoned her.

"I'm so annoyed with you," she said, stopping in front of him and setting a gift bag on the counter.

He craned his neck to look around her and tipped his head at the staff in a gesture that clearly told them to scarper. They did as they were told and the doors swung closed behind them.

"What are you doing here?" he asked.

She remembered Lewis's request for her to go easy on him and held back on her verbal assault.

"I wanted to see you," she said simply.

He reached for her hand, his fingers lightly caressing her palm. "I'm such an idiot."

"I can't really argue with that." She ran a hand down his cheek. "Why didn't you just ask me about Hayden?"

His eyes darted to her face. "What?"

"If you thought I was on a date with Hayden, why didn't you just ask me about it?"

"I..." He withdrew his hand and rubbed at his brow.

"Oh. That isn't the reason you've been ignoring me, is it?"

"I wasn't ignoring you."

"Right. You've just been busy." She sighed. "Please explain what's going on."

"Lewis mentioned you'd been out with Hayden, and to be honest, it didn't exactly fill me with joy to think of you out with him... but I assumed he'd got it wrong when he said you weren't over your ex."

"Of course he got it wrong. Hayden asked if we could meet up, and I wanted to hear what he had to say. But not because I had any thoughts about getting back with him. Things still felt unfinished between us, and before I started anything with you, I needed to draw a line under that part of my life. I went to dinner with him for closure." She paused and pressed her lips together. "Except then you went all weird on me, and it seems as though you don't want to be with me, anyway."

"I'm sorry."

"I don't know what you're sorry for," she said through gritted teeth. "Do you just not like me that much, or are you moving away? What's going on with you?"

"Why would I be moving away?"

She released a breath. "Lewis thinks you're looking for a new job."

"What made him think that?"

"Does it even matter? I want to know what's going on with us, not talk about my brother." Anger simmered inside her. "You've been giving very mixed signals, and if you're going to insist on playing games, then I'm just going to walk away now. I spent two years feeling like I'm not good enough because of my ex, and I refuse to spend my time wondering if you even have feelings for me..."

He shot off the stool to stand in front of her. "Of course I have feelings for you. I haven't been able to stop thinking about you for weeks."

"Then you need to explain what's going on in your head."

He looked her right in the eyes, then swallowed hard. "I guess you were right about me sharing some qualities with my family. There are things I need to tell you, but instead of talking to you, I just avoided the issue."

"What things?"

"Stuff about my past."

"Surely that's why people date – to find out more about each other."

"Yes, but..."

"But what?"

His arms circled her waist. "I don't know."

"Well why don't you just tell me, and we'll go from there. Or better yet, let's go to my place and we can talk properly."

"Yeah, okay." He looked so forlorn that she felt a pang of sympathy for him.

"Is it really such a big deal? Do you have some sort of criminal past you need to tell me about?"

A smile tugged at the corners of his lips. "Nothing like that."

"Good." She licked her lips, then pressed them to his. All her earlier worries melted away as he brought his hand to the back of her head and deepened the kiss.

The way he winced as he broke away wasn't a great sign.

"What now?" she complained.

"I can't go to your place this evening."

"Why not?"

His eyebrows inched upwards. "I have a date."

Anna only just refrained from rolling her eyes. "Is this a weird thing where you try to make me jealous and then tell me the date is actually with me?"

"No." He winced. "It's not with you."

"Are you trying to tell me you really have a date?"

He nodded and at least looked remorseful.

"You have a date with a woman?"

He nodded again.

Anna stared at him for a moment, then she really did roll her eyes. "Is it with an old lady?"

"Yeah." He smiled. "I always spend Christmas Day evening with Edie. Her family will have been over for lunch, but they'll have left by now. She saves me Christmas cake."

"I suppose if I have to lose out on you to anyone, I can cope with it being Edie."

Warren rested his forehead against hers. "She'll be waiting for me. I'd feel terrible not going."

"It's okay." Disappointing, but she'd get over it.

"Do you want to come?" he asked, eyeing her hopefully.

She didn't even have to consider it. "I'd love to."

"I should probably warn you that Edie may be slightly tipsy and she might crank the music up and insist on us dancing around the kitchen with her."

"I think I can cope with that." She reached around him for the gift bag. "I got you something."

Taking the bag, he sank back onto the stool and lifted out the gift in shiny red packaging. He eyed her curiously before tearing at the wrapping to reveal the wooden box filled with a variety of individually wrapped tea bags.

"So you can have a bit of luxury at home, too," she told him as nerves fluttered in her stomach.

"I love it."

"Do you?" It had seemed like a good idea before Frannie had eyed it up for the old women in her family.

"I really do. Thank you." He set it aside and took her hand. "I got you something, too."

"Yeah?"

Nodding, he pulled her onto his knee. "It's not wrapped," he murmured before his lips met hers.

Briefly, she got swept up in the kiss. Then she pulled back. "I thought I was getting a present."

"Yeah." He leaned in again. "Happy Christmas."

With a hand on his chest, she stopped him with his lips millimetres from hers. "Sometimes your teasing is just annoying," she said, while her mouth betrayed her by stretching to a wide grin.

"What teasing?"

"The type of teasing where you give me a kiss for Christmas."

"What's wrong with that? Don't tell me you're the materialistic type?"

"I absolutely am."

He curled his lip. "In that case, it's a good job I bought you an actual gift."

"Did you?"

"It's in my car. Tied with a ribbon and everything. Shall we go and get it?"

Her lips grazed his. "I'll just have one more kiss first, if you don't mind?"

"Go on then." He tightened his arms around her waist. "Since it's Christmas."

Chapter Forty-Seven

In the car, Warren turned the heat on before reaching into the back seat for Anna's gift.

Nerves fluttered in his chest as he handed it over. "It's not very exciting," he said automatically.

Carefully, she pulled at the ribbon and peeled the paper away to reveal the small cardboard box. Her gaze homed in on the sticker with the logo for the local potter, but she didn't react as she eased open the lid and drew out the mug.

"It's the same as yours." Her eyes sparkled as she turned the mug to read the writing. *World's Best Florist.*

He drummed his fingers on the steering wheel. "Do you like it?"

"I love it." She tugged on his shoulder, drawing him in for a kiss. "Thank you."

"You're welcome. I was thinking... if you wanted..." Another flurry of nerves hit him. He wasn't usually overly sentimental, and he was slightly concerned his thoughts would come out sounding pathetic.

"What?" Anna prompted.

"Nothing." He scratched at the back of his head. "I was

going to say that if you wanted, you could leave the mug at my place. That way, you won't be tempted to use mine."

"You're thinking I'll be spending a lot of time at your place?"

"Just hoping, I suppose."

Her smile was half-hearted at best.

"Sorry," he muttered. After ignoring her for a week, now he was moving too fast. "If you're still annoyed with me, it's totally understandable. I spent the last week caught up in my head, and it wasn't fair to you, but I really am sorry and I promise I'll make it up to you."

"It's okay." She shifted to face him. "I just don't want to be in a relationship with someone who shuts me out. I might seem like a pushover most of the time, but I won't put up with that for very long."

"Good. Because you shouldn't. I promise I'm done with hiding things." He paused for a moment. "I can tell Edie I'll see her tomorrow. She won't mind. We can just go to my place, or yours, and I'll explain everything properly."

"Thank you." She sighed. "It's Christmas, though. You can't bail on Edie."

Part of him wanted to insist it was fine to cancel his plans with Edie, but he also felt a stab of guilt at the thought of it. It was their little Christmas tradition, and she'd be waiting for him.

"Are you sure?"

Anna nodded.

"We only need to stay for half an hour. Then we can go to my place and I'll tell you everything."

It would be a relief to get it all off his chest. Hopefully, she'd be her usual understanding self when she knew the truth about him.

Half an hour later, he sat at his neighbour's kitchen table with

Anna enthusiastically explaining to Edie how her online shop worked.

"It's fascinating," Edie said over the Christmas music emanating from the speaker on the windowsill. Her gaze was fixed on Anna's phone, looking at her website. "Isn't it fantastic how you can set up your own business, just like that. It's very clever."

"Thanks," Anna said. "I've been thinking of expanding, but I'm not sure."

"Expanding how?" Edie asked.

"Into a physical shop." Anna bit down on her lip, looking suddenly vulnerable. "I have an appointment to view a place next week."

Edie's face lit up. "That's exciting."

"You made an appointment to view somewhere?" Another stab of regret hit Warren. If he'd been in touch with her, instead of shutting her out for the last week, he'd already know that.

"Yeah." She put her thumb against her teeth, nibbling on her nail. "Which sort of feels like a mistake. Maybe I'll cancel it. I haven't even made a proper business plan."

"You can at least have a look," Warren said.

"If you like the place, that will be good motivation to make a business plan." Edie patted Anna on the shoulder. "It sounds very exciting to me. I think we should have another glass of wine to celebrate."

"There's nothing to celebrate yet," Anna insisted but didn't protest when Edie refilled her glass.

Feeling slightly anxious about the conversation he needed to have with Anna, Warren had been intending to suggest leaving, but decided another drink would probably make the conversation easier.

"I'll turn the music up," Edie said, and Warren exchanged a look with Anna, whose cheeks were rosy from the wine.

"Warren was saying you two sometimes have kitchen dance parties."

When Warren gave Anna a reprimanding stare, she only beamed back at him.

"That's a good idea." Edie held out her hand to Warren as she shimmied across the kitchen. "Let's have a waltz."

Since he couldn't say no, he took a large swig of his wine and obediently twirled her around the kitchen to *Santa Baby* while Anna giggled away. With Edie and Anna having such a good time, he waited half an hour before suggesting they leave.

"That was fun," Anna said, slipping her hand into his for the ten second walk across the driveway. She was giddy from the wine and kissed him as soon as they stepped into his place.

"Not so shy any more, are you?" he said when he could get a word in between kisses.

"I'm not feeling very shy at all," she said, pressing her body against his and making all coherent thoughts fall out of his head.

"Wait," he said breathlessly. "We were going to talk."

"True." She kissed his jaw and then his neck. "But now I'd like to suggest we save the talking for later... or tomorrow. It's Christmas, and I can think of much better things to do than talk about your earlier life of crime."

He chuckled. "I already told you I was never a criminal."

"Good." She rubbed her nose against his. "That means whatever it is can wait."

With her hands creeping under his jumper and her fingers trailing up his back, he didn't feel as though he had much choice in the matter.

She pulled back, weaving her fingers with his. "Would you like to see my tattoo now?"

"Yeah." Beaming, he followed her into the bedroom. "I'd like that a lot."

Chapter Forty-Eight

Waking on Boxing Day with Warren's arms wrapped around her, Anna felt a deep sense of joy. She gazed at his features while her stomach turned somersaults at the memory of their night together.

She'd purposely distracted him from telling her whatever it was he'd been hiding. She should probably have heard him out, but at the time she'd been too hyped up on wine and Christmas cheer for any deep conversations.

If she was honest, she hadn't wanted anything to ruin the mood.

Now, she wondered what had got him so wound up. Presumably, she'd find out soon enough.

He didn't stir as she ran her fingers over the tattoos on his bicep, or when she eased herself out of his embrace.

Pulling on his T-shirt, she headed for the kitchen.

She made coffee for Warren in his favourite mug and used her new mug for herself.

Impatiently, she took a scalding sip before setting it back down and drifting into the living room, which wasn't as tidy as the last time she'd visited. Books lay strewn on the table, and one was open and draped over the arm of the couch. Picking it up, her eyes skimmed the content. Then she sank onto the couch and turned it over to read the title.

"Snooping again?"

Her head snapped up to Warren, who stood in the kitchen in a pair of boxer shorts.

"I don't think it's snooping if things are lying around. Also, it's not exactly private. It's only books." Once again, her gaze roamed over the titles of the non-fiction collection. "Why are you reading books about staff management?"

Warren pulled out a chair at the kitchen table, turning it to face her before taking a seat. "Because Lewis had a go at me for the way I run the kitchen. He doesn't like the way I manage the staff."

"And you didn't just tell him where to go?"

"No."

She caught the vulnerability in his eyes but couldn't figure out why he looked so defeated. "Why not?" she asked quietly.

"Because he was right – I don't know how to manage the kitchen." He scrubbed a hand over his face. "I don't know what I'm doing in that kitchen most of the time."

"Well, that's not true." She smiled through her confusion. "I've seen you in the kitchen. You absolutely know what you're doing. I've also eaten your food. Of course, you know what you're doing."

"What I'm doing," he said slowly. "Is winging it. Every single day."

She stared at him, waiting for him to crack a smile and make a joke, but his posture was rigid.

"Is it like an imposter syndrome thing?" she asked eventually. "Sometimes I feel like that when I'm doing a workshop or something… like I'm not really qualified to teach people anything."

He shook his head. "I'm genuinely not qualified. I told you I studied economics..."

"And then you went to culinary school," she finished.

"No. I didn't say that. You assumed."

"How did you become a chef, then?"

He massaged his temples. "I had jobs in kitchens and worked my way up."

"Okay. What's the problem with that? You don't need formal qualifications to be a chef, do you? If you can cook well – that's the main thing, isn't it?"

"Sort of. But it usually takes a long time. And people usually train under famous chefs." He looked at her sadly. "I fast-tracked myself."

"I don't know what you mean."

"I had all this debt hanging over me, and I was struggling to pay rent. To really progress in my career, I needed some kind of formal training, but I couldn't afford it, and I had too much pride to ask my parents for help. Not that they'd have helped me."

"So, what did you do?"

"I taught myself to cook. I found any free tutorials I could find online, and I read books."

"What's wrong with that?"

"Even though I could cook, no one would give me a break." He sighed. "So I started applying for jobs I wasn't qualified for. I was sure I could do anything if someone would just give me a chance. All I needed was someone daft enough to not bother checking my references. Or at least not the place where I claimed I'd been head chef."

Anna grimaced. "Lewis didn't check your references?"

"No."

"And you never told him?"

He smiled sadly. "This is why I didn't call you last week. I spend most of my life feeling like a fraud, and I didn't want to feel like that with you."

"You could have just told me."

"I planned on telling you. But telling you means I have to tell Lewis, and I got myself all tied in knots just thinking about coming clean. Lewis is my best friend, and I've spent years lying to him."

"Have you?" She placed the book back on the table and moved to sit on Warren's lap. "Lewis thinks you're a brilliant chef, and that's true."

"It's not the whole truth."

"My brother isn't stupid. He's meticulous in the way he runs the hotel. If he didn't check your references, it won't have been out of negligence or laziness. Or because he's *daft*," she added pointedly.

"I cooked for him in my interview," Warren said. "He said the food spoke for itself. I worked on a trial basis for a month."

"There you go then. You didn't get the job based on lies. You got the job based on your ability to cook."

"I think you're being pretty generous in your assessment."

She took his hand, entwining their fingers. "I really think you're making more of this than it is."

His thumb trailed a path over the back of her hand. "It's why I get so angry when the staff make mistakes. If the food is good, everything feels fine, but every mistake feels as though it might be the thing to reveal what a fraud I am."

"You're not a fraud." She put a hand on his cheek and forced him to look her in the eyes. "You're amazing at your job." A smile crept over her face. "So good that Lewis has spent the last couple of weeks panicking that you're looking for another job."

He eyed her sceptically. "Why does he think that?"

"He thinks he offended you when he talked to you about shouting at the kitchen staff."

"I wasn't offended – only worried that he'd finally figured out that I don't know what I'm doing."

"But you do know what you're doing."

"Winging it," he said again.

"No," she replied sternly. "You might have been winging it to start with, but you absolutely know what you're doing now."

"It doesn't feel like it."

"Michelin gave you a review, for goodness' sake! How can you think you're not good at your job?"

"I think I'm lucky they came on a day when everything was running smoothly."

"That's most days. And I thought they visited more than once."

"I think they usually come more often."

"Probably not a fluke, then. And kind of funny that you think Michelin don't know what they're talking about."

"It was great to get the review," he said.

"But you don't think you can get a star?"

"The restaurants that get Michelin stars are run by top chefs."

Standing, she went and got his coffee. Then stared pointedly at the writing on the mug when she gave it to him.

"I think it would be weird if they didn't give a Michelin star to the world's best chef," she said, smiling.

He set the mug aside. "I think it means more to me that your brother thinks I'm good at my job than a Michelin star would mean."

"Nice sentiment," she said, sitting on his knee again and draping an arm around his shoulders. "Fairly sure it's not true, though."

His lips twitched in amusement. "A Michelin star would be great. But it genuinely doesn't matter to me. I get to do a job I love, and I work with great people. That's enough for me. I just hope your brother doesn't fire me when he finds out I lied."

"There's no way Lewis would fire you." She ran her finger through the short hair at the back of his neck.

"Aren't you annoyed with me?" he asked, his forehead wrinkling.

"Why would I be?"

"Because I kept this from you. I outright lied to Lewis, but I essentially lied to everyone I've become close to since I moved here."

"You're being really hard on yourself," she said. "It doesn't matter to me how you got your job. I'm only glad you *did* get the job." She flashed him a flirty smile, and he tightened his arms around her.

"How am I going to explain this to Lewis?" he asked, burying his head in her neck as he hugged her.

"You'll figure it out. And you have a week for him to get back from London. I'd say worry about it in a week."

"Very wise," he said, drawing back to look her in the eyes. "I may need a distraction though, so I don't drive myself crazy worrying about it."

"There's always work," she said, stifling a smile.

"And when I'm not at work?"

She swept her lips over his. "I can probably distract you."

Chapter Forty-Nine

Anna spent three nights in a row at Warren's place. On the third morning, she woke with his arm draped across her. From his shallow, even breaths, she was sure he was fast asleep, but the moment she tried to slip out of bed, his arms clamped around her waist, drawing her to him.

"Where are you going?" he murmured into her neck.

"I was going to get a drink and then have a shower. It's already mid-morning."

"Where do you need to be today?"

"Nowhere," she said, grinning.

"Then there's no need for you to get up."

"I'll make drinks and come back to bed," she suggested, but he kissed her earlobe and then her neck.

Suddenly, getting up didn't seem at all important.

Half an hour later, they were propped up against the pillows, with Warren teasingly suggesting more places she might want to get a tattoo when her phone rang.

"It's my mum," she said, reaching over and checking the screen.

"Don't answer it."

"Why not?"

"Because I don't want your mum knowing we just had sex."

Anna snorted a laugh. "Weirdly, I wasn't planning on mentioning that."

"She'll know. She'll hear it in your voice."

Shaking her head, she pushed him off her and suggested he go and make coffee. Then she swiped the screen and greeted her mum.

"It's a bit late in the day to still be in bed."

In a panic, Anna moved the phone to check it wasn't a video call.

"How do you know I'm still in bed?" she asked, then caught Warren's smug look as he pulled on a pair of jogging bottoms.

"You just sound as though you're still in bed. It's not like you to sleep so late."

"I was about to get up."

"You're not working over the next few days, are you?"

"No," she said slowly, slightly concerned her mum was about to rope her into something she didn't want to do – which was pretty much anything other than spending time with Warren.

"Maybe you can do something with your sister. Check she's okay."

Anna frowned. "Why wouldn't she be okay?"

"She stayed at our house on Christmas Day. Overnight, I mean. Said she felt like sleeping in her old bed. And then she stayed another night, and another... didn't leave until this morning. And I think she'd have stayed longer if she didn't have to work. She's just been lounging around on our couch, looking miserable."

"That's weird." Usually, Carla had a social life that was hard to keep track of. If she wasn't working, she was out with one of her various groups of friends.

"She said she's tired from working so much over the last few weeks, but she seemed down. Not herself."

"She's been fine whenever I've seen her over the last few weeks." Which admittedly hadn't been often since they'd both been working a lot, but she really hadn't got the impression there was anything unusual going on with her.

"She acts tough. That's Carla's trouble. If she has a problem, she keeps it to herself rather than let anyone see her vulnerable."

"Unless the problem is a spider in her shower," Anna said with a small smile.

"What about spiders?"

Anna chuckled. "I was just thinking about her freaking out about the spider in the shower."

"When was that?"

"I don't know," Anna said. "Whenever she called you to help her get rid of it."

"She's a wimp when it comes to spiders, but thankfully she hasn't quite reached the level of calling us to remove them for her."

"But she said..." Anna's insides tightened. "She didn't call you?"

"I think I'd remember that! Did she call *you?*"

"No, I just... she said... never mind. I might be confused..." Except she was fairly sure she wasn't confused. "I'll call her and check she's okay."

"Thanks, love. Where are you, by the way?"

"What do you mean, where am I? I already told you I'm still in bed."

"You just don't sound as though you're at home..."

Anna opened and closed her mouth a couple of times.

"Never mind," her mum said. "You're not back with Hayden, are you?"

"No." She shook her head, desperate to insist she was at home, but not actually comfortable with the outright lie.

"I'll leave you to it, but call me if you get anything out of Carla."

"Okay." She ended the call in a daze. "How the heck did she know I wasn't at home?" she muttered.

"Did you tell her you were here?" Warren asked, appearing in the doorway.

"No. But apparently I didn't sound as though I was at home." She frowned. "There isn't any background noise, so how could she possibly know that."

"Fiona knows everything."

"She didn't know about the spider," Anna said under her breath.

"What was that?"

She massaged her forehead. "I have to go and see Carla."

"How come?"

"Mum's worried about her, and now I am too."

"Why?"

"I don't know for sure. I have an inkling, but I'm really hoping I'm wrong."

"Would you like to share? You're being cryptic."

"Sorry." Pushing the duvet aside, she scrambled for her clothes. "I have to go."

"Now?" He moved in front of her. "I rearranged things so I don't have to start work until later."

"I really have to speak to Carla."

"Okay."

"Can I shower here?"

"Of course." He stepped out of the way. "Are you okay?"

"I will be if Carla is."

Twenty minutes later, she gave Warren a hasty kiss goodbye and stepped out into the freezing cold. In the car, she pulled the seatbelt around her with one hand, and called her sister with the other. Carla answered after a few rings.

"Are you at work?" Anna asked.

"No, I'm at home."

"Are you going to work soon?"

"No, I'm not working today. Why?"

Anna turned the engine on and twisted the dial to put the heat on full blast. "Mum said you'd been at their place and had only gone home to go to work."

"I was supposed to work today, but I found someone to cover for me."

"Are you ill?"

"I'm okay," Carla answered ambiguously. "What have you been up to for the last few days?"

Anna winced. "Can I come over?"

"Now? Why?"

"*Why not?* I'd like to see you. I'm going to come over now."

"Fine," Carla muttered. "Just promise not to make comments about how much of a mess my place is."

"Promise," Anna said, and ended the call.

That promise meant she had to bite her tongue when she walked into Carla's flat in Bourton-on-the-Water, not too far from their parents' place.

"It's not that bad," Carla said, swiping a bunch of clothes from the couch to make space for Anna to sit.

"No," she said, eyes scanning over the collection of plates and mugs on the table, which must have been there a while since Carla hadn't even been at home for the last few days. "It's not so bad."

With a spark of amusement in her eyes, Carla flopped into the armchair, her legs hanging over the arm. "What's going on with you?"

Anna opened her mouth to make small talk before thinking better of it. "Have I upset you?"

"No. Why?"

"Because of Warren. I told you I liked him, and you didn't get in touch to see how that had turned out."

"I tried to ask how that turned out, but when I called you told me you were going on a date with Hayden."

"It wasn't a date."

She nodded. "I got that update from Lewis. He also seemed to think you were getting together with Warren."

"But you didn't get in touch to find out..."

"No, because it all seemed pretty obvious. If things hadn't worked out, you'd have been in touch."

That was true. Which now meant she felt even worse for not checking in – she wouldn't have hesitated to call Carla if she'd needed a shoulder to cry on.

"Do you like Warren?" Anna asked.

Carla gave a slow nod. "Definitely prefer him to Hayden. Not that I ever had a problem with Hayden, but I think there are better perks to you dating Warren. The food thing. We'll get well fed."

Anna eyed her sister sadly. "That's not what I meant, and I'm fairly sure you know that's not what I meant."

"I don't know what you're talking about," Carla said, but shifted in her seat, bringing her legs in front of her.

"You told me you only called Warren to help you with the spider because you couldn't get hold of anyone else, but you didn't actually try to call anyone else, did you?"

"Oh my god!" Carla's eyes bulged. "You checked with Mum and Dad to see if I was telling the truth."

"No. I made a joke about it to Mum, and she didn't know what I was talking about."

"I can't believe you! Why would you talk to Mum about it?"

"I didn't intend to, but I'm glad I did. Tell me what's going on?"

"Nothing is going on," Carla said wearily.

"The spider was just an excuse to get him to come over, wasn't it?"

"I really don't want to have this conversation." Carla pressed her head back into the chair.

"If I'd known you had a thing for Warren..."

"*What?*" Carla's eyes filled with tears. "You'd have stayed away from him?"

"Yes." Anna's heart squeezed. "Of course I would have."

"That would have been stupid."

"Why didn't you talk to me about this before?"

"Because I knew things would get weird. And for the record, I don't have a thing for him. I don't have any issue with you getting together with Warren. I'm happy for you."

"But I got together with Warren on Christmas Day, and since then you've barely left Mum and Dad's couch. Is that really a coincidence?

"Sort of." She wiped her fingers under her eyes to catch her tears.

"Carla!" Anna sat forward in her seat. "Tell me what's going on."

"It's so embarrassing," she sniffed.

"What is?"

"That I called him that night."

"You didn't actually need him to get rid of the spider?"

"No. That was just an excuse." She sat bolt upright. "But bear in mind, this was months ago. Maybe I had a bit of a crush on him, but I think mostly I was just lonely. It seemed like a good idea after a couple of glasses of wine, but he laughed at me, and I was mortified. And it's not as though I really liked him or anything. I swear I have no problem with you dating him."

"Then why are you so upset?"

"Because I don't know what I'm doing with my life. You and Lewis have everything together, and I..."

"You what?" Anna asked, confused.

"I spent most of the last month dressed as an elf," she said with a small smile.

"So? You enjoy doing that, don't you?"

"Yes. But I feel as though I just bounce from one job to the next, doing anything that seems fun, but with no proper plan. I don't know what I'll do long term. I need a career plan, but I don't have a clue what I want to do."

"You're twenty-three. You don't need to know what you want to do for the rest of your life. At some point, you'll figure it out."

"I feel like I'm drifting through life, and it's getting tiring. Plus, I've been on a spate of terrible dates recently, which is depressing."

"You didn't tell me."

"No. Because I didn't have the energy to make them into entertaining stories."

Anna felt a pang of sadness – her sister did tend to make everything into a quirky anecdote. "You could have just told me."

"I didn't feel like bringing you down. Especially not when everything is going so well for you. I think it's great that you're going to look at the premises for your shop. And I really am happy for you and Warren." She pressed her hands to her face. "Does he know the spider thing was just me trying to get him to come over? Because that's really embarrassing."

"No. He really thought you just wanted him to play exterminator." She grimaced. "Sorry he laughed at you."

"I actually think that was an entirely fair response. Can you please not tell him? I'd never be able to face him again."

She shook her head and moved to perch beside her sister. As she pulled her in for a hug, her eyes swept the room.

"What are we going to do about the state of this place?" she asked eventually.

Carla shoved her so hard she almost fell off the arm of the

chair. "I knew you wouldn't be able to keep quiet about the mess."

"It's hard to ignore," she said gently.

"Not for me. I'd planned on spending the rest of the day ignoring it while I watched TV."

"How about we tidy up and then spend the day on the couch?"

"You're hanging around?" Carla asked. "Don't you have anything planned with Warren?"

"No. He's working." It might not have been entirely true, but she was sure Warren would go to work as soon as she told him she was busy for the day.

He sent her a few messages over the course of the afternoon, obviously keen to know what was going on with Carla, but she kept her replies vague. At least he was in touch regularly. After his lack of contact the week before, it was reassuring that they seemed to be on the same page now.

When he messaged and asked if she wanted to come to the hotel for dinner, she told him she was going to hang out with Carla for the evening and would see him the following day. An hour later, the doorbell rang, and Carla hit pause on the TV remote.

"Who's that?" she asked, eyeing the door dubiously.

"How would I know?" Anna asked, shaking her head. "Maybe one of your friends checking on you since you've gone AWOL."

"I hope not." Carla hopped off the couch and headed for the door. She sounded a little confused as she spoke into the intercom but buzzed whoever it was up.

"Who is it?" Anna asked, joining her at the door.

"Food, apparently," Carla said, looking confused.

A moment later, Will, one of the hotel kitchen staff, appeared. "Warren said I could leave early if I dropped this off."

He handed a bag to Carla and disappeared before they could thank him.

"This smells amazing," Carla said, sticking her nose in the bag. "Told you there'd be good perks to having him as your boyfriend. You can never split up with him. You know that, right?"

"I have no plans to," Anna replied happily.

Chapter Fifty

Anna wasn't sure if the rate at which she'd gotten used to waking up with Warren was a good thing or not, but she missed him when she rolled over the following morning to find the other side of her bed empty. When she'd left Carla's flat late in the evening, she'd been tempted to go to Warren's place but had decided that a night apart wouldn't do any harm.

When he called her an hour after she woke, she smiled at the sound of his voice and didn't hesitate to agree when he invited himself over for breakfast. After that, he'd go with her to view the shop.

"How's Carla?" he asked, peeling his coat off after greeting her with a kiss.

"She's fine."

He followed her into the kitchen and leaned against the counter. "What's going on with her?"

Anna sank onto a chair at the table by the window. "She's just been working a lot. She's tired. And I feel kind of bad that I've been so caught up with my life that I didn't check how she was doing."

"But she's okay?"

Anna nodded. "Yeah. But let's not talk about Carla."

"Why not?"

She shrugged. "Mostly because every time we talk about my sister, it involves you saying how annoying she is, and I don't really feel like listening to that today." She'd meant to sound jokey, but the words came out full of bitterness. "Sorry," she whispered.

He moved to sit on the other side of the small table. "I'm very fond of Carla," he said slowly. "And I'd hate to think that I've done something to upset her."

"Why would you think you've upset her?"

"I just got the impression that maybe whatever is going on with her is something to do with me. A while ago you accused me of flirting with her, so now I'm wondering if she also thought I was flirting with her..."

"No."

"So I didn't accidentally lead her on or anything like that? I always thought we were friends with good banter."

"I think that's exactly what you are. And I know you're fond of her, but she's upset, and that makes me upset."

"But it's nothing to do with me?"

She gave a one-shouldered shrug.

He swore under his breath. "That time she called me about the spider... was there more to that request, and it went completely over my head?"

"I'm not supposed to talk to you about it."

"Right." He nodded, looking thoughtful. "When she called, I'd just got home from work, and it had been a stressful shift. I was kind of mean to her."

Anna nodded too. "I think you definitely killed any romantic notions she had towards you."

"Well, now I feel terrible." He scrubbed a hand down his face. "What should I do?"

"Nothing."

"Should I apologise?"

"No! I wasn't supposed to tell you any of this. Pretend you don't know anything. Besides, I really don't think it's an issue now. I guess she's just been reflecting on the year and her life, and she's stressing that she's lacking direction. She thinks Lewis and I have our lives all figured out, and she feels left behind or something. I think it's more about that than anything to do with you."

"Okay." He reached over and took her hand. "Should I stop teasing her?"

"No. Don't act differently around her or she'll know I said something to you. She'll be mortified... and then she'll be furious with me. Just carry on as normal."

"All right." He squeezed her hand. "What do you want for breakfast? We should hurry up so we're not late for the viewing."

"Sit down," she said when he got up. "I'm going to cook for you for a change."

"Yeah?"

She hovered over him and kissed him softly. "Thank you for sending dinner over yesterday."

"You're welcome."

❄

If Warren hadn't gone with her, she'd have backed out of viewing the shop premises. As soon as they met Greg Prince, the estate agent, she felt overwhelmed, and then completely out of her depth when he asked her questions about her interest in the building.

It wasn't as though it mattered what the guy in the suit thought about her business ideas, but she felt oddly pressured to say the right things. Thankfully, as they wandered through the downstairs of the building, Warren did a great job of making small talk.

"The upstairs was previously a flat, which was also used as an art studio," Mr Prince said as they followed him up the stairs. "It's completely open plan, but could easily be modified."

Anna walked around the large space. A bathroom and kitchenette were located at the back, and the large windows at the front let in copious amounts of light, which glinted off the polished wooden floor and brightened the white walls.

"What do you think?" Warren asked when she stood looking out onto the road.

"I'm not sure."

"This would be perfect for holding workshops and classes, wouldn't it?" He stood close beside her, his presence reassuringly calm. "And the downstairs is a good size for a flower shop. I realise I'm no expert, but it seems great."

"Yeah, it does," she said without enthusiasm.

Mr Prince looked at his phone, which lit up in his hand. "I'll leave you to have a look around at your leisure. I'll be downstairs if you have any more questions." He was halfway down the stairs when he answered his phone, and his voice faded the further away he got.

"Do you like it?" Warren said, touching Anna's elbow.

"It's a lovely building. And it would work perfectly for what I'd need."

He pursed his lips. "But?"

"I don't know." She scanned the room. "I guess I've had this idea of what I want to do for so long... and the reality of it is a little overwhelming."

"That's understandable. It's not as though you need to decide now."

"I couldn't if I wanted to. I didn't even make a business plan, and I don't know if I'd be able to get a bank loan."

"Would you want to get a bank loan?"

Her shoulders sank. "You think I should ask Lewis for the money?"

"It would save you a heck of a lot of interest."

"I suppose I would ask Lewis for the money." He'd give it to her without question – she didn't doubt that for a moment. "I'd probably apply for a bank loan first, just to see if the bank thinks it's a sound business plan. I'd feel better knowing that I could theoretically get a bank loan, even if I borrow the money from Lewis."

He put a hand on her shoulder, and his fingers crept up to caress her neck. "I'm sure you would make a success of it if it's what you want."

"Thank you." She leaned into him, taking comfort from his sturdy stature. "I need to think it all through."

Downstairs, they thanked the estate agent and got back in Warren's car.

"Have you got time to come in?" she asked outside her place.

Checking the time, he shook his head. "I need to get to the hotel."

"Thank you for coming with me."

"You're welcome. What are your plans for the rest of the day?"

She sighed heavily. "I think I'll make a start on a business plan."

"Good luck," he said with a small smile. "Will I see you later?"

"Do you want to come here after work?"

"I'd love to." He leaned across the console to kiss her.

Anna had her fingers on the door handle when she paused and turned back. "Have you been in touch with Lewis at all?"

"Yeah. I messaged him this morning to ask when he'd be back."

"And?"

"Tomorrow afternoon. Hopefully, I can grab him for a chat before the New Year's celebrations get into full swing."

"You could also wait and speak to him later."

He shook his head. "I want to get it out of the way. Then I can start the year with all that behind me."

"He'll be fine about it," Anna said, giving his arm a squeeze.

"I hope so," he replied, but didn't look at all convinced.

Chapter Fifty-One

It was probably the first time that Anna had arrived early to a party – but after spending a day and a half battling with her business plan, she just wanted to get out of the house.

Carla always claimed New Year's Eve was her favourite night of the year, so Anna had fully expected to find her at the hotel bar when she got there, but she was nowhere to be seen. After giving her a glass of wine, Ivy told her she should finish her shift soon, before moving away to serve more customers.

A quick glance around the dining room told Anna that most people were on dessert. That meant Warren should also finish work before long. She glanced at her watch and fought the urge to go into the kitchen looking for him – she'd already messaged him to say she was on her way, so he'd join her when he could.

The worst thing about sitting at the bar on her own was the speed at which her wine went down. At the rate she was going, she'd be drunk by the time anyone joined her.

Thankfully, it wasn't long before Warren appeared.

"You look good," she said, running a hand down the front of his dark shirt.

"Thanks." He gave her a kiss, but failed to focus on her. "Have you seen Lewis?"

"No."

"I'm going to check and see if he's in the office."

Anna clenched her teeth. "Nice to see you, too."

"Sorry. I just really want to talk to him before the evening gets into full swing."

"Fine. I'll just continue sitting here on my own."

"Where's Carla?"

"I don't know. I'll message her." She fumbled in her bag, then let out a low groan. "I think I forgot my phone."

She'd messaged Warren just before she was about to set off, and vaguely remembered setting her phone aside to put her coat on.

"You don't need your phone. Everyone you want to hang out with will be here soon."

He was right, but it did nothing to make her feel better. "Why do I feel as though this night is going to be a disaster? I was fed up with being at home, but now I'm wishing I hadn't left my couch."

"What's wrong?" he asked with a frown.

"I just had a stressful day. Apparently, working on a business plan isn't my happy place."

"I don't think it's many people's idea of fun." Again, he seemed distant, and he caught Ivy's eye across the bar. "Have you seen Lewis?"

"No. I thought he and Erin would be here by now."

"I'm going to check the office quickly," he said.

"Why don't you just wait and talk to him another time? Maybe when I'm not hanging out at the bar on my own?"

"I want to get it over and done with." He gave her arm a squeeze. "Carla will be here soon. And I won't be long."

"Fine. But I'm annoyed with you."

He gave her another quick kiss, apparently undeterred by her emotional blackmail.

❄

Finding the office empty, Warren made a hasty decision to catch Lewis at home. It would be easier to speak to him there anyway – away from the bustle of the hotel. After deciding to grovel to Anna later, rather than go back and tell her of his plan, he made a dash for the front door, then almost collided with Carla, who was coming the other way.

"Is the party that bad?" she asked. "You're running away already?"

"No. I just need to nip over to Lewis's place. I'll be back soon."

"See you later," she said flatly.

He felt a pang of guilt, despite Anna insisting that Carla's recent low mood wasn't because of him. "Are you okay?"

"Yeah," she said, continuing inside without glancing back at him.

He blew out a sigh, which fogged in front of his face and made him debate going back for his coat. It was only a five-minute walk, though. At a brisk pace, he could be there quicker than that.

He shivered as Lewis answered the door, dressed smartly in a pair of jeans and a shirt.

"Hey!" His forehead wrinkled in confusion as he opened the door wider. "I thought you'd be at the hotel. We're heading down there soon."

"I just came from the hotel," he said, swallowing hard as he stepped inside. "But there's something I want to talk to you about, and I wanted to do it before the party."

Lewis shook his head as he closed the door. "If you're

handing in your notice on New Year's Eve, I'm going to be so annoyed with you."

"Of course I'm not handing in my notice," Warren said, struggling to comprehend that was a genuine concern. When Anna had mentioned it, he hadn't taken it very seriously.

"Today? Or generally?"

"Generally," he said with force. "Why would you think I'm quitting?"

Lewis sucked in a breath and led the way to the kitchen. "Because you've been in a bad mood recently. More so than usual. And I know you weren't happy with me for commenting on the way you run the kitchen. Also, because I'm reasonably certain that at least one restaurant owner around here has been trying to poach you."

Warren lifted his eyebrows.

"They have, haven't they? If they're offering you more money, you know I'll match it."

Warren sank into a chair at the kitchen table. "I've had job offers. But I never considered any of them."

"Really?" The relief was clear in the sag of Lewis's shoulders. He opened the fridge and pulled out two bottles of beer. Without bothering to ask, he popped the tops off and handed one to Warren.

"Did you come to talk to me about Anna?" Lewis asked after sitting and taking a long swig.

"No. Well, yeah, but that wasn't the main thing."

"What then?"

Warren rubbed the back of his neck. "I lied on my CV."

"What?" Lewis asked, squeezing his eyes closed in confusion.

"When I applied for my job, I lied on the application."

Lewis stared at him. "That's what you want to talk about?"

"Yes."

"*Now?* After four years working for me?" He snorted in amusement and leaned back in the chair. "At this point, I assumed we were never going to have this conversation, but if you feel the need, go ahead."

Warren let his words sink in. "You already knew?"

"Of course I knew."

Stunned, Warren struggled to find words. "I asked you if you'd checked my references..."

"Yeah. If I recall correctly, I told you your cooking spoke for itself. I never said I hadn't checked your references."

Warren's eyes widened. "So you did check them?"

"Do you think I'm stupid?" Lewis cocked his head. "I wouldn't employ you without speaking to your previous employers."

"Oh my god," Warren said, dragging his hands through his hair.

"Your former employers spoke highly of you. I was only surprised to learn that you weren't the head chef at your last place. Or anything close."

Warren winced. "What did he say?"

"That you were hardworking and ambitious. His main issue with you was that you were too ambitious. He said you wanted to run the place."

"Why the heck did you hire me?"

"I liked you. Your food was far better than anyone else I'd interviewed, and I thought being overly ambitious probably wasn't a bad quality."

"But you knew I'd lied..."

"I thought being under-qualified would mean you'd work extra hard to impress me. Honestly, I thought you'd confess eventually, but you were great at your job and the restaurant was getting rave reviews, so I didn't think it was a big deal. After a while, it felt irrelevant."

Warren rested his elbows on the table and hung his head. "It never felt irrelevant to me."

"Why did you suddenly feel the need to tell me?"

Warren huffed out a humourless laugh. "Because I'm in love with your sister. I had to tell *her* the truth, which meant I had to tell you. Also, I think I just got sick of feeling like I was living a lie."

"That seems a little dramatic. At the end of the day, you're great at your job."

"I always felt as though I was faking it and was waiting for the day I got found out."

"I feel the same about the hotel," Lewis said. "I had big aspirations to manage a hotel one day, but owning the place still feels surreal."

"You actually have qualifications in the hotel business, though."

"Yeah. But the hotel fell into my lap." He shrugged. "As far as imposters go, I think we're both doing a great job of fooling everyone. Maybe we know what we're doing after all."

"Maybe," Warren conceded.

Lewis's mouth twitched at the corners. "Did you just say you're in love with my sister?"

"Yeah. But I haven't told her that yet, so you can keep it to yourself for the time being."

"She's going to be really impressed that you told me first."

"Maybe don't mention this conversation. At least not until your best man speech. She might think it's cute then."

"Best man speech!" Lewis grinned. "Are things that serious?"

"Do you really think I'd get involved with your sister if I wasn't serious?"

"No. Which is partly why I'd never have any issue with it."

"Partly?" he asked.

"I think you two are well suited – in a weird, opposites-attract kind of way."

"I don't think we're all that different. Not really."

Lewis nodded.

"She's not dating Hayden, by the way," Warren said, grinning.

"Yep." Lewis fought a grin of his own and took a swig of his beer. "Sorry about that. Apparently, I had bad information."

"It seems like it." He paused. "What were you saying before about matching any offers I'd got from other restaurants?"

"I thought you might bring that up again." He heaved in a breath and looked suddenly serious. "You know, if you ever wanted to move on to something else, I'd understand... I wouldn't like it," he added quickly. "But I'd hate to think of you staying purely out of loyalty."

"I'm not going anywhere," Warren said.

"I know you think you can't get a Michelin star if you stay at the hotel, and if that's something you want to pursue, it's understandable."

"That's not why I think it won't happen."

"Why then?"

"Because I don't have any significant formal training. Restaurants with self-taught head chefs don't generally get awarded Michelin stars."

Lewis's brow wrinkled tightly. "Most self-taught chefs probably aren't as good as you."

"It doesn't matter, anyway. I don't care about Michelin stars. I'm happy I get to do what I love for a living."

At the sound of footsteps, they both looked towards the door as Erin appeared.

"You could have told me you were starting the party already," she admonished with a smile. "I thought we were going up to the hotel."

"We are," Lewis said. "We were just having one drink here first. Do you want one?"

"I actually need to get back to the hotel." Warren drained his beer. "I'm already in trouble with Anna. I need to go and grovel."

When he stood, Lewis did too, and they embraced tightly. "Good talk," Warren said, chuckling as he released him.

"Wait, what did I miss here?" Erin asked.

"A lot of stuff," Warren teased, earning himself a playful punch from Erin.

Then her eyes widened. "Did you and Anna get together?"

"Yes," he said beaming.

She hugged him tightly. "I'm so excited, but I'd rather hear about this from Anna. Is she already at the hotel."

He nodded and they moved towards the door. Despite having said she wanted to hear about it from Anna, she still bombarded him with questions while they walked.

As he answered them, he grinned so widely that his cheeks ached by the time they reached the hotel.

Chapter Fifty-Two

At the bar, Carla sat alone with two glasses of wine in front of her, both almost empty. She didn't notice Warren as he sidled up beside her. He'd lost Lewis and Erin in the lounge where they'd been cornered by a couple of regular guests wanting to chat to them.

"Hey," he said, breaking Carla from her trance. "Are you okay?"

"That's the second time you've asked me that today," she said, lifting her eyebrows. "And considering I don't recall you asking how I am in the entire time we've known each other, I'm going to assume my sister has been blabbing her mouth off."

"She just said you'd been a bit down recently. Excuse me for being concerned."

"I don't believe for a second that's all Anna said." She stretched her neck as she looked at him. "For the record, I may have had the tiniest crush on you for approximately five minutes. I'd argue it was some kind of temporary insanity. It has nothing to do with my recent bout of being pissed off with the world."

"Good to know."

She rolled her eyes. "Please don't make this weird. You being nice to me might just be the last straw. I can cope with anything but that."

"Are you implying I'm not normally nice?"

"Normally you're a big, annoying oaf. Let's stick with that."

"You're pretty annoying yourself," he told her with a smirk. "Where's Anna?"

"She was annoyed with you and went home."

"See what I mean about you being annoying? Where is she really? Bathroom?"

"She went home," she said emphatically. "Because she realised you're a big, annoying oaf."

He glared at her until she grinned.

"Or... maybe she just went home to get her phone and then she's coming back. It might have been that – I can't really remember."

"When did she leave?"

"Ten minutes ago."

He glanced at his watch. "I might drive over there and give her a lift back."

"Good idea. Knowing Anna, she'll get home and decide she'd rather spend the evening on the couch in her pyjamas. Go and make sure she doesn't bail."

"Will do." He took a step away, then hesitated before backing up and wrapping his arms around her. "Glad you're okay," he said while she wriggled away from him.

"My sister is probably only suffering temporary insanity," she said. "Don't be too shocked if she comes to her senses and realises she doesn't want to date someone so irritating."

"Thanks. I'll bear that in mind." He gave her arm a friendly shove and told her he'd see her soon.

❄

Once she was back in the warmth of her flat, Anna lost enthusiasm for the New Year's party entirely. She picked up her phone and got caught up in a flurry of messages from her friends, all discussing their plans for the evening. Hayden's message in the group, describing his itinerary of four different parties for the evening, left her exhausted just reading it.

She fired off a quick reply, reminding them she'd be in the hotel as usual and inviting anyone who was nearby to call in. The message was entirely unnecessary, since her plans had been the same since she was about sixteen. Kylie and Mike occasionally put in an appearance, but everyone had their own parties to attend. She wished them a Happy New Year in advance and had just forced herself off the couch when the doorbell sounded.

"What are you doing here?" she asked Warren when he stepped inside.

"Thought you might like a lift back to avoid trudging around in the cold."

"Thanks. I was just about to set off."

"Carla was concerned you may have just made a sneaky exit from the festivities."

"Tempting as that is, I really did plan on coming back." She cocked her head. "Did you speak to Lewis?"

"Yes." He followed her into the living room and took a seat on the couch.

"And?" She picked up her coat, which was draped over the armchair.

"He was fine about it."

"I told you he would be. What did he say?"

He leaned his head back and chuckled. "He wasn't surprised."

"Really?"

"He knew all along."

"What?" Anna dropped onto the couch beside him. "How?"

"I think the major clue was after my interview, when he called my previous employer and found that I hadn't actually been the head chef there."

Anna pressed her lips together and swallowed her laughter. "I'm surprised he never mentioned that to anyone."

"I was definitely worried about nothing. Lewis really doesn't see it as an issue."

"Good. Now you can relax and enjoy the party tonight."

"Yeah." He put a hand on her knee when she made to get up. "What was going on with you today? You didn't seem very happy earlier."

"The business plan was stressing me out. I hate this kind of thing."

"It'd be worth it in the end."

"Maybe."

"I can help you with it next week if you want. I'll have some time off."

"Thanks." She patted his knee. "We should get going."

"Should we?" he said, sinking further into the couch cushions.

"It's New Year's Eve. We can't miss the party."

"I don't really see why not."

Anna felt a tingle of excitement at the prospect of skipping the party and staying home and cosy. "I don't know," she said, torn. "I told Carla I'd go back, and I'm still kind of worried about her."

"Carla's fine. I spoke to her before."

"What did you say?" Anna asked, jutting her chin out.

"Nothing." He raised his hands. "I was nice."

"Oh, great. So now she knows I said something to you."

His shoulders shook as he laughed. "Why is me being nice to Carla so shocking to everyone? I'm always nice."

"You didn't upset her, did you?"

"No! We joked around. She's fine. Ivy was about to finish

her shift, and Lewis and Erin are at the hotel. Carla will be fine, so if you don't want to go back, we can stay in for the evening. If that's what you want."

She narrowed her eyes and glared at him. "That's what you want, isn't it?"

"I'm very happy to skip the party."

"I'll bet you are, because everyone will think it was *my* idea not to go back to the hotel."

"I'll take the blame," he insisted, looking thoroughly amused. "I'll say it was all my idea."

"Staying at home does sound very appealing," she conceded, then eyed him warily. "You know that even if you say it was your idea, they'll still all think it was my idea to miss the party."

"Yeah." He smirked. "I realise that."

When she went to playfully slap his arm, he grabbed hold of her and pulled her down onto him, then caught her lips in a kiss.

"What do you want to do?" he asked eventually.

She kept her face close to his. "If you keep kissing me like that, I definitely won't want to go anywhere."

"Thanks for the tip," he said, eyebrows twitching mischievously before he pulled her closer and kissed her again.

It seemed as though they'd be having their own private party – and Anna couldn't think of a better way to celebrate the start of the new year.

Chapter Fifty-Three

The few teasing messages from Carla over the course of the evening reassured Anna that her sister was fine, and not upset by her and Warren skipping out on the party.

Once Warren left for work on New Year's Day, Anna's plan was to spend the rest of the day lazing around her flat. Maybe she'd meet Warren at the end of his shift if she felt like getting out of her flat.

When her phone lit up with a call from Ivy early in the evening, she answered it with a smile. They hadn't properly caught up since she and Warren had got together, and she assumed Ivy was keen to get information from the source. The thought of filling Ivy in gave her a thrill as she swiped at the screen.

"I need you at the hotel," she said. The panicked edge in her voice put Anna on high alert.

"What's wrong?"

"Nothing yet, but I'm fairly sure I'm about to have a problem with Warren, and you're the only person who can deal with him when he flies off the handle."

"What's going on?" Given the mood Warren had been in

when he left her bed that morning, she couldn't imagine there was much that would rile him up today.

"His parents are here," Ivy said.

Anna's eyes widened. Maybe there wasn't much that would rile him up, but she had little doubt that his parents could manage it.

"What do you mean?"

"I mean, Warren is in the kitchen and his parents are eating in the restaurant. He doesn't know, but if he glances into the restaurant, I imagine there's going to be an issue. From what Carla has told me recently, I guess it might not be a joyful family reunion."

"Oh, wow," Anna breathed.

"They're staying at the hotel," Ivy said in a rush. "They checked in earlier, and I didn't think much about the surname. I assumed I'd know if his parents had booked in for a stay, but his mum just let it drop that their son is the chef and they're here to surprise him."

"That's not good."

"No," Ivy agreed. "They insisted I keep quiet until they'd eaten, but I really don't want to be the one to tell him they're here."

"I don't blame you."

"Please can you get here quickly? I'm slightly hungover, and I can't cope with drama."

"I'll come," Anna said, already off the couch. "Try to keep Warren in the dark until I get there."

Fifteen minutes later, she strode into the hotel dining room. She gave Ivy a quick smile and made a beeline for Dennis and Jen.

"Hello!" Jen placed her napkin on the table and rose to greet Anna. "We're on a secret mission," she said, her silly grin causing Anna to wonder how much wine she'd drunk.

"Warren doesn't know you're here?"

"Not yet. We don't want to disturb him while he's busy."

Dennis raised his hand to beckon Ivy over, then told her to bring an extra chair for Anna.

"How long are you here for?" Anna asked while shooting Ivy an apologetic glance.

Jen took her seat again. "Just tonight."

"Not much happening with the business on the first day of the year," Dennis added. "So we thought we'd come and check out the place our son has devoted all his attention to."

"The hotel is gorgeous," Jen said. "Warren didn't mention that the place was so upmarket."

"And you never thought to look into the place he worked?" Anna muttered, annoyed that they were probably about to wreak havoc on the sense of harmony she'd been living in.

"Our room is lovely," Jen crooned.

"And *the food?*" Anna asked, her jaw tight as she loomed over them. "Did you already eat?"

"It was *very* good," Jen said.

"Yes," Dennis agreed. "That tasting menu isn't bad at all."

"Oh, my god." Anna dropped her chin to her chest as she sighed. "Warren's food is amazing."

"That's what we said." Dennis straightened his tie. "It really was decent."

"No!" Anna spat, aware of Ivy hovering beside her with a chair. "Those aren't compliments. When you speak to Warren, say the food was fantastic. Do not say that it's *not bad,* or *decent,* or any other mediocre adjectives. You can say delicious, incredible, mouthwatering... You should say he's talented and that you're proud of him. Do you understand?"

Dennis swilled his wine, with an amused glint in his eyes. "Feisty, this one, isn't she?" he said to Ivy.

"Apparently so," Ivy replied, chuckling.

Anna's gaze swept the busy room – lots of guests were on starters, some partway through the main course.

"I take it things are busy in the kitchen?" Anna asked Ivy.

"Yeah. I imagine it'll be another hour before things calm down."

"In that case, why don't we move to the lounge and have a drink there?" she said to Warren's parents. The suggestion was firm enough that it sounded more like instructions, but Dennis and Jen smiled approvingly.

Ivy told them there'd be a staff member in the lounge to take their drink order. Then she patted Anna's arm and mouthed her thanks before moving away.

In the lounge, Dennis ordered a bottle of wine. When it arrived, Anna felt a jolt of panic at the thought of spending an hour making small talk with them. Hopefully, the dinner rush might be over sooner than Ivy predicted.

For a while, they talked about the hotel and the area. With the neutral conversation and the wine, Anna stayed relatively relaxed. Until Dennis shifted the conversation, asking about her work, then she felt herself tense up.

"It's a very quiet time of year," she said, the words feeling practiced. "But after the Christmas rush, it's good to take a break. I'll start back at the flower shop later in January."

"And what about that idea of expanding to having your own physical shop?" Dennis asked. "Have you thought any more about that?"

She froze, pondering what to say. Part of her was tempted to brush the subject aside, but there was also a part of her that was desperate to chat it through.

Dennis and Jen probably weren't the right people to talk to. Yes, they were business people, but on a very different scale than anything she aspired to.

"I viewed potential premises a few days ago," she said, the urge to talk winning out.

"How exciting," Jen said, sitting forward in her chair. "How did it go?"

"Fine," she said weakly.

Dennis frowned. "The building wasn't suitable?"

"It was," Anna said. "It was actually perfect, but I just didn't feel much when I looked around it. I thought I'd be excited, but it left me feeling flat. Maybe it was just overwhelming – I'm not sure."

"Perhaps it just wasn't the right place," Dennis suggested. "You're absolutely right to trust your gut on these matters."

"The first place you look at is unlikely to be the right one," Jen said. "You may have to view lots of places before you find one that ticks all the boxes."

"Yeah." Anna bit her lip. Maybe she should leave it at that...

"It wasn't just the building though," she added after a pause. "I started getting into the business plan, and it felt all wrong."

"In what way?" Dennis asked.

"I don't want to do it," she said, a lump forming in her throat. "The idea has been floating around my head for ages, but the reality of it just depresses me. If I expand the business, so much of my time will be spent doing things I don't like. There'd be heaps more paperwork, and I'd need to employ at least one person, probably two. Managing people fills me with dread. And doing those things means less time doing the things I enjoy."

She realised she was talking a lot, but apparently after bottling it all up, she now couldn't stop. "I like working for someone else. I get to do the job I enjoy without all the responsibility that comes with being the owner. And even though my boss can be a little annoying, overall it works out well because I have time for my online shop, and for any craft markets and workshops I want to do. Things are pretty perfect as they are, so I'm not sure why I'm thinking of changing them."

She swiped at the corners of her eyes to catch the stray tears while cursing her lack of composure.

"I'm probably being daft," she said to fill the silence. "I'll look at it again in a few weeks, and I'll probably feel differently."

"I suspect you'll feel exactly the same," Dennis said calmly. "If you don't have the drive and ambition, it probably won't work out well. Expanding your business will mean putting in a lot more hours. If you're not willing to do that..."

"I'm not afraid of working hard," she said quickly.

"That's not what I meant," Dennis said, a smile teasing his lips. "I only meant that you have to give it your all."

He cast a glance at his wife, which seemed to express some private meaning. "I always wanted Warren to join the family business," he said slowly. "Partly because I'd like to work with my son, but partly because I thought he'd be very good at the job."

He shifted in his seat and shook his head. "I'm starting to see that having a head for business isn't enough – your heart has to be in it, too. Warren has done well with his cooking because he gives it his all. He wouldn't do that for the family business because it's not what he's passionate about. He's followed his own path, and I think that's admirable."

Anna's jaw had gone slack as she stared at Dennis. "He has done very well for himself," she muttered.

"I think it's the same with your business," he went on. "If you're happy with the way things are – and you're financially stable – maybe it's best to stick with that. At least for now. I can't imagine you'll change your mind in a matter of weeks, but maybe in a few years you'll feel differently. Or not," he added and reached for his wine.

"Yes," Anna said, and took a swig of her own wine. In the ensuing silence, she glanced around the room. "Maybe I'll see if things are slowing down in the kitchen."

Walking through the hotel, she felt slightly dumbstruck by the conversation with Warren's parents. And surprisingly lighter at the notion that she didn't have to expand her business if she didn't want to. Somehow, she'd felt she *should* do it, but she wasn't sure where that pressure had come from.

The kitchen was reasonably calm – with just the normal amount of chatter and bustle. Warren was in the centre of the room, his focus entirely on the two dessert plates in front of him, which he drizzled chocolate sauce onto with artful precision. He gave the waiter the nod to take them before looking up and spotting Anna.

"Hi!" The way his eyes lit up at the sight of her made her stomach flutter, as did the casual way he greeted her with a kiss. "This is a nice surprise. I know you said you might come in, but I wasn't really expecting you to."

"How's work?" she asked.

"Busy, but good."

"I'm glad." She smiled gently. "Your parents are here."

He cocked his head. "My parents?"

"Yes. Apparently, they checked into the hotel for the night. They ate dinner in the restaurant earlier."

He propped his hands on his hips as his eyes widened. "They ate my food?"

"Yes."

"There you are!" Ivy said, interrupting them as she rushed into the kitchen. "Are you okay?" she asked, a hand on Anna's arm.

"I'm fine. Why?"

"Kate said you were upset."

"Oh." She shook her head. "No. I'm fine."

"Really? Because Kate thought you were crying."

"I kind of was..."

"Oh my god," Warren grumbled. "What have they done now?"

"Nothing." She smiled up at him. "They were actually very nice. I got emotional, that's all, but not because of anything they said."

His gaze slid to Ivy. "Have you been dealing with them all evening?"

"Yeah," she said sheepishly. "They didn't want me to tell you they were here when you were busy."

"Well, I apologise for any offence they caused."

"They were fine," Ivy told him before turning her attention to Anna. "We need to get a drink soon and have a proper catch up."

"Definitely," Anna agreed before Ivy left again.

"I'll make sure everything is under control here," Warren said to Anna. "Then I'll get changed and come and find you. It shouldn't take long. That's if you don't mind entertaining my parents a little longer."

"I don't mind. We're just having a drink in the lounge." She kissed him again, then headed back to his parents.

It was only five minutes later when Warren joined them, pulling up a chair beside Anna and immediately reaching for her hand.

"This is a surprise," he said to his parents. "I'm sort of glad you didn't tell me you were coming."

"That's what we thought," his mum said. "We didn't want to put you under pressure."

"How was your dinner?" he asked.

"Excellent," his mum said proudly. "The salmon was cooked to perfection."

"It was all very good," his dad said. "It's a surprisingly decent wine list, too. Is that down to you?"

Warren nodded.

"It's not overly extensive, of course, but there are some good vintages."

"Thanks," Warren said flatly.

"Anyway," Dennis said. "I'm sure you don't need us to sit here and tell you how great you are at your job..."

Anna's whole body flashed with annoyance, because that's

exactly what they should do and she really thought she'd made that clear earlier.

"Now that you've made your final decision not to join the family business," Dennis continued. "We thought it only fair that we give you a little financial boost, as we did for your sister. We transferred some money into your account."

Anna's eyes bulged. Was that their idea of an apology?

She tensed, waiting for Warren to react.

"Thanks," he said curtly. "I might just grab myself a drink from the bar."

He hadn't gone far before his mum called out to him. "Why not get a bottle of champagne and we'll toast the new year?"

He nodded once and continued through the lounge.

"Maybe I'll see if he needs any help," Anna mumbled and rushed after him.

When she caught up with him, he was asking Ivy to get them a bottle of champagne and four glasses, and charge it to his parents' bill.

"Are you okay?" Anna asked, standing beside him while he scrolled on his phone.

"Yep."

"Really? You're not angry?"

"No. Why?"

"Because they're so dismissive! I don't know why they won't say they're proud of you and tell you that you've done well for yourself." Her voice increased in volume, and she made a conscious effort to keep her irritation under control while Warren continued to look at his phone. "They said nice things about you before. Your dad said he thought it was good that you followed your passion and that he admired you for following your own path."

She shook her head, wishing she'd paid more attention. "It was something like that. I don't understand why they won't say nice things to your face."

"I suppose the question is whether I'd prefer them to praise me and tell me they're proud of me..." There was a gleeful glint in his eyes as he angled his phone towards her and lowered his voice. "Or whether I'd prefer a hundred thousand pounds."

"No," Anna muttered, before snatching the phone. "They did *not!*" Her eyes bounced from his banking app to his face. "A hundred thousand," she whispered. "*One hundred thousand.*"

"Call me shallow. But I'm okay with that. They've never been affectionate or encouraging parents, so it would probably feel weird if they started now."

"So you'll keep the money?" she asked, eyes fixed on the phone screen.

"What else would I do? Do you think I should refuse to accept it on principle?"

"Maybe." She shook her head. "No. Keep it. Do something crazy with it."

"I'll save it. Maybe it'll come in handy one day." He shoved his phone into his pocket. "Or you can have it for your shop."

She laughed. "You can't just casually offer me a hundred grand!"

"I just did."

Her heart swelled, knowing he genuinely would give it to her. "I'm not going to open a shop."

"Why not?" His eyebrows twitched together. "Is that what you were upset about before?"

"I wasn't upset, but I was speaking to your parents about it. Making my business plan – and then chatting it through with them – made me realise it's not what I want. I'm happy as I am." She reached for his hand. "You also inspired me to make sure the career path I'm on is the one I really want to be on. I'm going to stick with what I love for now. If I ever feel I want to explore other options, I can reassess."

He nodded approvingly, then plucked the bottle of champagne from the ice bucket on the bar and popped the cork.

"We're supposed to drink that with your parents," Anna said, chuckling as he drizzled the fizzy liquid into two glasses.

"You know I don't like to be completely sober when hanging out with them." His eyes sparkled with mirth. "We'll have one glass here and then join them."

"Go on then," she agreed, taking a glass and touching the rim to his. The gentle ting rang in her ears as she took a sip and grinned madly.

"What are you celebrating?" Ivy asked from behind the bar.

"The new year," Warren replied, his intense gaze fixed on Anna in a way that gave her that wonderfully light feeling in her stomach. "And whatever adventures it may bring."

Epilogue

Three months later...

After only ten minutes at work, Ivy put her head into the kitchen and caught Warren's eye.

"Lewis wants to speak to you in the office," she said.

"What for?" Warren called from the food storage.

"How would I know?"

"Why can't he come in here and talk to me? And since when does he send you to fetch me?"

She shrugged. "He just said if I saw you, I should let you know he wants to speak to you."

"That sounds ominous."

A few minutes later, Warren knocked on the office door, then pushed it open.

"You were looking for me?" he said as he sank into the chair.

"Yeah." Lewis's eyes were on his computer screen while he scrolled with the mouse. "I received this letter this morning." He paused in what he was doing and slid a single sheet of paper across the desk.

The company logo jumped out, but the rest of the words were a jumble that Warren's brain couldn't quite fathom.

"What is this?" he asked, his voice oddly croaky.

"An invitation to Michelin's award ceremony."

That's what he thought he was looking at. His heart rate went through the roof. "Why are they inviting us to the awards?"

"The restaurant is being awarded a Michelin star."

"Right." He stared at the paper, still unable to get his brain to focus on the words. "Okay."

"I know you always said you're not driven by awards and accolades, and I'm actually starting to see why."

"How do you mean?" he asked, his words sounding hollow.

"Someone from Michelin called me for a chat yesterday. Partly to warn me of what to expect when the new guide comes out next week, and it's all official. He told me to be prepared that our online booking system is likely to go down due to too much traffic."

"Really?" Warren asked dumbly.

"Yes. He was talking about how much busier we'll be and how important it is not to let standards drop. Apparently, some restaurants don't cope well with the boost in customers and the high expectations of those customers..."

Warren was barely listening. "We're getting a Michelin star?"

"Yeah. And you know what I never really considered?"

"What?"

"Once you have a star, you have to make sure you don't lose it. The inspectors will continue to visit to make sure we maintain standards. Imagine the disappointment of having a star taken away. That would be worse than never having one, wouldn't it?"

Warren stared at him, not sure what he was babbling on about.

"A Michelin star?" Warren said again.

"Hard to take in, isn't it?" Lewis said. "Let it sink in and next week we'll get together for a planning session of any changes we'll need to make. I'm thinking we'll need to take on more staff, both in the kitchen and out front in the restaurant. From now on, every meal coming out of that kitchen – be it breakfast, lunch or dinner – has to be of the absolute best quality. That goes for your days off, too. Everyone needs to be at the top of their game."

"Of course." He opened and closed his mouth a couple of times. "Who knows about this?"

"Just us. And Erin."

"You haven't told the rest of your family?"

"No. I didn't know if you'd want to tell Anna yourself."

"Yeah."

"You don't mind me telling the rest of the family?"

"No."

"I thought we might hold off on telling the kitchen staff. Wait until the guide comes out, and it's all official."

"Sure. Whatever you want. We should celebrate, though. Maybe we can do something with the family this weekend? I can get Liam to take care of the kitchen."

"That's the other reason I don't want to mention it to the rest of the staff yet. Erin and I are away in Madrid for the weekend."

"Oh, yeah." Warren shook his head – he knew about that.

"So we'll tell the staff next week and then organise a proper celebration. I don't want to tell them and then fly off to Spain – I'll look like a pretty crappy boss." He grimaced. "Sorry I can't celebrate with you this weekend. If it were anything else, I'd cancel, but we booked the trip ages ago and we've been looking forward to it."

"No worries."

"I got you something," Lewis said, reaching under his desk

and producing a bottle-sized gift bag. "I know the star is awarded to the restaurant and not the chef, but it's really down to you, and I want you to know how much I appreciate all your hard work and dedication."

"Thanks," Warren said, slipping the champagne out of the bag.

Maybe he had more in common with his dad than he liked to admit, because he couldn't help but think that if Lewis truly appreciated him, he would have chosen a decent champagne and not a cheap supermarket brand.

"When do you leave for Madrid?"

"Tomorrow morning. I hope we get a bit of blue sky. I really need a break from all this grey and drizzle."

Warren frowned. He'd just found out he was being awarded a Michelin star and Lewis was drivelling on about the weather. It all felt slightly surreal. "Yeah," he muttered. "Have a good trip."

"Thanks."

In a daze, Warren headed back to the kitchen, then felt utterly lost. What was he supposed to do now? Just carry on with work as normal?

He stepped out of the back door intent on calling Anna, but was distracted by Lewis posting on the family messaging group. The picture of the letter from Michelin popped up, along with the caption, *'Exciting news! Guess who's getting a Michelin star?'*

The flurry of replies made him smile.

He tried to ignore the niggling annoyance that Lewis hadn't given him time to tell Anna himself.

His phone rang before he could think too much about it.

"Oh, my goodness!" Anna sounded slightly breathless. "How long have you known about this? Why didn't you tell me yourself?"

"Good question. Apparently because your brother beat me to it. I only just found out. No one else knows."

"It's so amazing! I'm not at all surprised, though. Haven't I been saying all along that you'd get a star?"

He tried to contain his smile. "I think you should congratulate me, not say, 'I told you so'."

"Sorry!" She laughed loudly. "Congratulations! We need to celebrate. Let's get everyone together over the weekend. Liam and the rest of the kitchen staff must be over the moon, too."

"They don't know yet. Lewis wants to wait and tell them next week. He's off to Spain tomorrow."

"Oh, yeah. I forgot about that. I'll call Carla and my parents and we can do something with them at the weekend."

"That sounds good."

"Let's have a drink tonight as well."

"I have a really bad bottle of champagne we can drink."

"A what?"

"Never mind." He shook his head. "I'll see you after work. Can you meet me at my place? I want to tell Edie."

"Yes. She'll be so excited."

And she *was* excited. Sadly, he didn't get to see her immediate reaction to the news, since Anna had accidentally told her before he arrived.

The week went on like that – with everything just a little underwhelming. Considering he'd genuinely never thought he'd get a Michelin star, it was funny how his expectations suddenly weren't being met.

The proper excitement would come the following week, though, when it was officially announced and splashed all over social media. Not telling the rest of the kitchen staff felt fairly excruciating, but at least he had their reactions to look forward to. It was their achievement too – once he could share it with them, he'd no doubt stop feeling so flat about the whole thing.

Walking into Anna's place after work on Thursday evening, he immediately spotted the trepidation in her features.

"What's wrong?" he asked, giving her a kiss and sitting beside her on the couch.

"Don't freak out," she said, gripping a cushion in front of her.

"That's never a good start to a conversation."

"Mum called this morning to say she's got the flu."

"Maybe that explains why she hasn't been in touch to congratulate me," he said under his breath.

"What?" Anna frowned. "She's messaged you, hasn't she?"

"Yeah." She'd sent him several messages – he just thought the situation warranted a phone call, but that was the mood he'd been in since he got the news about the Michelin star. No one seemed to react quite how he'd like them to.

Anna narrowed her eyes. "So Mum won't make it for dinner tomorrow, after all."

"Us and your dad then," he said sulkily. At least Nicholas had called him and made a big fuss.

"Carla feels terrible, but she can't just cancel when she's agreed to dog sit."

"Yeah, I know. It's fine."

"So I thought maybe we'd just do something completely different."

"What's the plan?"

"Remember, I said not to freak out..."

He lifted an eyebrow and waited for whatever was coming next.

"Your parents are very excited."

"No." He shook his head. "No way. I'm not celebrating this with my parents. It's not happening. We'll do something just the two of us."

"It's one night of your life," she snapped. "And you always said the Michelin star wasn't a big deal to you, anyway. What does it matter how we celebrate? I spoke to your mum today, and she suggested we drive down to Bath tomorrow and have a night there with them. She'll get Rachel to come along and cook, and we can have a nice evening with them."

"I'd rather just not go out. I'll tell Liam he doesn't need to cover for me after all, and I'll work over the weekend as usual."

"I already told your mum," Anna complained. "Plus, we can go into Bath on Saturday and get some supplies I need for my candles and greetings cards."

"So this is not actually anything to do with celebrating the Michelin star? You just fancy a weekend trip?" He regretted the words instantly. "Sorry," he said, running his hands through his hair.

"Do you really not want to go?"

Of course he didn't want to go. Didn't she know him at all?

"We can just have dinner with them," she said quietly. "Then disappear off to the hot tub with a bottle of champagne..."

He rubbed his eyebrow. "Yeah, okay. Whatever you want."

❄

Warren should probably have fought his case harder, but he'd never got over his issue of not being able to say no to Anna. Something he should probably rectify to avoid getting himself into situations like this one – driving down to his parents' place on a Friday afternoon and feeling as though there was hot lava inside him, waiting to erupt.

After the week he'd had, there was no way he'd be able to deal with his parents calmly. He was even struggling not to snap at Anna, and she was the one person who could never normally get under his skin.

"Are you okay?" she asked, her words slicing through the tension in the car.

"Yes," he said tightly, the first time he'd spoken in an hour.

"You're very quiet."

He gripped the steering wheel tighter. "It's been a stressful week."

"Why?"

He shrugged, wondering how she hadn't noticed he'd had a tricky week. "It's just been a little disappointing. A Michelin star should be a highlight of my career, but I guess it feels pretty underwhelming."

"You always said you didn't even care about getting one."

"That's not what I said."

"Yes, you did."

"I didn't care about *not* getting one!" he fumed. "Getting one is quite a big deal. It would be nice if people would acknowledge that."

"Sorry," she whispered. "But you've spent the last year telling everyone you didn't care either way, so maybe that's the problem."

"Surely *you* know how much it means to me?" A lump formed in his throat as his ribs squeezed his lungs. "*You* know how hard I've worked for this. It would be nice if *you* were proud of me."

"I am." Her voice sounded brittle, and he wished he'd kept his emotions bottled up, but after a week of doing that, he seemed to have reached his limit. "Of course I'm proud of you."

"I don't understand why you thought it was a good idea to meet up with my parents."

"Because they're really proud of you..."

"Of course they are! Now that I have a Michelin star for them to brag about. But I'm not interested in celebrating with the people who *only* care about the big achievements."

"I'm sorry. I thought it would be nice."

"Whatever." He shook his head and rummaged in the centre console for the fob for the automatic gates as they came into view. "I'll just drink a lot and ignore them. My usual plan."

"Warren." Anna put her hand on his arm. "I'm sure it will be fine."

❄

This was a spectacularly bad idea.

Anna's heart was beating so furiously that it felt as though it might burst out of her chest. The atmosphere in the car had been stifling since the moment they set off, and as Warren parked under the security light in the driveway, the tension hung around him like fog.

"Why is the house so dark?" She craned her neck to look up, but there wasn't a single light on in the house.

"I guess they're not here yet," Warren said, switching off the engine.

"They said they'd be here from lunchtime." She checked her watch. "It's seven o'clock. What time are we going to eat if they're not even here yet? Also, do you have a key?"

"Yes. I have a key." He peered out into the darkness. "I'll call Mum."

He didn't speak much during the conversation, and Anna couldn't make out anything Jen was saying. After a few grunts from Warren, he ended the call.

"They're not here," he said, pulling on the door handle and stepping out of the car.

"What time will they arrive?" Anna asked frantically, trying to keep up with him as he grabbed their bags and strode to the front door.

"Tomorrow," he said. "Lunchtime."

"What?" Anna's eyes widened. "Why?"

"Because apparently you arranged to have dinner with them on Saturday and not Friday."

"No!" Anna stood close beside him on the doorstep. "I said Friday. Definitely. I know I said Friday."

"It doesn't matter now," he said, walking inside. "They're not here. It doesn't make much difference who messed up the plans."

"Sorry," Anna said, her insides tied in knots as they walked through the grand entrance hall, which looked stark and barren without a Christmas tree dominating the space. "Maybe it's a good thing," she suggested quietly. "You didn't want to have dinner with them, anyway."

He threw his keys on the table, dropped their bags, and headed down the hall. Halfway to the kitchen, he swung back to her, his eyes filled with rage.

"Maybe it *would* be a good thing if they genuinely got the days mixed up, but I think we both know there will have been some work thing that came up."

"I don't think that's true," Anna murmured, but he spoke over her.

"At least their behaviour isn't surprising," he shouted. "What really gets to me is your mum didn't even bother to call me. And I had one lousy message from Carla, who apparently thinks some random dogs are more important than celebrating with me."

"Warren," Anna said, tears filling her eyes, which she had no control over.

"No!" he snapped. "You can't make this okay. Carla should have called me! And your *brother,*" he fumed. "It's like he went on a quest to find the cheapest bottle of champagne he could find!"

"Yes," she said, her hands shaking from the adrenaline rush. "I think that's exactly what he did."

Warren looked as though he was about to continue his rant, then registered her words. His forehead creased. "What?"

"I think he purposely bought you terrible champagne."

Warren stared at her as she moved past him. The door was

already ajar, but she pushed it wider and stuck her hand around the corner to flick on the lights.

"Surprise," she said weakly.

It didn't quite go as planned. There was a stunned silence as Warren stepped into the doorway, only broken by Josh jumping out in front of him.

"Surprise, Uncle Warren!" he shouted, arms stretched out. "Well done on your star."

"What's going on?" Warren put a hand over his mouth as his eyes scanned the room, decorated with a star theme and filled with all his friends and family.

"Do you know what the best thing about this is?" Carla said loudly, waving her phone in her hand as she moved beside Anna. "I started recording the moment I heard the front door open, so I have that entire rant recorded." Her eyes flashed with mirth. "Now, just for a laugh, let's try that entrance again..." She flicked the lights off and counted down from three before hitting the switch again.

This time, 'surprise' rang out in a loud chorus as the room flooded with light.

Warren looked at Anna. "You had this planned the whole time?"

She only nodded in reply before Liam and the rest of the kitchen crew jumped around Warren, congratulating each other raucously.

Then he got caught up with everyone else – Edie, and Ivy, his family, and Anna's family. She watched him move around, looking slightly stunned and very emotional.

By the time he made his way back to her, he was more on the emotional side.

"I'm *so* sorry," he said, lifting her off the floor as he swept her up in a tight hug.

"That was the worst car journey I've ever been on," she said, snuggling into his neck. "Of course I'm proud of you!"

"That's quite clear now." His forehead wrinkled deeply. "I shouldn't have shouted."

"You were upset."

"I still shouldn't have shouted."

She pulled back to look him in the eyes. "You shout when you're emotional. I don't particularly like it, but I'd never want you to hide your emotions because you think I can't handle it."

He rubbed his nose against hers. "I love you."

"I love you too."

Carla appeared beside them and cleared her throat loudly.

Warren winced as he looked at her. "I'm sorry about my rant."

"I was really touched," Carla said with a hand at her chest. "Of everyone to disappoint you this week, mine hurt you the most!"

"I was so annoyed that you didn't call," he said, his cheeks flushing.

"Mum and I were under strict instructions not to call you," Carla explained. "Anna thought we'd let it slip about the party." She leaned her head against his shoulder. "It was really horrible not calling to congratulate you."

He looped his arm around her shoulders and squeezed. "What happened with your dog sitting job?"

"There wasn't one. We made that up."

"What about you?" Warren called to Lewis, who hovered nearby. "I thought you were supposed to be in Spain."

"You got a Michelin star!" Lewis said. "We cancelled the trip."

Warren hung his head. "All that stuff you were saying about the Michelin star causing more work..."

"It was so hard to keep a straight face." He rolled his eyes. "Those Michelin stars are such a problem!"

"And the champagne!" Warren said, beaming.

"I thought I'd gone too far there. I almost cracked up

laughing at your look of disgust when you pulled it out of the bag."

"I hate you all!" Warren growled as he pulled Lewis into a hug.

"I spent most of the week feeling as though I was about to have a cardiac event," Anna said when he draped his arm around her shoulders. "This is the last time I ever throw a surprise party."

"We only have one Michelin star so far," Warren said cheekily. "When we get the second and third, I'll be expecting the same thing then."

"You can have a party. Just without the surprise element. My nerves can't take it."

Warren kissed her forehead, and the tender gesture made all the stress worthwhile.

As he drew away from her, his eyes shot to Lewis. "Who the heck is taking care of the restaurant tonight?"

Lewis shrugged. "It's closed for the night."

"You're not serious?" Warren's eyes bulged. "You closed the restaurant?"

"Only for one night. Given the circumstances, I'm sure people will understand. I offered vouchers to anyone with a reservation."

"What about the hotel guests? What are they supposed to do?"

Lewis laughed. "Liam made a batch of soup and sandwiches for anyone who's desperate, but they can also go elsewhere to eat."

"That's a really bad way to run a business," Warren said, shaking his head mockingly. "Do you even know what you're doing?"

"No. I've absolutely no idea." Lewis's eyes sparkled with amusement. "What about you?"

Warren shook his head. "I'm winging it."

As her family moved away, Anna looped her arms around Warren's waist and rested her head against his chest. "You've done a really great job of fooling everyone," she teased. "Even your parents are convinced you're great at your job." Lifting her head, she gazed up at him. "Your mum is over the moon, you know. And your dad. Not just because they get to brag. They're genuinely happy for you."

"I know," he said grudgingly, then cast a quick glance to where his parents were chatting with Edie. "Where's everyone staying, by the way?"

"Some people are staying here, some in a hotel. Your mum and Lewis organised all that."

"Everyone went to a lot of effort."

"Because they're all very proud of you."

He sighed and drew her closer, looking deep into her eyes. "Explain to me how I got so lucky."

Warmth pooled in her stomach, knowing he wasn't only referring to career achievements, or to the bustle of friends and family around them. Over the last few months, their relationship had flourished, and every day she marvelled at how right it felt.

As the sound of their family's laughter drifted around them, she pressed her lips to his.

"I think I got pretty lucky, too."

Also by Hannah Ellis

<u>Christmas in the Cotswolds</u>

Not Just for Christmas

A Chef's Kiss for Christmas

<u>The Lily Larkin Series</u>

Death on the Rocks (Book 1)

Malicious Intent (Book 2)

A Poisonous Plot (Book 3)

Dead in the Water (Book 4)

The Sunken Truth (Book 5)

Artful Deceit (Book 6)

<u>The Isles of Scilly Series</u>

The Weekend Getaway (Book 1)

A Change of Heart (Book 2)

The Summer Escape (Book 3)

The Potter's House (Book 4)

An Unexpected Guest (Book 5)

<u>The Hope Cove Series</u>

The Cottage at Hope Cove (Book 1)

Escape to Oakbrook Farm (Book 2)

Summer at The Old Boathouse (Book 3)

Whispers at the Bluebell Inn (Book 4)

The House on Lavender Lane (Book 5)

The Bookshop of Hopes and Dreams (Book 6)

Winter Wishes in Hope Cove (Book 7)

There's Something about Scarlett (Book 8)

The Single Dads Club Series

It Takes a Village (Book 1)

Riding the Waves (Book 2)

Playing for Keeps (Book 3)

Rules of Engagement (Book 4)

The Loch Lannick Series

Coming Home to the Loch (Book 1)

The Castle by the Loch (Book 2)

Fireworks over the Loch (Book 3)

The Cafe at the Loch (Book 4)

Secrets at the Loch (Book 5)

Surprises at the Loch (Book 6)

Finding Hope at the Loch (Book 7)

Fragile Hearts by the Loch (Book 8)

New Arrivals at the Loch (Book 9)

The Lucy Mitchell Series

Beyond the Lens (Book 1)

Beneath These Stars (Book 2)

Always With You (Standalone novel)

The Friends Like These Series

Friends Like These (Book 1)

Christmas with Friends (Book 2)

My Kind of Perfect (Book 3)

A Friend in Need (Book 4)

Hannah has also written a series of children's books aimed at 5-9 year olds under the pen name, Hannah Sparks. The first book in the *Land of Stars* series is entitled *Where Dragons Fly.*

Printed in Dunstable, United Kingdom

73501422R00214